Voice Over

CÉLINE CURIOL

Translated from the French by SAM RICHARD

Original title: Voix sans issue
Copyright © 2005 by Céline Curiol/Actes Sud
First English edition 2007
Published under arrangement with Actes Sud, Arles, France
English translation copyright © Sam Richard

Translated from the French by Sam Richard

LIBRARY AND ARCHIVES CANADA CATALOGUING IN PUBLICATION

Curiol, Céline
Voice over / written by Céline Curiol ; translated by Sam Richard.

Translation of Voix sans issue.
ISBN 978-0-7710-1816-9

I. Richard, Sam   II. Title.

PQ2703.U75V6313 2007   843'.92   C2007-903827-1

We acknowledge the financial support of the Government of Canada through the
Book Publishing Industry Development Program and that of the Government of
Ontario through the Ontario Media Development Corporation's Ontario Book
Initiative. We further acknowledge the support of the Canada Council for the Arts
and the Ontario Arts Council for our publishing program.

Liberté · Égalité · Fraternité
RÉPUBLIQUE FRANÇAISE

CONSULAT GENERAL DE FRANCE
A TORONTO

This work, published as part of the program of aid for publication, received support
from the French Ministry of Foreign Affairs and the Cultural Service of the Consulate
General of France in Toronto.

Typeset in Fournier Reg by M&S, Toronto
Printed and bound in Canada

This book is printed on acid-free paper that is 100% recycled,
ancient-forest friendly (100% post-consumer recycled).

McClelland & Stewart Ltd.
75 Sherbourne Street
Toronto, Ontario
M5A 2P9
www.mcclelland.com

1 2 3 4 5   11 10 09 08 07

For Mémé

Yes, it is rather an ambiguous voice and not always easy to follow, in its reasonings and decrees. But I follow it none the less, more or less, I follow it in this sense, that I do what it tells me. And I do not think there are many voices of which as much may be said. And I feel I shall follow it from this day forth, no matter what it commands. And when it ceases, leaving me in doubt and darkness, I shall wait for it to come back . . .

SAMUEL BECKETT, *Molloy*

They have known each other for a long time. She has never quite been able to recall the moment when they met, the place, the precise day, whether she shook his hand or they kissed on the cheek. Nor has she ever thought to ask him. She does have a first memory, though. As she was climbing into her coat in the narrow hallway of an unkempt apartment, she had caught his look of distress. The woman he had flirted with all evening was refusing to leave with him. He was trying to persuade her with a barrage of words, which fell to pieces before the face of the majestic creature. She thought the idea of suddenly being deprived of the object of his affections must have been more than he could bear just then. And seeing him this way, in love, had moved her. She had slipped between the two of them and said, I'm off. But he had not replied.

She still remembers his hair and his hands. In her mind, she retains a distinct image of their thickness and colour, their size and shape. Because to touch these parts of him is perhaps what she most spontaneously desires, is what for her would open up the path to intimacy.

In the window of the wine shop, each bottle has been set at a slight angle to those on either side. No prices are marked on the labels; she decides to go in. To help her with her choice, the man behind the counter wants to know what dishes will be served at dinner. She doesn't dare tell him that they won't be eating, she fears he'll take her for an alcoholic. I've been invited, I haven't been told anything, she says, improvising an answer to counter the hint of reproach dawning in the man's eyes. I'll take some white and some red, I suppose, she adds by way of conclusion. He picks out three bottles; she accepts at once. He wraps them in shiny paper, sets them down vertically in a bag. Back outside, she walks along with the promising rattle of glass in her arms.

She has sat down at a deserted outdoor café. From the heights of his over-elongated spine, an ashen-faced waiter takes her order while checking to see that nothing has changed on the terrace of his little domain. The espresso arrives with the bill. The coffee is cold and bitter. In spite of her exhaustion, she has no intention of missing the party: that would show she was unworthy of his friendship. No doubt one of the guests will have remembered to take along candles. It would be a shame if he had nothing to blow out, no wish to make, no icing to lick off the little plastic holders – he who is so keen on celebrating his birthday. Honouring a person's arrival into the world has never seemed to make much sense to her, but in his case she can understand. What is a birthday? A mark on time to reduce it to human scale. The waiter is closing up the cash register, he wants his coins. The palm of his hand is a tracery of jumbled lines imprinted by hundreds of adroit actions repeated every day. All of a sudden, she has an urge to put something on it other than metal, perhaps her own hand.

Her apartment smells of varnish and incense. She takes the wine bottles out of the bag, lines them up on the kitchen table. A moment's hesitation, and then she opens the bottle of white, pours herself a glass, and waits for the hour when she will leave for his house.

People are talking in groups around a chair or a sofa. There's laughter, joking, merriment; everyone's loosening up without too much trouble. The wash of conversations follows her from room to room, the voices modulating, bursting like giant bubbles against her ears. Already, her head is spinning. Someone asks if she's seen the corkscrew. She shrugs; the muscles in her jaw are a bit stiff. Drinks are

handed to her; she's made to clink glasses, to take sips.
There are more and more unfamiliar faces, and she hates
being the one to make the first move. An overexcited girl
with dyed blonde hair knocks into her coming out of the
toilet. She tries to catch her aggressor's eye to let her know
that the gesture has not been well received, but the girl
ignores her, heads straight for the living room. She bolts
the door, gathers up her dress, and sits down clumsily on
the seat. She yawns; her head weighs a ton and a half, and
it's not yet even midnight. When she emerges from her
hiding place, he is in the hall. A woman has just arrived
and has her hands around his waist. Her name is Ange.
The woman is almost as she remembers her, but slightly
more friendly than at their first meeting in the doorway.
They exchange a smile. Yes, she tells herself, they do make
a nice couple. He has won his bet: the rebellious angel has
been conquered, and here she is at his big annual party. It
is only now that she sees the white wings sprouting from
Ange's back. A harmless pair of little wings, of a down soft
enough to cure the worst insomnia. He has touched those
wings, and that is what has drawn him to her. Who could
resist a pair of wings? She, too, would like to be able to
touch them, to find out the sensation they leave. But she
isn't the type who could interest an angel – even one with
crumpled wings. How's it going? She gives a nod. That's
when she remembers the reason for her presence. Happy
birthday. She says the words in a tone that makes them
sound more like an excuse than a wish. He comes up to her,
takes her in his arms. She stiffens, unwilling for him to

hold her in that way. She wants to tell him that certain gestures are not to be granted so lightly, especially not in such
mundane circumstances. You have to move cautiously,
wait for the right moment. The grip of his arms is firm, his
hands are spread out like stars and press into her back. For
one brief moment she manages to let herself go, then,
quickly, the arms release her, but the mark is already made.

She has a drink on the sofa, next to a man she doesn't
know. She remembers vaguely the song and the clapping;
it was Ange who'd remembered the candles. The man
beside her is not moving a muscle. She presses gently
against the arm that is flung out along her thigh. The
man's eyes blink – as for the rest of him, not a twitch. He's
beginning to worry her, staying frozen like that. I can tell
I've made a big impression on you! The words slipped out.
His face remains impassive. Aren't you feeling well? Her
question provokes no response. The man seems to have
abandoned his body, a hollow shell of flaccid flesh, as if he
has catapulted his spirit to a place where no one can dis-
lodge it. His eyes see nothing, not even the spot on the wall
in front of him, which he appears to be staring at. Only his
nostrils continue to quiver. She notices that he is freshly
shaven. A few hours earlier, he passed the blade of a razor
over his cheeks, sketched out bands of smooth skin in the
foamy whiteness. His skin is unlined, his lips dark and
chapped. Something to drink, you'll feel better, no need to
get so worked up, we can talk it over, there's always an
answer . . . She casts about for the words to shake him out
of his lethargy, but all that comes are phrases warped by

alcohol. How to guess the cause of the state he is in? Even depressed people don't do that. She doesn't do that, not that – imitating a dead body in that way, it's enough to give you the creeps. She takes a sip of wine. No one else has noticed the lifeless body on the sofa. A man wrestles open a bottle, a couple kisses by the window, a woman patiently cadges a cigarette, a trio burst into laughter. No one is aware of anything other than the person he or she is speaking to. And so she wraps her fingers around the man's unresisting fingers. She lifts his heavy hand and places it on her belly. For an indeterminate length of time, she keeps it there, its warm weight upon her.

From the far end of the room someone has spotted how she has borrowed her neighbour's hand. When she pushes it away, the man still doesn't react. She remains seated on the edge of the sofa, drinking from someone else's plastic cup. Inside her, things begin to clash and shift, to become confused and, before long, unbearable. She can no longer fight back the need to cry. Preferring that no one find her in that state, she takes refuge in the kitchen. He is leaning against the refrigerator, talking to someone who is rinsing glasses at the sink. On seeing her come in, he says something that she doesn't catch. She sees his mouth form the words, but the buzzing in her ears blocks out the sound. Don't tell me you let the angel fly away? He looks baffled. She feels her eyes cloud over. Why did you let her go? The man by the sink leaves, clutching the wet glasses awkwardly between his fingers, saying, flying high, I'd say. Have you been crying? There's a dead man on your sofa, and I'm making no impression on him. She wants to meet his gaze, but she can't quite bring his eyes into focus. Here. He holds out a glass of water, and she wets her lips. And it is then that she loses control and glues her mouth to his. For a brief moment, she feels their tongues collide. She barely has time to realize they are having their first kiss when she catches sight of the angel and has to back away.

There isn't a sound in the apartment. She is on the couch, the apathetic man has gone, it's early afternoon. Around her are littered empty glasses and gorged ashtrays. In the toilet, she finds a Heineken bottle standing in a corner. The mess is even worse in the kitchen: ripped-open crisp packets, knocked-over plastic cups, a nauseating stink of beer; stains of every kind on the grey, tiled floor. Her head in a fog, she surveys the remains of the party: it looks as if people had a good time here but rushed off before she got a chance to join in. Clearing up would be a good idea, no doubt he'd thank her for it. She gathers the empty, discarded items and puts them into a large plastic bag, which she seals as tightly as possible. Crouching over the tiled floor, sponge in hand, she scrubs away at the stains, attacking the smallest ones with excessive vigour. And while trying to restore the tiles to their original colour, it comes back to her: the kiss. She giggles, like a child delighted at a piece of mischief that has gone unpunished. She closes her eyes. She wants to remember details – the texture, the temperature, the thickness of his lips – but all that remains is the sensation: that of something warm and nourishing, solid almost, passing from the depths of her throat down into her chest. She wishes she could tell him how good that kiss felt. Behind the closed door to his bedroom he is with Ange, asleep, his body wrapped around hers. Is the sensation of a kiss the same for Ange, the same for him with her? Whatever he makes of this impromptu coming together of lips, she had better not be here when the couple gets up. She breaks off her frantic scrubbing, puts on her coat, and leaves.

The rue Charlot leads to the boulevard du Temple. Music is floating down from a tinny portable radio set four or five metres above the pavement, on the edge of a construction scaffolding where three workmen – three Frenchmen of North-African origin, as she has learnt to call them – are rhythmically striking the facade of a building with their tools. One of them spots her. He whistles, and she smiles. Hey, wait a second, he yells during a pause in the song. She walks on, but her mind lags behind. She is waiting at the foot of the scaffolding, watching as the agile man lets himself down the metal poles. Straightening before her, he pulls off his gloves, tells her his name. They go to a café or perhaps straight to a hotel. Make love like in that American film she saw at the cinema, where the lead actress, throat bared, tugs down her singlet and murmurs, Do me good. Her partner helps her off with her clothes, removes his own, positions himself behind her, penetrates her, and their two bodies start to pitch and toss violently. Several times they change position; she, moaning with

pleasure, he, intent on his mission, not uttering the slightest sound, dignified male that he is. The film was *Monster's
Ball,* and not *Monster Balls* as she'd called it when buying
the tickets. *Balls* in English, the ticket clerk had pointed
out, means testicles. She had felt ridiculous.

Saturday. A week has gone by with no news. It's a bit odd,
but she doesn't want to call him. That would cast a strange
light on their slip of the lips. On the phone, she wouldn't
know where to begin. There is nothing she wants to say in
particular, except to ask him the question she asks herself.
But do you ever examine the reasons for a kiss? Either
you ignore it or you move on to the next stage; as a rule,
you refrain from making any comments. All week she has
worked evenings, from two o'clock to eleven. To get home
from the gare du Nord she takes Line 4, towards Porte-
d'Orléans, then changes to Line 1 at Châtelet if it is too
late. He had advised her not to get out at that station or to
go up the rue de Rivoli on foot. According to him, it got
dodgy at night. A friend of his had been mugged around
there at about two in the morning while taking money out
to buy cigarettes. A guy had jabbed the barrel of a gun into
his back and had taken him off to a place somewhere in the
suburbs. A forty-five-minute trip on the RER, with some
nutcase sticking a revolver into his ribs. She was sure that
afterwards no one asked the victim, whose life was nothing
more than a soft minuscule ball that his aggressor could
squeeze at will, what had gone through his mind in the

course of those forty-five minutes. When he failed to return, his girlfriend had gone to the police, who found it hilarious: a young chick coming to them to report the disappearance of the guy who had just screwed her! They didn't believe in the evaporation of the party in question; they assumed that he had skipped out on purpose. Have you called his house, miss? And how about his friends? He just went to get some cigarettes, she kept repeating. Privately, the cops went on thinking it all a big joke, and she was unable to convince them of the gravity of the situation. The boyfriend came back at nine the next morning, deathly pale, frozen stiff, physically unhurt but emotionally a wreck. He had spent three hours in a vacant lot with a gun pointed at him, waiting for a bunch of other guys who never turned up. Eventually, his aggressor had told him to beat it, but not without first relieving him of his wallet and jacket. Now, when she walks down the rue de Rivoli, she often imagines the sensation of the cold barrel pressing into her clothes, the fear raging in the pit of her stomach, the thought of death penetrating her every pore: each second cancelling out the one before, presenting itself as the last. She does her best to heed his warning; she watches out for silhouettes in the dark and avoids going that way alone at night.

Saturday night. A student she met the week before has invited her to a cabaret night in a dance studio near Bastille. Quite a few people are already there when she arrives.

Armchairs and folding chairs ring a vacant space intended to serve as the stage. She threads her way to the bar at the back of the room and orders a vodka tonic, which she drinks in small sips, perched on a high stool. The mixture is too strong. People press up against the counter, then leave again with several glasses that they hand round to the others in their party. She is the only person seated at the bar; no sign of her host who has apparently failed to show up. The women, in skimpy low-cut tops, keep bursting into laughter, dragging on their cigarettes at regular intervals. The men make an effort to keep them laughing, even as they check out the new arrivals. A few glances flutter around her, but no one makes up his mind to come over and talk.

A figure in a long black wig, dark glasses, and fake fur coat has just entered the studio and is advancing in her direction. With a languorous gait, the transvestite pushes his way through the crowd, making for the bar. He slips off his coat. A slim, androgynous body. Fascinated, she tries to distinguish what is male from what is female. She attempts to make out the eyes behind the dark glasses and locks of hair. Sensing her gaze, he turns his head. His voice is husky, his eyes still invisible; he has the smile of a woman, teasing, affectionate. He's a singer, he's appearing in the show. His name is Renée Risqué. This brief introduction over, he stops talking and from behind his tinted lenses appears to size her up. I have a proposition for you. He needs a woman to come on at the start of his act and hurl herself at him, screaming the words, you promised me. It

will make for a great opening, he reckons, and lead him
straight into his first song. She shakes her head emphati-
cally, laughing: I'm too shy. He calls over the barman, has
their drinks refilled. How about after that one? And he
takes off his glasses. His eyes are very pale, made-up. He
reminds her of someone, but of someone she has never
met. You'll have to pretend to be incredibly jealous, almost
hysterical, that's important, you understand? His will be
the third act; she'll have to come on a few seconds after
him, and then do exactly as he has just explained. Is that a
yes? Yes. Renée leaves her to go off and get ready.

The lights have been dimmed; a powerful projector
illuminates the stage. A man has stepped up to the mic and
announced the names of the artists about to perform. As
the first sketch gets underway, she finds herself unable to
follow. Her stomach churning, she plays with her glass,
picturing herself on stage: taking her first steps into the
spotlight to confront a drag artist, a practised exhibition-
ist, now playing opposite a poor girl paralysed with fear,
who has to blurt out a line as trite as you promised me and
sound convincing. Why on earth had she felt obliged to
accept? In her own life she can't recall ever having said
you promised me. If the staging were up to her, she would
say the words in a tone that was flat, calm; saddened, yet
bitter too. But certainly not screaming. However, her fake
anger would guarantee the comic effect; the audience
would laugh not thanks to her, but as a result of the contrast between her screaming and Renée's calm composure.
A man in drag and a woman having a lovers' quarrel – that

was rather ludicrous to begin with. If her voice broke with stage fright, she would make do with gestures. Act number two. Two girls in pink tutus, their mouths gleaming red, hail each other in an elaborate series of acrobatic mini-routines. She tries to put *you promised me* out of her mind, along with all the various ways to say it. . . . Renée. That's not his real name. And once she gets offstage, then what? Can you even envisage an affair that begins with the words *you promised me,* yelled out in front of a hundred-strong crowd, in a tango studio at the back of a shabby court-yard, to a man dressed in women's clothes? Her drink is too strong; the music, omnipresent. In such an atmosphere audacities of every kind seem permissible, even believing that you're in love. Applause. The two ballet dancers have finished their act. She gets down from the bar stool and walks mechanically towards the stage. No one in the assembled gathering guesses that she is the jealous, rash, and pathetic woman who comes to have it out with the per-former. She stations herself at the edge of the stage to await the arrival of Renée Risqué.

The words burst out, violent. Her field of vision shrinks, and for about twenty seconds all she sees is Renée's mouth, tensed, his eyes wide in feigned surprise. Then she hears the laughter, the first chords from the guitar, the song starting up. A man pulls her back and makes her sit down in the front row. You can let go of me now, she tells him, her fists still clenched. Around her people are staring, intrigued. Impossible to remain among all these admiring and sorry looks. She feels emptied, as though she has lived what has just happened. She goes back to the bar and orders another vodka tonic. The voice of Renée, the puppet without strings under the coloured spotlights, is everywhere now. She imagines his body naked, from his made-up face down, his cock thrusting forward as though in painful negation of the black on the rims of his eyes. He is wooing the audience, male and female alike. Inventing for them a cavalier, sarcastic character, an all-round charmer, one able to look into the void without ever falling in. Enthralled, the audience begs for more, but the prince aerialist reveals himself immune to flattery and makes a dignified exit. He comes back into the room just as the last act before the interval is beginning. Hands reach out to him as he goes by, he is congratulated, he responds with strained smiles. She forces herself not to look in his direction. They could just as well leave it at that, especially since he doesn't seem the sort to say thank you. But he comes over, just as she had hoped. After kissing her on the cheek, he orders two more drinks under the insistent stare of the barman whose excessive courtesy she fears he will find seductive. They clink glasses. Sitting up on her stool she casts a sidelong glance at Renée and catches him eyeing her breasts. Why me? He smiles. Because I wasn't expecting you, darling. The last word stings, and in spite of the perfunctory way it was said, she can't help reading it as a sign of affection. Do you want to go back with me? With the mannerisms of an actor in a third-rate action film, he has pulled off his glasses. All she can see are his clear pale eyes, far more human than the rest of him; childlike, expectant, too gentle to remain exposed. Her silence becomes consent. Renée replaces his glasses, downs the contents of his drink, and takes her by the hand. She grabs her things, catching the barman's look of disappointment on her way out. Whether the hand in hers is that of a girlfriend or a potential lover, she is no longer sure. What they will do at his place, she has no idea; anyway, *his place* was not the term he used.

When she starts to walk, she becomes aware that she is drunk. His hand guides her around the vibrant bodies planted in the studio, out over the paved courtyard, now cold and deserted. Few people in the street: it must be late. At the edge of the pavement they stop to wait for a taxi. Above all, she mustn't allow this pause to give too much room for thought; be bold, don't retreat. An image of him asleep against Ange's silken shoulder appears in her mind for a few seconds before dissolving into the gelatinous mass of her brain. They are rolling forwards. She has no memory of getting into the taxi now gliding along between the facades of unlit windows. Waves of orangey light from the street lamps crawl up the windscreen and are whisked off overhead. The rear-view mirror holds the driver's alert gaze; other vehicles are passing them. She has opened the window a crack, the fresh air helps her to sober up slightly. Renée is talking and waving his hands, turning his head in her direction from time to time. All of a sudden he no longer strikes her as mysterious or attractive, instead just terribly alien. She doesn't give a damn about what he is saying and lets the words fade without holding on to a single one. She knows now that it is not a question of her

listening, only of her following. A great deal of air lies
between them, and their two joined hands can do nothing
about it. They are both realizing that they don't have the
slightest need of each other. How to describe her presence
in this taxi, alongside a seasoned female impersonator, on
her way to an unknown destination? Misplaced? Point-
less? She thinks about how she could give him the slip. Tell
the driver to pull over, mumble an excuse, and ignore
Renée's vexed stare. But she does nothing of the sort. The
ambition that has possessed her all evening is holding her
back: to pursue what she has started to the very end.

She is sitting on a navy blue sofa. The windows are
shrouded by thick curtains. On a shelf stands the framed
photograph of a man in his forties. Sleep is beginning to
exert its gentle hold. Renée has served her a drink; some
kind of liqueur, she doesn't catch the last word. It'll make
her feel better, he announces as he comes over. He is
without his glasses now and avoids meeting her eye. Tiny
beads of sweat pearl his forehead. He straightens the magazines that are strewn across the low table, adjusts the
flowers in the vase; all this in a series of automatic, measured, and precise gestures. Then, without warning, he
takes a firm hold of the top of his long mane and tugs. The
black wig stays in his fist. A down of fine hair covers his
skull. A lot less sexy, no? He finds that hilarious. The
mouth, nose, and eyes are still there, but the top of his head
has now shrunk. His most certain feminine attribute, his

luxuriant head of hair, is an inert mass on his knees. Without it, his shaved skull resembles a convict's. She senses that with his face freed of its surrounding curls, he is revealing to her an intimate part of his body, without the slightest embarrassment. There are certain situations in which a man and a woman end up looking the same. She can't help noticing Renée's last remaining signs of femininity: the makeup, the way he crosses his legs, holds his cigarette. She clings to these arbitrary distinctions, not wanting him to revert fully to being a man. He has his head down, he combs the hair of the wig with slender fingers, then his eyes stare off into the distance. She worries that it will all go wrong now, that he'll realize the inappropriateness of their presence in this apartment. To rouse him from his torpor, she pipes up, I really liked the songs. Of course you liked them, how many singers like me have you heard? And he mimes flicking back a now-absent strand of hair. They exchange a look. He leans in to kiss her. The wig slips to the carpet. She has never kissed lips with lipstick before. She feels the hands undoing her clothes; wants to resist because she understands now that this is not what she came for. But the arousal in her nether parts draws her to Renée. He stands to remove his own clothes. The torso is smooth. Her eyes fix on his groin to see what will appear once the boxer shorts are off. The thin legs flex; the piece of cloth drops to the ground. Before her is an erect penis. He says, I'll be right back, before coming right back with a condom already on. He lies down on top of her. Briefly, the smell of rubber dominates then blends in with the smell of the room, of their secretions. She doesn't move. She wants it yet doesn't want it; or rather wants it with a woman who has a penis. A woman like the one she thought she had met. She wants it with the knowledge, the sensitivity that she imagines such a creature would possess. But what penetrates her is a man, who comes with a single brief sigh. The thin body collapses on to the breasts he hasn't touched. She may have come, but she isn't sure. Gently, she caresses Renée's back. For a minute they lie motionless. Then Renée gets up, removes the condom, picks up the wig. Come to bed, darling. Again the word stings. She does as she is told.

She is woken by the hushed variations of a voice. Sitting up on the edge of the bed, she spots her clothes carefully folded on a chair. Her tongue is furred, her head aches; slowly she gets into her clothes. Spruce and already dressed, Renée is on the phone. A silent good morning, a gesture in the direction of the table as the lips mouth *help yourself*. On the table are the tea, the orange juice, and the croissants. The perfect breakfast. All that's missing is the husband, she muses. Sitting down, she pours the tea into a cup and blows on the steaming liquid. The black hair of Renée's wig dangles and shifts against his back during the course of his telephone conversation. The long silences, punctuated by the word *yes*, prove that the person at the other end of the line is either very talkative or very upset. I'll come, Renée keeps saying; yes, I'll come, I promise. You promised me, she whispers to her unheeding cup, reproducing her indignation of the night before. Renée turns round, looking falsely annoyed at being stuck on the phone while his guest is up and about. She picks off a piece of croissant, chewing it diligently to reduce it to a saliva-soaked paste, which she doesn't swallow but goes on chewing. Eventually, Renée hangs up; what remains of the croissant goes straight to her stomach. Is it good? I'm going to have to leave pretty soon. His words come out detached, devoid of purpose, leaving her with the unpleasant impression that it is her mother who is talking to her. She imagines him with an apron round his waist. Renée is already putting on a jacket and writing his number down on a scrap of paper. He asks her if she can get a move on. They're outside his building; she doesn't recognize the surroundings. I'll call you, he says, kissing her cheek. He points out the way to the nearest métro station and strides off in the opposite direction. As she passes a dustbin, she throws away the slip of paper.

She walked by the métro station but didn't go down into it. She continued walking without knowing the way, letting her intuition guide her. She made a few conscious detours so as not to arrive home too quickly. She didn't see many people out, then remembered it was Sunday. In a bistro, she sat for a long time over an insipid coffee, staring at the glass of water that they had been reluctant to serve her. Sitting at a Formica table behind a window filled with grey light, she did nothing. She didn't watch the passersby, since there were hardly any to speak of. She remained motionless, while inside her chest a kind of acid swirled, alive with currents. Afterwards she got up for no other reason than to continue walking. Images played over her body, passing right through her. They followed an order she could not control, but whose logic could only be hers. It was not a process that could be mastered but a dream logic without absurdity, as if she were improvising a sequence on an infinite keyboard, every note of which corresponded to a crucial moment in her life. She listened: contractions, surges, waves. She was gliding from one emotion to the next, although none had any real focus. She was colliding with things that were painful, pressing her lips to disembodied mouths. She was kneading slack, thick skin that wasn't hers. She was crawling on beds of perishing flowers whose perfume was that of a beloved person. She was twisting about in every direction searching for a pair of eyes that would recognize her, rolling around between blue thistles that tickled the tender soles of her feet and made her laugh impatiently. She was walking. When she reached her landing, it all suddenly stopped. She had to make a conscious gesture to find a key to open a door. Then there was only a single reality.

A small red light is blinking in the semi-darkness of the living room. She takes off her shoes and coat, stretches out on the carpet. She is tired. From the floor, the furniture looks gigantic; its straight edges map bands of blackness across the walls. She reaches out an arm and presses the play button on the answering machine. The recorded voice lodges itself in the corners of the walls, in the folds of the pillows, under the high and the low table. The voice says it is calling to see how she is, that it hopes she enjoyed the party, that it has something to offer her, that she has to call back. There's a beep, followed by silence. Inside her something swells, triggering a sense of well-being. Her finger is still on the button. She presses, and the voice repeats the message. She ought to go on listening until it no longer has any effect on her. Create the antidote through repetition. So that in case he eventually starts talking to her in a direct way, she can survive. After hearing the message four times, she takes her finger off play and picks up the phone. She barely has time to say a few polite words before Ange, in top form, monopolizes the conversation, without the least intention of relinquishing it. This weekend they're having a dinner party at their place, his place, Ange corrects herself, they would really like her to come. She doesn't know what to say; she is disappointed. A dinner party to which others will be invited, and once again she is denied exclusive access to him. When at last Ange stops talking, she screws up her courage and asks to speak to him. He's gone out, says Ange, but she'll pass on the message. She hangs up. There is still no light on in the room. She lies down on the bed, fully dressed. The last sound she hears is the gurgling of her stomach.

She undresses, showers, gets dressed again, and goes out. The platforms in the métro are packed with commuters champing at the bit. Ready to push aside anyone that gets in their way, they charge forward when the doors open, pouncing on the handful of free seats. Their only master is time. Everything they do is fast, to claw back the fleeting minutes, as if they stood to gain a bonus by pushing back the end of their lives. She is wedged upright between two stony shoulders that have no intention of budging to give her more room. She can smell the reek of strong scent, feel someone's breath on the back of her neck, the tension of mute, sweating bodies packed into a narrow carriage, bodies too close to inspire in one another anything but a mutual sense of suppressed revulsion. She shifts a little to keep the blood flowing in her legs. Someone gives her a dirty look for not knowing how to keep still, for disrupting the smooth progress of the journey. Inside the station, commuters are gathered around the departure boards. Many are alone. They're waiting for a number or a letter to appear before rushing off to the platform from where they'll set out. She recognizes the voice of her colleague announcing the 07:10 TGV as she heads towards the small door marked STAFF ONLY, which they refer to as the stage door. The last time she took the train was over two years ago. She can't remember the exact date, only the price of the return ticket. Six hundred and twenty-four francs to go from Paris to Montpellier and back, to bid goodbye to a friendship. Montpellier was where Marion lived. Perhaps she still lives there. She doesn't know. Has made no attempt to find out, not since the day she held Marion in her arms before boarding the train and promised to keep in touch more often. Call me. Yes, yes; you too; of course. At the time they believed what they were saying. And yet, in that instant, she also knew that it was goodbye, that the parting would be final. A dissonance in their voices, their stares, a suspect rush of mutual warmth – and she understood that their friendship was ending for good. It made no difference whether she said it or not. Take a good look at her, she had told herself, because you won't see her again. She wanted to take with her a particular image of her friend; the last image seemed critical. And so she had tried to commit Marion's face to memory. Today she wonders if it might not have been that look, taken by Marion to mean that she should leave, which led to their breaking off relations. Perhaps. Behind the window of the train that has been in the station too long, there is Marion with her yellow T-shirt and tiny bag, clutching her sunglasses. That is when she realizes there is nothing harder than looking into someone's eyes through the window of a train. It's no longer possible to touch that person, no longer possible to talk. There is only the look in the eyes, the intuition that the other person's feelings more or less match your own. And seeing the expression on Marion's face had made her want to cry, Marion who was condemned not to follow the train, to stand stock-still on the platform, to recede until she disappeared from within the frame of the carriage window. They were both smiling for all they were worth, struggling to contain that ridiculous pressure expanding the walls of their chests. By the end, they were just doing one thing: waiting for the damn train to leave. She had almost forgotten it was the last time. And the moment the carriage jolted into motion, the relief. At last Marion was gone from behind the window; her eyes were no longer there, tempting her to climb back out and explain what by now seemed inevitable. There was only an unvarying succession of houses, then fields, then hills. The serenity inspired by a world now devoid of human forms, a world that was but did not seek to be. She clearly remembers how there had been no one next to her. She vowed eternal gratitude to the SNCF ticket-seller who chose that particular place for her. She imagined him at his computer screen, telling himself that he could save the little lass from being squeezed in or getting bothered at lunchtime by some person in the next seat taking out his sandwich of soft bread and moist ham. She imagined that the ticket-seller had recognized her voice and granted her that small favour. Delighted, she had lifted the centre armrest. Two whole seats to herself. Relief at leaving Marion behind had lasted a good hour. Travelling through space without moving from her seat no doubt catalyzed that feeling of buoyancy. Gazing out at the landscape sucked back by the speed, she had dozed off. The need to take stock became apparent only when she awoke. Sleep had given her back a clear head.

Marion was the only one who knew what had happened to her. Before they reached adulthood, she had told Marion about the rite of passage. At the time, she referred to it in that way for she was trying to extract from the event a kind of pride. No doubt in order to bear it, to believe that its only consequence had been to help her grow up faster than the others. They had never spoken about it again, not since she told Marion the first time in the drab surroundings of a school playground. But was *tell* the right word to use in this case? She had hurriedly, somewhat randomly, strung together a series of words describing what she thought had happened to her. With a mixture of conceit and disgust, she had described what she had seen, felt, and said, and it was perhaps then that she could have grasped the magnitude of the event. In Montpellier, she had realized that Marion had forgotten nothing. The three days they spent together had been slow and heavy going. There had been enough time to understand who her friend had become, and with such a person, she could not share her past and sustain relations in the present. For as long as the conversation had moved between matters of little importance, she had not noticed. But as often happens when people live and sleep in the same room, vigilance slips; living at such close quarters soon becomes trying unless you agree to go beyond mere pleasantries. And the moment they ventured down that path, she had sensed her own secret steering her friend's remarks. Though no mention of it was ever made, it crept into Marion's thinking, formed the basis of the logic she was using to size up her guest. As if Marion could no longer conceive of her except in terms of that central piece of information, the event confessed to years earlier. The more they talked, the harder it became to bear, and the more Marion kept returning to it, both of them coming to realize, with each passing hour, how little they had in common. Marion thought she could use the rite of passage to find a path back to intimacy, whereas for her part, she dreaded the slightest, even tacit mention of the episode. Ever since that visit, neither she nor Marion had made any attempt to get back in touch.

In front of her is the microphone. To her right, the computer. A new message has just appeared on her screen, with the number of the train, its destination, its time of arrival, the platform where it has pulled in. She presses the red button at the base of the microphone. The three notes of the mini-arpeggio ring out. Over to her. To talk, she uses her other voice, the one she draws up from the depths of her throat, that gives her the authority of an SNCF announcer. Articulating each syllable, she feeds the impatient travellers the details that will enable them to find their platforms.

At 4:45 p.m., she leaves the office, passes through the stage door in the reverse direction. If she had a mask, she would have chosen that moment to put it on. With a sweeping, pathetic gesture, like Renée with his dark glasses. It would be a plastic mask, held on by a piece of elasticated string, in the likeness of Everyman. Who would do the same job she did, but who would then get to live another life every evening. Unfortunately, the only masks on sale in the shops are those of celebrities. At the end of the day, the station concourse – a vast structure with a part-glass roof, lit from below by the nimbus of orange-tinted globes – always seems to take longer to cross. The travellers haven't really changed places: only their identities have changed. The ones rushing head down for the exits are those long accustomed to lonely arrivals. They are generally travelling on business and never go anywhere without a clear aim. The rest of the crowd wanders about with their noses in the air, looking for signs or a familiar face. The only people who approach strangers are the tramps. One night, she remembers seeing one of them land a couple of slaps on a guy who'd been waiting at a café terrace with his girlfriend. The couple was enjoying a quiet kiss when the tramp came over to ask for money. He could hardly get his words out, was emitting guttural sounds in a language that no one could grasp except him. The boyfriend had shaken his head without so much as a glance. The tramp went round behind him, then clapped the filthy palms of both hands down hard on the two healthy pink cheeks. Astonishingly, the boyfriend relied only on his voice to ward off his assailant, who hurried away, limping. A beefy security guard set off in pursuit.

It seems that tonight the tramps are not out to cause a stir. They are wandering among the travellers as usual, gauging with practised eye each one's willingness to part with a few euros. Outside the brasseries in front of the station, foreign tourists are studying the menus, perplexed. She walks along the boulevard Denain. At a bakery, she stops to buy a pain au chocolat with almonds. One small piece at a time, she consumes the soft, greasy confection, which she chews with the skill of an expert. Once the pastry is finished, she goes into Promod. The only people inside the store are women, their eyes riveted on the clothes hanging on rails at various heights. Pounding techno-music complements the decor, making for a reasonably tolerable whole. By the entrance to the store, a young security guard is shaking his thick thigh in time to the beat. She observes him and wonders where his thoughts are sending him: to a bar, a half lager, to a football match, a serial on TV . . . After Work. She walks over to the displays. With one hand, she slides the hanging clothes along their rails. No one is talking around her. She picks out an item at random, checking its size. She makes her way over to the fitting rooms, where a young woman briefly asks her how many articles she has. The cubicle is cramped; with the curtain drawn, she has her nose pressed up against the mirror. On to the single coat peg she piles the jumper, price tag still dangling, her jacket, and her tank top. Ten seconds later, the small bundle collapses to the floor, where she leaves it. She slips on the black jumper and surveys the result. Tugs it down, pulls up the sleeves, adjusts the neck, twists round to see the effect from the back, assessing whether any added appeal might be derived from the combination of this jumper and her chest. But everywhere the material is creased, too loose, makes her seem ugly. Needless to say, no eighteen-euro jumper is going to turn her into a model, and she concludes that it's her body whose proportions are wrong, not the jumper. She slips back into her clothes — clothes she has worn long enough for them to fit. Outside the changing room, there is no sign of the salesgirl. She rolls the jumper up into a ball and stuffs it into her bag, then proceeds through the displays, her eyes fixed on the automatic glass doors. She keeps her pace steady. She knows the alarm will go off soon. The shoppers pay her no heed, not yet realizing that it is she who has made off with a measly eighteen-euro jumper from Promod. You earn your own living, don't you, miss? The security guard hasn't spotted her yet either; his thigh is still moving to the beat, his eyes locked on to the beer he is going to drink two hours and forty-six minutes from now. She is coming up to the detector panels. The guard turns his head, sees her; she purses her lips but keeps on walking. The techno-music slowly leaves her ears and is replaced by the din of car engines. She can now feel the tickle of fresh air on her face. She is out, the alarm has not gone off, she is safe. It takes her several seconds to grasp what has just happened. She hardly dares smile, for fear that a passerby will catch her expression and report her on the spot. The métro entrance is in sight, no one is going to point the finger now. An act gone unnoticed, lost amid a thousand others, missed by an infallible electronic device. Defiance in the face of technology and science, the system failed. Pardoned without even having been convicted. Only in her own eyes will she have been, at one time in her life, a black-jumper thief.

Back home, she wolfs down a bowl of pasta garnished with bits of onion and tomato. Dinner over, she takes the jumper out of her bag. The security disc is tightly affixed to the wool. She fails to see how she might get it off. Giving up, she folds the jumper and puts it away with the rest of her things. Later, she dozes off in front of a TV serial in which the heroine, a woman in her forties who looks ten years younger onscreen, can't make up her mind between her taciturn husband on the one hand and her childish lover on the other, because she loves them both equally but not in the same way. Love. There is something about that word that makes her sick to the core. She prefers to go it alone, without someone to make her believe he can raise her above reality. Love bears the mark of whoever gives birth to it. You only truly recognize it once, the first time, whether it's tender or painful. Hers, her first love – it has taken her years to admit – was hardly enviable.

Once a man had told her to go see a shrink because when she'd felt his penis inside her, she couldn't go on. In a calm voice she had simply said, pull out. No shriek of panic, no pleading. Blushing, the man had pulled out. For a while they lay there, side by side. It was then that he told her she ought to see a shrink. After that he got dressed: would she mind telling him when she changed her mind? And off he went. It didn't occur to her that he could be upset; she believed him.

He calls on Thursday. She realizes that she has been waiting for him to phone. How are things? He never presents himself as if he were sure he is the only man who calls her. She likes that mark of familiarity. Fine, and Ange? Fine. She confirms that she will be going to the dinner party. Several of his friends will be there, he informs her. One of them is really nice, you'll see. His voice becomes that of a travelling salesman: a tacit way to let her know he thinks the man in question ought to be to her liking. Soon he'll be listing this person's qualities to her. She feels like asking if he also offers home delivery. But instead she says nothing. As does he. The mood has changed; she senses his embarrassment at the other end of the line. About what happened the other night, I'd had a bit to drink. There, he's mentioned it. Not to tell her that he enjoyed it, but for her to rid him of his guilt at desiring another woman. A few banal words and his heart slots back into place. The message seems clear: what happened was just one of those things. By making it clear from the outset that the kiss could only have bothered her, he's denying her the right to have the least feeling in his regard. For him, there is no question, their brief moment of intimacy had been simply a consequence of his drunkenness. She takes a breath. No offence taken; I was the one who kissed you. See you tomorrow. Then she hangs up.

The following afternoon, on her way back from the gare du Nord, she drops by a stationer's. She chooses a sheet of wrapping paper. Multicoloured lines on a grey background. The paper is smooth and has a satin finish. The man behind the counter rolls it into a slender tube, over which he slips an elastic band. Leaving the shop, she wonders how she should hold it. It could be a sword or a walking stick, or a magic wand. She ends up tucking it under her arm. Because, obviously, what she is carrying is a baguette.

Ange is in mid-conversation as she opens the door. She seems pleased to see her and gives her a kiss on both cheeks before ushering her into the hallway. The fragrance of boeuf bourguignon fills the apartment. Her arms are still in the sleeves of her jacket as Ange takes hold of the collar to hang it up. She says, I'm late, but gets no answer from Ange. She keeps her handbag with her. The zip wouldn't work after she put the package inside, trying not to crumple the wrapping paper, which was already damaged at the corners. Ange is about to charge into the living room, majestic in her high heels, when she holds her back by the arm. I have something for you. As best she can, she extracts the package from her bag. Ange's eyes fix on the multicoloured lines as her fingers eagerly press the wrapping paper. Seconds later, the paper is on the floor and in Ange's large hands the jumper suddenly resembles a small furry black animal. Ange likes it – she hasn't seen the Promod label yet, not to mention the magnetic security disc. Ange puts the jumper down on a chair. I'll introduce you. He has appeared in the doorway to the kitchen. He smiles at her, but Ange already is leading her off to present her to the other guests.

There are four men and two women. Some are standing, some are sitting, as if they were posing for a photograph. When she follows Ange into the room, they freeze, look her over, size her up, and she finds this collective evaluation irksome. She kisses the women, shakes hands with the men, which they always find a bit surprising. But that's how she prefers it; she doesn't have to explain. It's always the same: whenever she touches a person for the first time, her eyes have a tendency to look off to the side. But now she makes an effort; she wouldn't want them to assume immediately that she is shy. Ange enunciates first names. She recognizes her own but doesn't remember any of the others. She doesn't do it on purpose: her memory refuses to register that kind of thing the first time round. Ange invites her to sit down. Somewhat laboriously, the conversations get going again. The two women perched on the sofa offer her embarrassed smiles. No excess emotion, no sudden effusions: they're figuring out how to interact under the circumstances. She looks at third fingers and counts two wedding rings. Which leaves only two possibilities as to who the guy she is supposed to like might be. Ange presses a glass of white into her hand, then, just as quickly, beats a hasty retreat to the kitchen, where he must be busy stirring solids and liquids in a large pot. As for her, she has no right to see him until he is good and ready. His hair must smell of onion and bay leaf, his forehead of the salt from his sweat. In the meantime, she turns her attention to the two bachelors. Neither one pays her any attention, engaged as they are in a discussion that requires

[33]

all the seriousness they can muster. One has a slight stoop, gesticulates a lot; the other has metal-framed glasses and from time to time runs the tip of his tongue over his lips. The couple sitting on the other couch has stopped talking in low voices. They are inspecting the contents of the room, he from the right, she from the left, to be sure they won't miss a thing. A real bit of teamwork. They'll compare notes when they go to bed: what they liked, what they might eventually buy for themselves. Even so, she detects a hint of boredom stirring in her neighbours. Her silent presence is beginning to be embarrassing. It won't be long, she senses, before someone tries to draw her out. She takes a sip of white wine so as to seem busy. The husband sits up and leans slightly towards her, about to ask a question. At which point Ange sweeps into the living room, barks out, dinner's ready, and makes everyone jump. She suddenly feels like saying to Ange, who is increasingly agitated, that they're not deaf, but instead she just sketches a faint smile in the direction of the husband and wife to show that she has noted their intention to enter into oral communication with her.

Everyone heads meekly over to the table. Ange assigns the places; someone points out that there are nine people present and it won't be possible to seat men and women alternately. She hangs back and takes a quick look inside the kitchen. He has his hands in the water, his head tilted back as he blows strands of hair from in front of his eyes. After a few seconds, he realizes that she is watching him. He gives her a wink and whispers, I'm coming. I'm coming: a promise that has the effect of an order. If only there were just the two of them, she wishes, in this archetypal early twenty-first-century kitchen. Because now she understands *I'm coming* to mean *Leave me alone*, and not *I'll be with you in a second*. She retreats. The outside world has suddenly shrunk, and the inside has become dense and enormous. She tells herself that she must look like the Michelin-tire man. But no one seems to mind. She proceeds robotically over to the table and, without thinking, flops down on to an empty chair. She doesn't realize straight away that she is the one Ange is speaking to. The tone of voice is impatient. No, not there, that's my place. Ange points a commanding finger at another chair at the end of the table. She says nothing. She gets up and slips between one of the husbands and the man with the stoop. There now remains just one empty seat, directly opposite hers, reserved for the chef, who at last makes his entrance. A thunderous chorus of *ahh* from the guests, the metal sound of cutlery. Each plate contains a small triangle of toast, a dollop of crème fraîche, and a slice of smoked salmon. She is going to have to force herself. Smoked salmon is served at one out of every two dinner parties she is invited to. She recalls the supermarket slogan: "Chic and cheap." It feels as if she is chewing an oily piece of salted rubber. This show-dinner is starting to get on her nerves. As she sits there eating her slice of dead fish, trying not to feel sick, the guests resume their conversation, now that their stomachs have been gratified. They are discussing one couple's most recent trip. To Iran. The woman keeps going on about how she had to wear a veil over there. The others adopt sympathetic demeanours; as for her, she seems to have found it rather amusing. She even tells Ange and the other woman that if they ever decide to go, she'll give them the address of the shop where she bought the cloth for the veil.

The plates are now empty; Ange is clearing the table. After retreating to his laboratory under the watchful eye of his partner, he returns with a steaming casserole of boeuf bourguignon. Everyone holds out a plate to the chef, who serves the food himself. She takes advantage of the profusion of outstretched arms to give the porcelain a discreet wipe with her napkin and rid it of some of the salmon taste. Hardly has she done so when the man with the stoop grabs her plate and declares in a loud voice, Ladies first. Here then is the young man who has been reserved for her. Charming; perhaps he'd also like a round of applause? Someone says, it's crazy how Le Pen . . . General approbation, use is made of the words *alarming, worrying, sad.* They all seem to have given the problem quite some thought. She notes that they take pleasure in agreeing. That strikes her as a bit sterile. Timidly, she puts her question: Out of interest, do you have many French people of North-African extraction among your acquaintances? Looks fly in all directions. I mean, it's a strange term, *French of North-African extraction.* One of the husbands fixes her with an annoyed stare. I really don't see the connection. Neither do the others apparently. She looks to the end of the table for support, but he is leaning over to

Ange and not looking in her direction. The husband is back on the attack, his tone more aggressive. And you, miss, do you know many? She can't stand people who use the word *miss* to remind you that you are less mature or more unmarried than they are. It's not miss, actually, she would like to shoot back. That would have put him in his place. Luckily, Ange, ever the perfect hostess, enquires if everyone is enjoying the delicious meal lovingly concocted by her boyfriend lover fiancé partner sweetheart, i.e., the guy she allows herself to be groped by. But since everyone is waiting to hear if the girl at the end of the table knows, might one go so far as to say frequents — what was it she called them? — French people of North-African extraction, Ange's question goes unanswered. Do you like it? asks Ange again. Everyone makes *mmm* sounds with their mouths; compliments are made to the chef and to his hostess. A moment of true harmony. But the husband has not lost the scent: from the look in his eyes, she sees that he regrets not being able to sink his teeth into that piece of woman whose discretion gives him the right to pick on her. The conversation resumes, but she is no longer following.

She thinks back to her dream of the night before. In a sunlit street, elegantly dressed young women are pushing prams. There is a small crowd of them, all advancing at the same pace. They are filled with a quiet joy, which seems to suit them. At first, she can't make out what they're pushing in front of them. Finally she turns, her point of view changes, and she sees what's in the prams: children, all too big to be ferried around like that; their limbs gathered in, folded tightly in front of them to fit between the metal struts of the pram; children dressed in military fatigues and all of them holding in one arm, against the length of their bodies, a machine gun practically as big as they are. She could perhaps tell them about that, but discussing dreams at dinner parties is not done. In one gulp, she finishes off her glass. She sees the hand of the man with the stoop reaching out for her plate, on which some tiny puddles of a rich, dark sauce remain. Or did you want to mop up with some bread? Without waiting for her to reply, he whisks her plate away. She wonders whether to pretend to laugh or reward him for his effort. No thank you, she replies politely. She notices the table is being cleared; he hasn't looked at her since that wink in the kitchen. Ange gets up with the pile of plates, he follows her out. With the couple momentarily gone, the delicately spun bonds among the guests start to fray. The two husbands lower their voices and turn to their wives; the two bachelors slowly light cigarettes; for a few moments, everyone abandons his or her social role, enjoys a well-deserved mid-performance break. For an instant, she fears giving in to the physical urge to rush out the door. That bloody silence is starting to get to her. They're acting in a seven-man locked room drama, and it feels as if she's the last dead woman who has yet to grasp the rules of hell. She pours herself another glass of red wine, which she forces herself to sip for appearance's sake. Someone decides to open another bottle to put everyone more at ease. Since they all know each other already and she is acquainted only with the hosts, she senses there will be no escape: she is in for a full-blown interrogation. With everybody listening religiously as though her life were somehow thrilling. And sure enough, the guy with the stoop makes an exceptional effort and asks her what she does for a living. By chance, the question falls during a lull in the conversation, and the entire group feels invited to stick their noses in: the six others wait for the rather unassuming girl at the end of the table to speak up; damn it, it's about time she contributed to the discussion. They are in such a hurry to find out what box to put her in. She imagines the husband must be rubbing his hands under the table, delighted at this perfect opportunity to go back on the offensive. All eyes are on her: a court waiting to hear the correct answer. She isn't quite sure that she speaks their language any more. There is only one way to find out. I'm a prostitute.

She said it so well, with a mixture of professional pride and personal regret, that the others believed her – she sensed it at once. There is a brief freeze-frame. The man with the stoop feels a bit of a jerk now that he has his answer. He manages a polite rejoinder, all the same: And have you been in the business long? Maybe he's not quite so lacking in imagination, after all. Quick as a flash, her voice steady. Ten years, I started young. Even the virulent husband is taken aback; a few more details and he could almost feel sorry for her. She knows that none of the four men will dare ask her how much she charges. Besides, they have ceased to look upon her with kindness: she is no longer innocent. Only the two women continue to regard

her with curiosity. And then, all at once, a heartfelt cry
from the wearer of Iranian veils: life can't be easy for you.
It isn't sarcasm or disdain, but sincerity, and it plunges all
present into what, from the outside, appears to be intense
introspection. At which point he returns with a strawberry
tart, Ange, and nine dessert plates. Ange enquires about
the subject of their conversation. She then realizes that she
has overstepped the mark. I was talking about my work,
she says eventually, as the others maintain an obstinate
silence. Yes, it's unusual, says Ange, people always forget
that's a job, too. Frowns from the guests, surprised by such
tolerance on the part of their hostess. Silence reigns as
Ange nimbly divides the tart into near-equal portions. The
sugary taste in the mouth helps the dinner to continue as if
nothing had happened. No one else deigns to show any
interest in her now; the man with the stoop hasn't even
dared lay another finger on her plate. One thing is for
sure, there won't be any more questions. She wonders how
many of them will remember the interlude that briefly disturbed the course of their evening. There was a prostitute
at Thingamabob's the other night; she seemed like a nice
girl. She imagines herself as an anointed saboteur of the
social order. A single word from her and she had switched
identity in their eyes: reality had cracked in a place they
never would have suspected.

Before leaving, she went to the toilet. On opening the door
to come out, she found the husband standing in front of

her. Laughter was emanating from what seemed to be a very distant living room. At first she thought the husband was waiting his turn, but he made no move to enter. He took her for a different person; she had snared him with an unpremeditated lie. With dexterous movements of his thumb, the husband keyed her number onto the screen of his mobile phone; he asked for her first name again before entering the toilet.

She kisses air, pressing her cheek to each guest's in turn. Ange, tipsy, falls into her arms before he accompanies her to the front door. She is on one side of the threshold, he is on the other. He reels off end-of-evening phrases: thanks for coming, did you have a good time, I hope you enjoyed the food. She nods, understands that they won't mention the kiss again. A mishap unworthy of further thought. Now all that stands between them is the false impression he has formed of her, but she feels unable to persuade him otherwise. The battle would be lost in advance if she were the one who decided to lead it. She turns towards the stairwell. I'll call you. The door banging shut drowns out the last syllable. As she leaves the building, the street is deserted except for a couple walking in her direction. The woman is pushing an empty pram. A few paces behind her, a man is carrying a baby in his arms. As the man passes in front of her, the child gives her a little wave.

She thinks of her own death. As if it were a cessation, the sudden interruption of a current, the annihilation of what she is. At any moment. She concentrates on the physical duration of time. Each instant could be the last, yet each instant, once over, becomes a reprieve. And one by one, the instants pass, nothing happens, or rather everything does: she doesn't die. As if waiting for the impact of a shot that will be fired from an unknown direction and hit her in an unknown place, she forces herself to remain still to try to feel the imminence of her death. All she perceives now is her own breathing – automatic, beyond her control, capable of being smothered every time she inhales. She might have stopped breathing, swallowed her last gasp of air: she might have croaked without even realizing it. The exercise brings on a twinge of panic, but afterwards her confidence returns and she feels less vulnerable. She wonders what the last image she sees will be, what fleeting morsel of the world will flicker in front her eyes before it vanishes. She would never know what image sat on her retinas at the zero hour of their countdown to decomposition; she would never know what message was being relayed by the last nerve impulse to enter her brain. As a child she used to imagine herself dying, then coming back to life to spy on the reactions of those closest to her. She enjoyed imagining the consequences of her death. The scene was always constructed more or less along the same lines. Those who had known her were crying, telling each other how much they had loved her, and from this grief, which she pictured in all sorts of ways, she drew strength. She was getting her revenge on them; her dying was their punishment. Much later she found out that this mode of behaviour wasn't peculiar to her. Psychologists have a term for this childish instinct, which is supposed to disappear when you reach adulthood.

She is still in bed, studying the outline on the wall of the sun's rays filtered through the window, when the phone rings. His voice. She can't believe that he's calling her so soon, less than twenty-four hours since they last saw each other. From the clipped, cut-off sound of his words, she can tell that he is annoyed. Because of the jumper, no doubt. Ange can't have appreciated the fact that a piece of plastic was left attached to the material, and he is now going to order her to find a way to get that damn security disc off. He already must have spent the entire morning wearing himself out, directed by Ange's nervous commands. No, I'm not asleep. It's about last night. She senses that he is troubled, which makes her uneasy in turn. She could come clean with him about her shoplifting from Promod, but she fears the effect that learning of her spur-of-the-moment crime would have on him. It's about what you told the others. He says that all his friends really believed that she was a prostitute. It can't have done them any harm to meet one. Did you think you were being clever? He finds it pretty odd to lie like that, for no reason. Such is the paradox of a lie: so long as everyone equates it with the truth, they're prepared to accept it, but the moment a lie is discovered to be a lie, it's seen as a personal insult. Why should there always be complex reasons for lying? Truth, that endless Chinese box, is not terribly attractive. A lie at least has the merit of being complete and is often far more coherent than its opposite. Apparently she has succeeded in putting off the man applying for the post of boyfriend. They believed me, after all; I must really look the part. From the sound of his breathing in the receiver, she senses that he has relaxed slightly. And this subtle change in mood indicates that he got the message. Her heart reminds her of its presence: something simultaneously shrinks and expands inside her chest. Neither one of them speaks. She waits for him to come out with the usual words, the ones that restrict her to a clearly defined category, the female friend. But this time silence no longer seems enough for him to push on with his usual, preformatted phrases. They remain silent, as if to absorb the transformation that is taking place. And through this interruption in the automatic rhythm of their verbal exchanges, she has the sense that, for the first time, they understand each other. For the first time – she can feel it – the thought of a relationship with her has crossed his mind. Eventually he says, Ange is calling me, I have to go.

For a long while she continues holding the phone, half out of the sheets, her head back on the pillow. One by one, she connects the images that have lingered behind her eyes, the spectres of distant things. A dreamlike association that she can nevertheless control. The bit of excess skin on her grandmother's neck which she would push at with her finger, intrigued, whenever the old lady took her in her arms; the two straps and the metal buckles of her enormous satchel which once she shrugged it off, would leave her feeling as light as a feather; the unease she felt in the damp corridors she had to walk down to get to the cellar; her frenzied, heart-clenched dance behind the closed door of her room on the afternoon she saw that her underpants were stained with an unfamiliar blood; the igloo she started but never finished because the temperature climbed too fast; the mad dash in an ambulance after she cut her hand open while slicing the Gruyère; the steep climb up the stairs to get to her lesson with Mademoiselle Rousseau, who would complain whenever she crossed her legs while playing the piano; the hours of detention spent gazing out hypnotically at the magnificently empty playground; the filaments of the climbing rope that would work themselves into her palms while her irate gym teacher yelled at her to get her arse moving; the ridiculous slippers she'd kept on by mistake to go to high school; the comment at the bottom of her report card, year after year the same: inattentive, could do better; the mighty slap she'd received from big Caro in a corner of the schoolyard; the exquisite fur of the neighbour's cat as it grazed itself against her legs every afternoon when she came home from school. The pink room in her grandparents' house. She immediately shuts off the projector in her mind and rubs her hands over her face. The sun has sunk down behind a building; she shivers.

The more use we make of our memories, the more they turn into fables, which we keep turning over in our minds so as to not forget who we are, their moral serving as our solace or our torture. But let us continue.

Eleven-thirty a.m.; she still has some time. She walks up the street towards the market. Between the two rows of parallel stalls, the crowd moves slowly. Shoulders twist right and left, boring a path through the throng. The market gardeners, with their ruddy, florid complexions, plunge sturdy fingers darkened with vegetable dust into the mounds of produce. In a booming voice, they call out the prices. With rapid, precise gestures, they juggle the colourful, organic forms with the tarnished weights of their scales, the tiny coins and notes, which they lob into a small box set prominently in the midst of their wares. In an open-sided van, a refrigerated Punch and Judy show, a woman in a white apron, her fingers sheathed in plastic, is delicately removing from her display, as if they were precious stones, small round goat's cheeses, wedges of creamy Brie or rich Comté, fresh eggs, slabs of butter sliced off with cheese wire. She wraps each customer's order in wax paper. Standing amidst buckets of floating flowers, a man and a woman, their index fingers streaked with cuts from garden shears, are picking out delicately flowered stems to make a harmonious bouquet, which will then be wrapped in cellophane and showy ribbons and conveyed upside down to a mother or wife. For her, they are the last remaining survivors. People who still know the earth's moods, who know that carrots don't grow on trees, that cheese doesn't come ready-made from the udders of cows. She loves the resistance and the solidity, the tenacity of these

visitors from another world, a world where they don't need
to pile into underground train carriages, to breathe in
exhaust fumes, or to pretend they don't hear the amorous
panting of their neighbours coming through the wall.

She has spotted a box of raspberries. She slips her way
among those warily surveying the goods laid out before
them. The stall holder calls her my pretty one and hands
her the box wrapped up in brown paper. She reaches inside
the bag, eager for the soft, sweet fruit. She gobbles the
raspberries one after another in rapid succession, leaving
drops of pink juice on her fingers. She walks down several
streets, scanning the buildings for signs of human presence,
before being sucked into the warm sickly breath of a métro
entrance. Just as she is going through the turnstile, she feels
a body insert itself against her back so as to pass through
the two metal bars at the same time. She is instantly thrust
to the other side, and doesn't get a chance to see the face of
the man striding off down one of the long side tunnels. For
a few seconds she is left stunned by this contact, as brief as
it was powerful. She turns instinctively down a corridor
lined with advertising posters, which she scans with a sideways glance, without slowing her pace. Just then, a name
on one of them catches her eye. She knows that name,
knows it because it's hers. She stops, rereads the first and
last name buried in among a list of other names which
mean nothing to her. Those are her names, all right. A
group of travellers jostles past her, annoyed at finding a
stationary body planted there. The poster is for a play that
is opening the following week. The names of the lead

actors are printed in thick white letters at the top of the bill. Also listed are the producers and the technicians who have worked on the show. Red lettering has been reserved for the box-office phone number. She rummages in her bag. She takes out a lidless black ballpoint and uses it to scribble down the number on the raspberry-juice-stained brown paper.

The platform seems rather empty. Maybe the group that overtook her in the corridor just now, which seemed to consist of many people at the time, has found unlikely hiding places along the narrow concrete strip which is only long enough for four minimalist benches. Or else they have gone on their way, as a dense frantic mob, through secret passageways of the Parisian transport network. Her footsteps ring out under the tiled vault. Up ahead of her, a small crowd has gathered and is silently staring down at something on the ground. She moves closer. At first she thinks she's looking at a large, bulging canvas sack. But the sack has shoes and hands pressed together under a creased, grimy face. For a moment, she does what the others are doing: she observes the man lying on the ground. There is a barely dried bloodstain on his temple. She shoots an alarmed glance at the people around her, but for all their signs of agitation, they remain engrossed in their detailed scrutiny of the man. They seem fascinated, mesmerized by the spectacle of the totally lifeless body, which, deep down, they find repellent. The man's immobility strikes her as more and more suspect. She reaches out a cautious hand in the direction of his shoulder. The travellers take several steps back, their eyes swivel by several degrees. The voice of one onlooker comes straight at her. Do you know him? Asked as if it were a warning, the question almost causes her to have doubts. Quick, mustn't get distracted by the reproachful tone. (The film would be a Franco-American co-production. In this scene everything takes a sudden turn for the worse: the young heroine is discovered next to the body, which she has touched – it can't be said often enough, when you find a dead body, keep your mitts off. A passerby raises the alarm, the police find out that she and the dead man had been lovers; to cut a long story short, the guilty party – there is always a guilty party – is her.) What difference does that make? She can't see what difference that makes. And says so to the young nosy parker, who proceeds to chew his lip, either because for him it does make a difference – obviously it does, someone you know and a complete stranger can hardly be the same thing, how can you say otherwise – or else because it doesn't make any difference and it is he, who arrived on the scene before her, who should have reached out to touch the man's shoulder, just as she is doing now. She brings her fingers down on the almost adhesive surface of the coat. Tentatively, as if the mocking head of a clown might suddenly rear up at her, frightening in its gargantuan laughter. She presses through the layers of clothing to touch him, a piece of skin, muscle, bone, so that he, in turn, can feel someone there by his side. After maintaining the pressure for a few seconds, she draws back her hand. The body is not moving. As if she has just performed an act of exemplary courage, those around her begin talking again. (Script changes: the American side of the co-production is now in charge; no way can they leave the ending as it is. The heroine finds the body just in time for the emergency services to get to the scene and for the man – who through a series of clever flashbacks we discover was her lover – to escape death.) Someone asks if he's moving, someone asks what's the matter with him, someone asks . . . A shiver passes in a wave up through her scalp. Pursing her lips and ignoring the questioning stares, she manages to get to her feet and pushes through the circle of onlookers. She strides back off the way she came. She meets no resistance; the corridors are empty. Passing by the poster, she is tempted to check if her name is still printed on its glossy surface. She goes all the way back up to the ticket windows, where there is no queue. Inside, two men in khaki-green outfits bearing the RATP logo are in plenary session. The window is transparent, as transparent as a clean window should be, but the men appear not to see her through it. Bringing her mouth closer, she says in a loud voice that there is a man down there who is not well; they ought to send someone along. Her words smash into the glass partition, dribbling down it in long, invisible streaks. Inside the ticket office, the two human puppets continue to hold forth, voluble specimens of a species soon to be extinct. She is not in the métro but in a museum, where, as everyone knows, it would be ridiculous to talk to any of the stuffed creatures in the display cases. She gives three short raps; the two heads turn. One head, wearing the expression of a cashier on a bad day, leans down to the opening at the base of the window. There's a man on the platform in terrible shape; can someone go and help him? Between the time it takes for her to see that he has understood and for him to start talking, she's gone. The RATP employee knows, he'll do what's necessary, she's told him, he doesn't need her. And so she flees, because she finds it all very upsetting – not the man slowly expiring in his dirt and misery, but the living ones insensitive to the urgency of death.

She walks aimlessly along, leaving the market behind her. She could cry if she wasn't worried that sobbing would slow her down. Something is happening back there; she ought to have stayed on as a witness. She walks, no longer seeing the pavement, the buildings, the cars, the pedestrians, the mopeds. No matter the city, no matter the age, there are transitional moments when a person exists by default, by pure reflex. It ought then to be possible to fall asleep on the spot, to let that moment of floating pass, and to launch oneself into orbit around everyday life. The street runs into a small, three-sided public garden. She pushes through the metal gate. There are three marble benches. A fishbowl with a goldfish swimming inside has been placed at the end of each one. No one around. The gravel crunches underfoot. The fish revolve at varying speeds, at times bouncing off a translucent obstacle and, in a fit of pique, shooting back the other way. From above, they seem very slender; from the side, bloated, almost obese. She looks around for who could have set the three fishbowls down in this unusual spot, but she seems to be the only person here. Tugging up her sleeve, she plunges her fingers into the large bubble of water. The fish wriggles away, working its fins to avoid the hand that has just burst in on its world. She feels like catching the delicate slippery body, hauling it out of the water and contemplating the mouth opening and closing in the suffocating air. Once, at the seaside, she'd observed a fish that had been thrown down on the shingle after being caught. A terrible, fascinating sight. Blood was trickling from its gills; now and then its body would squirm. She'd crouched down and with her finger had given the animal's scales a timid caress. She had asked if it couldn't be put back in the water. The fisherman had laughed at her. It's just a fish, they're made to be eaten.

Someone is calling out to her. Just what does she think she's doing? She pulls her hand out of the fishbowl at once. A woman, who must have been lying in wait behind a bush, is striding towards her. Addressing her as though she were a prize idiot. It's an *in-sta-lla-tion*, not a finger bowl, looking is fine, but no touching, do you understand? Her hair in dreads, an orange band around her forehead, a ring in her nose, the woman is about to knock her down. If she had a sword, she'd have pulled it out already to slice her into little pieces. Your installation is really great. The anger drops from the woman's face. Artists live at the mercy of compliments, which is why she doesn't understand them very well. Don't worry, I'm going now. Actually, the artist would be happy for her to stay and share a few more favourable impressions of her work, maybe even ask her questions about where she gets her inspiration. She'd be happy now to give her permission to dip her fingers in, let her art become interactive. Accessible to ordinary folk like her – isn't that the criterion all creators must live by? She has heard what the artist is saying but has no real opinion on the matter.

Rue de Buci. Large signs up on all the shopfronts: EVERY-THING MUST GO. CLEARANCE SALE. UP TO 50% OFF. Enticing phrases to coax you inside. She pauses outside Vanilla Girls. Chocolate, strawberry, and raspberry are also available. All the flavours you could wish for, gentle-men. To be consumed without moderation, but must be kept refrigerated. She goes inside. Five young women work their way along the hangers like automatic sorting machines, taking out an occasional garment to check for manufacturing defects. Each displays remarkable powers of concentration: the fruit of years of practice begun in early adolescence. A female voice is singing in English. She catches the word *love* and the word . . . *love*. The sales assistant is wheeling packs of clothes from one side of the store to the other, taking them around for some fresh air. She spots a dress for forty-nine euros. Not really her style, but it could cheer her up to see herself looking different, not to recognize herself in the mirror. Can she try it on, she asks the assistant, who brushes by her at top speed and, without stopping, points to the rear of the shop. The garments in critical shape have to be moved urgently for fear they will suffer irreversible decay. In a corner of the shop, a curtain hangs from a semicircular rail. The curtain is narrow. Through the space between the fabric and the wall, she can see large sections of the shop. People can see her. She ought not to give a damn, since everyone here is of the same sex. No need to be shy, you're all built the same, her gym mistress would shout in the changing rooms at school. Except that she had breasts, whereas the others still had only the insignificant volcanic burgeonings of nipple. She undresses, keeping her movements to a minimum to stay hidden. She gets her head and arms in, but once the dress is on, she can't do up the zip at the back. The makeshift fitting room doesn't have a mirror. She steps out, with her back exposed and the dress gaping at the front, to get at least some idea of how she looks. A split second later the salesgirl is upon her, ramming up the zip with an iron hand. She barely has time to draw a breath: her chest will never be the same shape again, that's certain. She senses that the other women in the shop are peering at her. The salesgirl is recuperating by the till. It's very nice, don't tell me you don't like it. She doesn't like it, but she doesn't say so. She already knew that pink doesn't suit her. Besides, it's a colour she detests. And the length is wrong. As for her breasts, squashed at the front, plumped up at the top, they resemble nothing so much as a fine pair of soufflés still in their baking tin. The ruse hasn't paid off.

Even dressed like that, she still looks the same, only worse. Forty-nine euros, it's a bargain, the shopgirl calls out, before flying to the rescue of other endangered garments. Get back behind the curtain now that she's gone. She flaps her elbows, trying to catch hold of the zip. No way is she going out there again. After twisting herself into four or five different positions, release. She hurriedly gets back into her clothes and abandons the dress. She throws a quick glance outside. The shopgirl is standing guard a few metres from the shop entrance. She makes a run for it, ducking at the first display stand she comes to, and finds her way, hidden by a mound of heaped-up clothing, to the exit.

She crosses the carrefour de l'Odéon, then walks up one of the three streets leading to the Théâtre de l'Europe. She is surprised to find in this part of the city an erotic book-shop with no sign. In the window, books of photography featuring pictures of women in bras and G-strings on the front covers; novels and reference works. The thought of going in is tempting but makes her feel uneasy. Peering between the piles of books, she tries to catch a glimpse of what is happening inside. Two young men are leafing through magazines. Enthroned behind the cash register is a fairly stout woman in her fifties. The presence of the woman strengthens her resolve. She makes her silent entrance; neither of the two men turns round; the woman, on the other hand, greets her arrival with an amused stare. She must look like a self-conscious child walking into a place she has been forbidden to enter. Not daring to touch a thing, she goes over to the shelves and tilts her head to start reading the titles and authors' names, which she immediately forgets. Except for one: Marie Nimier. The name rings a bell, as if it were the name of an old friend, or the pseudonym she could have chosen for herself if she had been a writer. She takes down the novel and reads the first page. The story begins with the overwhelming attraction one woman feels for a man. A passionate love *which makes one want to worship everything about him, even the worst parts.* What is the worst about him? For her, best or worst has no meaning. She doesn't think of him in those terms, apportioning him into two columns and adding up the sum of his good and bad qualities. In the novel the man wears a silver ring, which the woman sees as an integral part of his body. Whatever the object of her obsession owns is turned into a fetish. In fairy tales, a magician's power comes from a ring. Rings are exchanged at weddings; a ring is affixed to the leg of a carrier pigeon. For the first time she wonders what his penis might look like. But she has no way of telling; each is unique, a signature whose overlapping lines are hard to decipher even when the person is known. All she can do is refer back to the ones she has seen and that she remembers. That game of adolescent girls: trying to find out whether the length and thickness of the male organ corresponds to the size or thickness of any visible part of the anatomy. The feet . . . the nose . . . the ears . . . the hips . . . the big toe . . . the wrists. It turned out there was an exception to every rule.

Place de l'Odéon is deserted, except for a man filming the exterior of the theatre. With one eye pressed to the viewfinder and the other closed, he doesn't notice her. On she goes.

The Jardin du Luxembourg and its hodgepodge of tourists. Rings of chairs arranged as if for the conversations of invisible characters. It's up to anyone out for a walk to imagine, according to the layout of these metal remains, what went on here before his arrival. Grey-haired men and women sit alone, gazing into space, or hunched over a newspaper, the articles and photographs depicting the world's latest carnages. And then, suddenly, heads look up. The sun's rays pierce through the dome of clouds; the contrast in the landscape sharpens. A paradoxical light that lessens the threat of a storm and yet still makes it seem likely, a light that has the coldness of metal and the sharpness of a blade, a light on which nothing feasts but which everything reflects, which strikes only at strategic points. Apocalypse. From a distance, the trees look like a long row of stone blocks miraculously suspended in mid-air. She enters the shaded path; the complex filigree of the branches appears overhead, the sky starts rustling, the mineral turns vegetal. She emerges on the other side of the park. Two thick lines of spindle trees frame a strip of sky.

Place Saint-Sulpice. Projectors are being set up for a photo shoot. Kids on Rollerblades orbit the fountain like multicoloured electrons around a nucleus of glistening water. Up the steps to the church, push through the heavy door that leads into the sanctuary. A young woman with blonde hair enters at the same time she does. Hurried steps, dip of the thin fingers into the holy water, sign of the cross. A man with torn trousers has fallen asleep at a prayer stool; his head lolls back at an angle. Walls, floor, roof, columns, statues, everywhere the same granite hue. She tries to keep her shoes from clattering over the flagstones: excessive noise could bring down the entire building. She doesn't believe in God, has never felt the need to, has never read a religious book. But churches are something else. Their tranquility, their dark cool air, their solemnity are a respite for her.

The Rue de l'Université. An old woman with gnarled shaking hands is talking to herself, then addresses her as she walks by. The woman in the blue cape! The poor thing isn't all there, she's lost her marbles, and continues to repeat, the woman in the blue cape, her liquid gaze directed at the end of the street. So as not to hurt the old lady's feelings, she turns round: there really is a woman in a blue cape, making her way quickly across the street. The mocking tone comes through the yellowed teeth: that one there was a nun and went to bed with a man; now she's got nothing. The old woman shakes her head, all but adding serves her right. At the age of twelve, after a guided tour of a convent somewhere in the middle of the countryside, she considered taking holy orders. No one said a word about the vow of chastity, not even the guide. What appealed to her was the silence of the stonework, the calm of the inner courtyards. Shutting yourself away forever was like hurling yourself into space. She longed for the challenge of absolute silence. She wanted to know what thoughts she would have after a few months, after a few years without uttering a single word.

Back home, 5 p.m. in Paris. Get herself a sponge and dog-gedly tackle the inside of the fridge or the top of the cooker? Play some music and sweat to the rhythm as she goes about getting rid of those greasy rings? Switch on the television and watch some programme? Listen to the radio and sort out the pile of bills on the living room table? Make a phone call? To whom? She has done all these things before; she knows what sensations they produce. She'd like to come up with other, more distracting activities, but right now, nothing occurs to her. And so she stays on the couch, unable to make up her mind. She rubs the tiny piece of skin next to her nail over her upper lip until the phone rings. She knows that it's not him, not twice in one day, not after what happened this morning. She picks up. Hello, it's Maxime. She doesn't know the voice or anyone named Maxime. She's about to say, you've dialled the wrong number, but Maxime goes on. We met last night at the dinner party, you gave me your number. I wanted to invite you for a drink.

She regrets not buying the pink dress, which would have been an excellent costume for the role she is getting ready to play. In any case, she still needs to wear a dress – that feminine symbol, the inverted corolla. Only one passes muster, short, red, and simply cut. Quick check on the state of her calves: passable in soft light, not so great to the touch. Hair removal is no small business. Excluded are creams and those electrical devices supposed to extract the hair by its root; they leave a lot to be desired, she tried all of them a long time ago. She doesn't have time for an appointment at the beauty salon. Besides, that never really worked for her, on account of the nagging feeling of being at the doctor's: the long sheet of paper crumpling under you as you lie down, the harsh light revealing the skin's imperfections. The shame is not appreciably different when she is lying on her stomach and senses the beautician appraising the appearance of her rump barely shielded by a pair of panties that are never up to standard. She is sure she presents a pitiful sight to those eyes accustomed to seeing so many fit and toned women, who look good even before their treatments have started. Her first weeks in the capital, she knew no one. After she got knocked down by that car, she had hobbled her way to the emergency room of a hospital. Looking after herself was her responsibility, young woman of eighteen that she was, suddenly in charge of a life, her own. At the hospital, only curt instructions — no prizes for having taken care of herself and got that far safely. A nurse sat her on an examination table and rolled up her trouser legs. And that white witch's first words: you might want to shave them now and then. These days, she couldn't care less. But this evening, she has to be impeccably turned out: so a few strokes of a razor blade it is; too bad if in three days' time hair density per square centimetre will have doubled. Powder for her eyelids, black eyeliner, some red lipstick – she redraws her face, taking care to accentuate her features.

Lots of people in the métro. Lethargic and tyrannical young people. Couples of every kind picking a quarrel or wrapping their arms around each other. A few skittish old coots keeping out of harm's way. An agitated young man is talking loudly, chopping the air with his arms in front of a pair of hippy types, male and female, who watch him expend his precious energy at a dizzying rate. I got me a gun, ya see; I got a gun. His audience of two looks on, impassive. I mean, I could blow y'all away, know what I'm sayin'? The future killer produces the onomatopoeic equivalent of three gunshots. But . . . I ain' gonna. Is he bluffing? She wouldn't bet on it. Elsewhere on the platform people are turning a blind eye. The kid is telling anyone who will listen that he's done time, and on the word *time*, his eyes lock onto hers. She looks away, wisely directing her gaze clear of this lunatic. Hey, you! The rumbling of the approaching train swallows the rest. She heads the other way and takes advantage of the jostling crowd to slip into one of the carriages. As his face passes by the window of the door, the ex-prisoner of the French Republic sticks his tongue out at her.

The rendezvous is at the Hotel Lutétia. Carpeting, golden lamps, geometrically patterned rugs, wax-polished furniture, staff that glide rather than walk. A man in a dinner jacket comes over to her, as welcoming as if they had spent their holiday together on the same beach. He motions solicitously in the direction of a second man, who wears a multicoloured striped shirt and black trousers, and who advances briskly towards them. Good evening, glad you could come. A tender flexing of the vocal cords, nothing like his irritation of the evening before. It hasn't taken him long to change his mind. His eyes are bright, wide open to take her in more fully. He makes no comment about her appearance, no doubt fearing to seem vulgar. With an expert hand placed in the hollow of her back, he guides her to their reserved table. A bottle of champagne in a silver ice bucket, a cigarette smouldering on the rim of the cut-crystal ashtray. He suggests they make themselves comfortable on a cream-coloured divan. He hands her a drink, they touch glasses. To your presence here today. She puckers her lips. She must look a sight – she always finds compliments annoying, even false ones. He offers her a cigarette and retrieves his own. He has a small, tight mouth, the air of a hunter assured of victory. Around them, several men in dark suits reading newspapers; the rustle of turning pages barely interferes with the piece of classical music flowing into the room. A hushed atmosphere. She senses him observing her neck, then her chest. She brings her eyes back to meet his in order to block the offensive. I don't even know what you do. He works at the ministry. The MFA . . . sorry, Ministry of Foreign Affairs. Did you graduate from that program – the ENA? Why is she asking that, of course he did. Where else would he have studied, it's hardly complicated. No one's perfect, he replies, and laughs to himself. Then, pronouncing his words very clearly: Do you follow international politics at all? She feels like biting him, she detests that kind of trick question. A no, and he'll spend the rest of the evening looking down his nose at her; a yes, and she'll have to give her informed opinion. She mentally rehearses the names she remembers, particularly American names, since they're the only ones that ever get mentioned. Bush, Powell, Rumsfeld. She often thinks that they would all make excellent names for pets. Bin Laden, and his life on video; Saddam, whom all journalists refer to by his first name, probably because they think they know him. She remembers two other names as well: Taylor and Mugabe, two African dictators. And then there's the Brazilian president with his pretty nickname that goes well with his left-wing positions. Yes, she knows a bit about international politics. As for him, he's working on Iraq. A major policy area, fascinating, France's position precisely mirrors his own personal convictions. What more could he ask for? I love my job. At least someone is happy with his lot. The Americans, we'll wear them down eventually. He finishes off his drink. And the Iraqis? He smiles at her as if she were a naive child. Oh, he hasn't forgotten the Iraqis. You're slightly naive, but I suppose that's normal since you see it all from the outside. He then proceeds to sing her the praises of French diplomacy taking the voice of the nation to the four corners of the world. She ought to appreciate the fact that *her* government is defending the interests of *her* country. And what did you tell your wife, that you had a meeting with the minister, a Saudi prince, or a Russian spy? He has trouble exhaling the smoke of his cigarette without coughing. He should have known that with a profession like hers she'd be rather cynical at bottom, and he caresses her forearm with his index finger. She feels like coming out with two or three choice inventions, stuff her supposed clients would have done to her, that might dampen his ardour. But she holds back. You're a friend of Ange's? She nods. Yes indeed, Mr. Diplomat, a very good friend, we share the same tastes. He must be wondering how Ange ever could have met such a girl.

He offers to take her to a private club with its own terrace. An irresistible proposition, he must think, for any woman with a passion for billing and cooing outdoors in temperate climates, a deft nod to romanticism. Taxi. The driver lowers the window to ask if the ride will be long enough to be worth the trouble. Someone has left a business card on the back seat. *Olivier Chedubarum, Photographer, 01 52 29 07 18.* She slips it into her bag. Sharp clack as the driver automatically locks the door. Through the rear window, she catches sight of a man in a hooded tracksuit moving with a supple stride. His face is black. Don't like seeing 'em round these parts. Stepping sharply on the accelerator, the driver sets off. Streams of red lights and yellow lights against the backdrop of a sleeping city. Walled off behind a surface of glass, with the help of the nighttime calm, each remembers a past when things were different. Inside the car, silence from the bodies of three strangers who have nothing to say to one another. She sees a woman holding a poodle's leash in one hand, clutching her jacket to her chest with the other. Farther on, a man is letting out a stream of urine into the corner of two walls, his feet spread wide. At place de la Concorde, she hears the sound of a zip. Reluctantly she turns her eyes away from the large lightning bugs that have transformed into street lamps. Mr. Diplomat has his fly open. She reads the words *Calvin Klein* on the wide elastic band of the boxer shorts stretched over his abdomen. He caresses the back of her neck. She knows what he is waiting for. His eyes pant; he feels sure that he is within his rights. She has no idea what the going rate for a blowjob could be. Her role is starting to get to her. I don't do it in taxis. She leans into his ear and closes the zip. He looks irritated but doesn't dare complain. He tells the driver to go faster.

In the main clubroom, wall lamps project long cones of orange light onto the brickwork. Wafting into the glow, cigarette smoke appears to solidify. The rest of the room is swathed in a suggestive penumbra. Electronic music. He has ordered two cocktails: a red sludge, its alcohol content nearly undetectable. She asks him where the toilets are. Four women are looking at themselves in a mirror that spans the entire wall above three washbasins. Low-cut flowing dresses, close-fitting trousers, gold jewellery, expensive-smelling perfumes. They are inspecting them- selves: eyebrows, nostrils, corners of the mouth, spaces between their teeth, breast elevation, armpit odour. They could almost have stepped out from a fashion advert. Perhaps they'll take her for the bathroom attendant. All the cubicles are occupied, toilets are flushing at full blast, bladders are emptying in the clockwork expulsion of liquid steadily poured for them by their attentive escorts. Even princesses have to go to the bathroom. She waits to one side to avoid being made party to the conversations. She listens in. I bought it today, very nice, on sale at Armani, I just love the smell of this soap, you have lovely hands. A tall, stunning blonde with a mane of pale curls and an aquiline nose is going on about herself. She's feeling totally depressed, she's found work, didn't dare refuse it, but actually it pisses her off; it's not like Bernard needs the money. Out she goes with a sigh, perfect and dignified. As the door swings shut, shoulders are shrugged. Apparently things between her and Bernard aren't all sweetness and light, which is why Lydia accepted the job, for the security. She goes into one of the cubicles. She hitches up her dress, tugs down her knickers, and notices a dark, metallic-smelling stain on the black material. She has a brief vision of herself disturbing the super-bimbos gathered in their marble temple to ask for their help. Too awkward. She unrolls a length of toilet paper, folds it into several layers, and places it between her legs, then pulls up her knickers to hold it all in place. Very sexy for her role as whore. She returns to the room, collects her bag under the diplomat's questioning stare. Do you need anything? She gestures no with her hand as the word *Tampax* flashes through her mind. She rejoins the queue; in the cubicle she eventually finds several tampons at the bottom of her bag. The pink-and-white wrapping is a bit torn. In any case, it's not as if she has a choice.

A fresh round of alcoholic fruit juice has been put in front of them. She feels the limits of her body dissolving. Under the effects of the drink, she passes from a solid to a gaseous state, lighter but taking up more space. She is expanding into the atmosphere. Can Maxime see her condition from the outside, she wonders – that she's losing density and gaining volume? He said something. Pinned down by his words, she has to interrupt her transformation, her mind has to organize the mad molecules that have begun to stray around the room. A girl like you, I'm surprised you haven't already found yourself a rich husband. She shrugs, imagining newspapers headlines: FRENCH FINANCIAL MARKETS SEE SHORTFALL IN WEALTHY HUSBANDS. I can see you with an older man, someone in his fifties would be perfect for you. His mouth increasingly resembles the mouth of a fish; he opens it slightly whenever he is pleased. An older man. She grips the edge of the table. Pink room, piano, spring mattress, pink, bed, room, springs, piano . . . He wasn't fifty at the time, more like forty. She asks Maxime if he likes older women. Not any more. His mouth makes a little moist sound. When I was eighteen I was, let's say, initiated, by a women twice my age. He'll let her in on a secret. At the time, she was sleeping with Villepin. He sits back on the couch, taking a drag from his cigarette. I had the same mistress as Villepin, aren't you impressed? He grabs her knee. His wife is not at home.

The apartment is vast. Room after room of polished parquet floors and white walls, a multitude of halogen lights to keep the night at bay. The tall windows framed by garnet-coloured drapes. Not an object out of place, as if no one lived here. The props are backstage; they're rehearsing the scene before the other actors show up. He's in the kitchen, the plump sound of a cork being pulled from a bottle. She stands in the centre of the living room as if visiting an art gallery. Most of the paintings are abstract or schematic representations of female bodies. The lines dip and straighten, form a head of hair, then a breast, a buttock. Look long enough and there emerges a complete woman contained within her curves. He has put on some music. Loud. Annie Lennox. The walls of the room reverberate in time to the modulations of the voice. The song reminds her of something, but exactly what she can't say, a moment of elation that only the carelessness of the young can produce. He is back from the kitchen. As if she had a choice to make, he holds a glass out in one hand, a slender wad of five 50-euro notes in the other. She notes the slight rise of his Adam's apple. Tomorrow, she's sure, he'll tell his closest colleague when they go for a drink after work that he got himself a nice little prostitute for the night. Briefly he stays there, both hands extended. She doesn't move. He goes to put the money and the wine down on the low table. She hears the clack of parquet tiles underfoot. The straps of her dress slip off her shoulders. Her breasts emerge; she feels an intense vulnerability. He has taken off his shirt, his body tanned by five weeks of holiday on the Mediterranean coast, his muscles toned by four hours a week in a large gym. She thinks of pigeons strutting about, circling each other, heads nodding. Yes, yes, yes, peck the air, peck the ground. Always behind the female so as not to see each other's pleasure, above all, as little noise as possible in order to remain civilized. She sways slightly. Tomorrow she'll remember the feel of the polished floor under the soles of her feet. The absence of smells in the bathroom reserved for important guests; all trace of them removed by a cleaning lady who comes in twice a week. He has taken hold of her breasts, is kneading them enthusiastically, biting the base of her neck. She imagines a fish's mouth suctioned to her skin. Her dress has slipped down to her feet. At the far end of her limp legs, the floor seems more distant than normal. He has taken off his clothes and is pressing his naked body against hers. His penis slips between her thighs. She closes her eyes.

And then she remembers. I've got my period, she says. The rubbing of skin against hers stops. He moves back, he hasn't understood. You have what? My period. Four dry syllables, clearly articulated. I was wondering how long you would keep this up. The tone is not aggressive but almost indulgent. She doesn't follow. I was wondering why you wanted to pass yourself off as a prostitute. She bites her lip. She'd like to be the woman who served as the model in the painting opposite her. If he were a painter, they wouldn't talk; she would just stand there naked before him; he would ask her no questions; her story would be read on her body. There is a pause between tracks on the CD. Still she can't manage to utter a word. Maxime places one hand around his still-erect penis. Really, you're not tempted? For the first time she glances down at it, finds it graceful, fairly in keeping with his face. If she hadn't been unmasked, she might still have gone through with it; ashamed of her pathetic ruse, though, she no longer feels up to the task. The silence thickens. Finally, he relents and laughs, but the laugh rings false. In that case, you'd better leave. He goes to fetch the money from the table and slips it into her palm. Financial transaction between a pair of fat naked worms. Just to show you I'm a good sport. He picks up her dress, which she slips back on while he phones for a taxi. This remains between us, of course.

Outside, it is raining. The windscreen wipers clear the water in great sweeps. The car is double-parked. The white light of the taxi sign streaming in the downpour. The purring of the engine merges with the sound of the rain. The interior is overheated. Good evening, madam. Speaking clearly, she gives her address to the driver's dark silhouette. Mist has started spreading across the windows. Revealed by the condensation, a three-pronged star has shown itself at her side. The start of a drawing. The previous passenger had given in to the temptation of the fogged surface, but didn't have time to finish. She adds a fourth, longer line, and two tiny ovals at the bottom: a flower for the person who will take her place. She realizes that her fist is still clenched. She opens her hand. The banknotes are moist; they appear to have had a good sweat. A fifth of her salary for having her period. Not one to bear grudges, Maxime; diplomacy has its merits. Around the mouths of the street lamps drops of rain materialize. Falling at the same speed, their trajectories parallel. On the facade of every building, two or three rectangles are giving off yellow light. Miniature homes, safe behind their panes of glass. If circumstances had been different, she would now be in Maxime's arms, all set to fall asleep in the comforting presence of another's body. The thought has nothing to do with the man, only with the weather, which brings out a yearning for the quiet contentment of domesticity. (She's the lone heroine in one of those old black-and-white movies. At some point, it's always raining. She's just escaped the base intentions of an amoral seducer. She hasn't come out of it too badly; the audience can feel reassured about her future. The words *The End* appear on the screen.) It occurs to her that she only sleeps at a man's house by accident, and on top of that, it's never the same man. Are there many other women like her in this city, she wonders. The thought crosses her mind briefly, she might not be normal. Playing a prostitute has made her long for marital happiness. The fragrance of chopped beef simmering in the frying pan, the affectionate peck on her cheek as she rinses vegetables in the sink, the sense of security. For an instant, she is convinced that she belongs to this pre-fabricated picture of conjugal bliss. The driver has put the windscreen wipers on at full speed. What a downpour! He spoke as if he were alone, and she was glad that he felt at ease with her, that he found a discreet company in her presence. She feels close to this man who doesn't ask questions, who looks after her without her needing to demand anything. She is in his car, in the rain, and there is nowhere else she could be. She has not really chosen it, but now she is here, and it is up to her to make the moment her own. She thinks of him. Ange is out of the picture. There's just the two of them. Somewhere. They're sitting side by side, gazing out in silence at an open landscape, together in a way that only they can be.

Here you are. Through the rain-streaked glass she recognizes her entranceway. Heavy double door, A768B. She folds the five banknotes in two and hands them to the driver. She scrambles out to pre-empt his reaction, feeling cold liquid on her scalp, as if the rain were passing through the roots of her hair into her very brain. Closing the door to her building, she hears the slam of the taxi door. A word is caught between the two sounds.

She goes to bed, unaware of what she is doing, and wakes up in a sweat. In the nightmare, her clitoris had been cut off with a razor blade. She saw nothing, felt nothing. She was lying on a white towel, which absorbed the fresh, red blood. People around her were watching the thick, shameful liquid flow from her genitals. She made no move to put a hand over the wound; like those around her, she was watching her groin, where the red drops kept forming, spreading across the fabric below. She felt terribly ashamed, had no idea how to explain to them that it had nothing to do with her. It wasn't in that precise spot that it hurt, but all over, a sort of generalized gnawing pain. She no longer knew exactly where the blood was coming from.

She had started to talk. She said, it's not my period, apologizing so that they wouldn't think there was anything natural about what they were seeing. I've been wounded. The towel needed changing, but she didn't dare ask. Any more than she dared ask them if she was going to receive treatment.

She slips her hand between her thighs. She's wet. She draws back the duvet. There are spots of blood on the sheet.

Mid-afternoon, and she is in front of a cup of coffee, leafing idly through a magazine. On the back page she comes across Nestor Karma's horoscope. A photograph of the astrologer's relaxed face appears in the top left-hand corner of the page, no doubt as proof of his credibility. She wonders if it is easy to earn a living by writing horoscopes. She is no longer quite sure what her sign is. She at once rules out those that don't seem to suit her, like Virgo, Scorpio, Aries, or Taurus. Pisces or Cancer might do. She eventually notices that the dates of birth corresponding to each sign are given: hers is Aquarius. *This week coincides with a period of optimism and positive feelings. So long as you are prudent, that will be of use in numerous situations. Yet you must remain extremely vigilant. You have a tendency to see the whole rather than the parts, and a lack of rigour could spoil your plans. So pay great attention to details. Read all the words, even those printed in small letters. Make an effort to be meticulous and success will come knocking at your door.* She isn't sure that she has paid much attention to detail in recent days. She closes the magazine. Glancing at the cover, she realizes that it is more than three weeks old. Water under the bridge.

She gets a sudden urge to call him. She'd like to mention her encounter with Maxime, not to go into specifics, but to admit that she had seen him, in case he came to hear about it from someone else. But how to justify to Ange her calling on a Sunday? She has never called on a Sunday before, and, as a rule, never calls at all. Ask her if the jumper fits? Compliment her on the dinner party? In any case, Ange must be irritated with her if she's been told about the prostitute story. Angels never lie. And she isn't at all sure she can manage to talk about her meeting with Mr. Diplomat without him misinterpreting her story. For a while, she wanders around the apartment attending to minor chores: hanging up her black dress, rinsing the bath, washing her cup. All these objects used only by her, objects she arranges and rearranges at whim, with no other choreographer to intervene in this ritual ballet. She is sole captain of the ship. On checking the contents of her bag, she finds the brown paper stained with raspberry juice. She hesitates, then dials the number of the theatre. Six rings; she is about to hang up when a breathless voice yaps hello into the receiver. It takes her by surprise – she was convinced that no one would answer on a Sunday. She is no longer sure why she is phoning. I saw my name on your poster and I just wanted to know . . . Impossible. Ill at ease, she takes the plunge. I wanted to book two seats for the play. Saturday, yes, that's fine. My name? She can't possibly give her own name; they'd assume she was the other one and wouldn't take her seriously. Ange Karma. Karma, *K-A-R-M-A.* In the centre, yes, that would be fine. She'll need to collect the tickets half an hour before the start of the performance. She hangs up and realizes that she said two. What's the name for that again? A mental slip. In any case, one seat or two, it doesn't make much difference. She wasn't paying attention, that's all. Just then she thinks back to the real Karma's predictions. Pay attention to details. Which leads her to one conclusion: she has to go there with someone, and that someone can only be him. All she has to do is find a way to ask. She could send him a letter, but it might not arrive in time. The best option would still be to call. She just needs a good excuse.

She decides to make herself something to eat; the act of cooking might help her to think. She cleans and chops up a few mushrooms, fries them lightly in the pan before adding two eggs that she has beaten with a fork. While the omelette is cooking, she switches on the television. She changes channels several times before coming across the faces of two adolescent girls. The first has her hair in braids. The second one's teeth are covered in a complex piece of metal equipment. The two girls, both white, are chewing gum in near unison. They're answering the camera in English with heavy American accents, their voices are dubbed. Listening to them, she eventually gathers what the report is about, the pressure American teenage girls feel to give their boyfriends blowjobs. If you

[75]

don't do it, says one of the girls, it's like your reputation
suffers, you know. The other says, and afterwards the boys
won't talk to you, everyone does it, it's nothing special.
Images follow of pupils settling down at their desks, then
of a busy school playground. A quick shot of a boy and
girl having an inaudible conversation, neither one touching or looking at the other, but both clearly very engaged.
Back to the two girls. Oh, I've never slept with a boy, one
says laughing, and it ain't gonna happen anytime soon.
The other says, when you suck them off they're happy,
that way they don't want anything else. She switches off
the television. She doesn't know what to make of what she
has just heard.

Like all adolescents, she had tried to define her own
identity through defiance or conformity. To imitate the
behaviour of an admired group or individual is a way to
avoid one's own contradictions. But whatever escape
mechanism is chosen, it's open to abuse. As an adult, one
forgets. She has forgotten. The rite of passage has only
come back to her in small chunks. It has taken her several
years to piece together what really happened.

All human beings end up believing in the uniqueness of
the events that traumatized them. So we try to hide our
scars in order to evolve beyond what they made of us, even
if we never stop dwelling on them. Others must have lived
through the same thing she did, but she isn't aware of
having met any of them; nor has she tried to seek them out.
Marion is the only person she has ever confided in, her sole
second-hand witness. For that same reason, they broke off

all contact. What Marion remembers is only a distorted echo of what she was told. As for herself, she has only her own version of events and at times doubts that the experience was real. At such moments, she tells herself the incident is one of those personal myths invented to justify excesses and wild behaviour. It would be wrong to keep talking about it at her age; it would serve no purpose. And talk about it to whom? The person concerned? He would claim she was lying; after all these years, he would manage to destabilize her. She smells something burning. She rushes to the kitchen, where the omelette has turned into a blackened mass. Angrily, she shuts off the cooker and tosses the frying pan into the sink before turning on the cold water. Steam whooshes into her face. She goes to the living room to fetch her things and leaves the apartment.

A métro took her to Les Halles. She went down into the station, got on the train, got off the train, and left the station in a kind of trance. She is now sitting on a bench, opposite a merry-go-round turning to the doleful strains of an accordion. Parents are placing small, anxious-looking tots on horses that have coats of white varnish, false bulging eyes, muzzles frozen in a cruel rictus held by two leather straps. Some of the children are fastened to their mounts as a precaution. The adults step back while an attendant in a tracksuit comes round to make sure the kids have paid. The machine shifts into motion. On a bench next to hers is a couple. Sitting slightly apart. Neither one of them is talking. Their attentive eyes follow one of the children, then freeze on the spot where the child vanishes from sight for a few seconds before they retrieve him visually on the other side to make sure he hasn't fallen off or run away. The man and the woman each raise a hand in the direction of their offspring, whose face becomes progressively more pale with each turn. By the tenth revolution the face passing before them is red and tense. The two little hands are still gripping the golden rod, the child is petrified. Powerless and seized by panic, the man and woman look on as the supposed fun turns to torture. Do something, says the woman, still trying not to look at her companion. He shrugs. The merry-go-round has to keep turning until the end. Only then can the woman rush forward, arms outstretched, to rescue her poor little boy, who bursts into tears in her arms. Look, darling, none of the other children are crying. She gets up from the bench just as the couple begins to quarrel.

She is heading towards Place Carrée. It sounds as if someone is calling to her from a few metres behind. The voice grows louder, more insistent, forces her to turn round. Seeing that he has managed to get her attention, the man steps closer, even as she continues walking. He is of North-African origin, his voice is slightly hoarse, his breath smells of tobacco. He wants to know if she'll have a coffee with him. Without looking at him she shakes her head and keeps on walking. He shuffles quickly alongside her to keep the expression on her face in view. It's my birthday, I'm forty today. Happy birthday. She quickens her pace, but he doesn't give up. I never thought I'd make it this far. The apparent sincerity of the declaration causes her to turn again. He has black eyes, several days' stubble. He wanted to do something out of the ordinary on his birthday, invite a stranger for a coffee. She has an appointment, she can't stop. Please. His persistence eventually forces a smile out of her, but she keeps walking. Why me? The question slipped out. By asking it, she's created an opening and will find it that much harder to get rid of him. But as with Renée, she couldn't help wanting to know why, out of all the dozens of women he has seen, she is the one he has decided to approach. Because she doubts he could have put on a similar act for others before her. I saw you by the merry-go-round, you looked a little sad. She wants to believe that he's telling her the truth. She slows down. Ten minutes then, but that's all.

They sit down at a table at the nearest outdoor café, in the same way you'd slip into the nearest hotel – never mind the number of stars, the price of the rooms – so as not to let the moment pass. Despite its banality, their brief exchange has had an effect on her; the world around her no longer seems quite the same. Influenced by the presence of the unknown, her senses are picking up new signals. His name is Momo, and he empties two packets of sugar into his coffee. He doesn't ask her name. He lives around here, he's unemployed. 'Cause finding another job at forty is tough. There's too much racism in France. Not that he's criticizing France, but even so. The young people who live in the suburbs take things a bit far, but they're not given a chance, you gotta see what happens when they go for an interview. Okay, so he's not that young any more, but he

knows tons of people like him, younger people, and they go
out and try. But after ten shots they give up. And then they
start pissing people off, 'cause they feel like they're not
wanted. Sure, there're always some real troublemakers,
but there's not only them. She finds it hard to keep listening because she doesn't have any particular opinion on the
matter. The story is already starting to go wrong; they've
got off to a bad start. He fixes her with a stare as she
watches his hand creep across the surface of the table.
You're not a bad looking woman. She wishes he hadn't
said that; suddenly she sees the world as it was before. Are
you embarrassed? Grimacing, she shakes her head. Do
you have a boyfriend? She wishes she were no longer
there; she knows now that he hasn't picked her out from
the crowd and that she is sitting with him only because
she has been naive enough to accept. She hesitates, a yes
would work to her advantage but she doesn't want to use
cowardice as a shield. No, and I don't want one. Momo
sniggers. That's not true, a woman always needs a man.
She finds generalizations tiresome, even if they have a
reassuring effect. All she has to do is to get a man, any man,
and keep him, so long as he has the word *man* written on
him in big letters. If you don't show a man you need him,
he won't stay with you. Barely ten minutes since they met,
and he's already giving her advice. Just because she's the
only one to have accepted, he thinks that gives him the
right to say what he likes. Is he saying that to her personally, she feels like asking, or is this his usual charm routine?
She holds her tongue: if she starts attaching too much

importance to what he says, she could be there for ages. She tells Momo that the ten minutes are up and that she has to go now. Please, it's my birthday. I'll buy you another coffee. Either this man is desperate or she's giving the impression that she needs him. She is about to leave when she feels a hand on her shoulder.

He is standing by the table with Ange on his arm. She ought to say something, but everything inside her has merged into a single organ and already that is making breathing difficult. In front of her, Momo, frowning, annoyed at the unexpected interruption; above her, Ange's mouth, which she fears is about to open. Everywhere else, his eyes. A fluid passes into her veins and at once stimulates and paralyzes her. Making the most of a Sunday afternoon, are we? Unstoppable Ange, all the more menacing because she sees nothing but the obvious. In a series of rapid glances, similar to the way people look at a meal they're not certain they will like, he sizes up Momo, who for his part doesn't take his eyes off her, trying to figure out who these people are, disturbing him at such an inopportune time. Aren't you going to introduce us to your friend? Ange can't bear to be left out. She says all three of their first names. Ange leans enthusiastically down to Momo, imparts two kisses on his cheeks, and then kisses her. He extends a hand to Momo. She gets a wink, an exact copy of the one he gave her in the kitchen and whose meaning she has yet to grasp fully. Ange falls prey to an irresistible urge for coffee, she'll also take the opportunity to nip to the ladies room, and given that they haven't quite finished, she thinks it would be nice to join them. Momo pulls up a chair for Ange, no doubt thinking that the presence of another couple can only contribute to the success of his seductive tactics. What could be better than an example right in front of you? He sits down next to her: How are you? Okay. The waiter comes to take their order. Four espressos. Silence descends once more. She ought never to have left her apartment. Momo takes out a cigarette. If you feel like smoking a joint afterwards, I don't live far from here. Ange returns, looking as fresh as someone who's just stepped out of a shower. She hopes they weren't interrupting anything. I was just explaining to mademoiselle here the importance of letting a guy know that you need him. She wishes she could vanish under the table. Ange thinks Momo is right, and to prove it she strokes her own man's thigh. The cups are set down on the table. The tinkling of spoons on porcelain and bitter liquid imbibed in small sips. Three coffees in fifteen minutes, she's not sure it's the best way to stay zen. Momo is of the opinion that Ange looks happy, and it's a pleasure to see. It feels to her as though she's fallen into a trap; this scene has been written with the sole aim of making her uncomfortable. She wouldn't be surprised to learn that the three of them had got together to engineer this supposedly accidental meeting. Momo and Ange have found common ground; they're chatting like old friends. Just then, she remembers Ange Karma, the play, the two tickets. She understands

that this conversation, which theoretically should under-
mine her position, is actually the best opportunity she
could have hoped for. She thinks of the word *courage* in
order to give herself some. Her mouth has shrunk; inside
it, her tongue weighs several tons. She counts to three,
then leans towards him to be sure Ange won't hear. I've
got two tickets for a play on Saturday night. There's a
pause, as he keeps his eyes on Ange; only his lower lip
quivers slightly. Okay, I'll call you. She wants to leap up,
to let her body move to express the joy she's feeling. But
she has to remain seated even as a frenzied dance begins
inside her. This time, the world really has changed.

For a long while they say nothing. The conversation
between Ange and Momo eventually dries up. Their eyes
now roam between the empty cups and the passersby. The
despondency of a Sunday afternoon drawing to its close.
Vague existential questions roil in minds assailed by the
looming spectre of a new week. Gearing up to return to
the relentless cycle: five days of work, two days of rest.
She forces herself to ignore the brazen glances coming
from Momo, who can't keep still any longer. Perhaps they
ought to go and smoke that joint now, he says. It's his
birthday, after all. The information appears not to move
the other two as much as it had moved her; they don't even
ask Momo how old he is. Ange is tired, they're going to
head home. She doesn't feel much like going to Momo's
by herself. She makes an effort to seem sorry, she too has
to work tomorrow. Momo looks vexed. That's unemploy-
ment, you get the chance not to work Mondays. He still

doesn't seem altogether convinced of the benefits of his situation. She finds it touching, though – this forty-year-old man so in need of company, who struggles against his solitude. Okay, but she won't stay long. Two pecks on the cheek for Ange. Just as she presses her cheek to his, he whispers, I'll call you soon. To keep her agitation in check, she looks into his eyes for confirmation of what appears to be a promise. He has already turned away, with Ange on his arm. She no longer has the least desire to smoke anything at all, but Momo, who has perked up considerably, gestures to her: this way.

There is no name on the door, which Momo opens with a single twist of the key. The television is so loud that it practically sucks the oxygen out of the apartment. Kamel, Momo calls out and as if by magic the host of the program shuts his trap. A narrow dark corridor leads to the main room, which barely manages to contain a sofa, a low table, a loft bed, and a gigantic television set. On the screen, an audience sitting in a studio is applauding, docile, open-mouthed. Behind small name cards, three august contestants are tasting their thirty minutes of fame. Kamel gives her a brief nod, then flops back onto the padded sofa. On the glass-topped table is an open carton of orange juice, some cigarette papers, a clear plastic bag with some dark green herbs inside. Momo invites her to sit down and goes off to the kitchen to fetch two glasses. Kamel changes the channel and stares at a cute young thing in a short skirt who has just appeared onscreen. Even without the sound, the young woman's gesticulations manage to convey the drama of the situation. She casts a quick glance at Kamel, who ignores her completely. She can still see daylight outside through the gap in the drawn curtains. Momo hands her the glass he has just filled with orange juice and then asks Kamel if he isn't bored with watching TV. Kamel shrugs, without taking his eyes off the young starlet now locked in a kiss with a stunning-looking man. Kamel puts the sound back on, and as Momo rolls the promised joint, the three of them let the serial draw them in. To speak would seem superfluous, even misplaced. Momo takes two drags on the long slender cone of red-tipped paper, then hands it to her. She inhales the smoke, easing herself farther back on the couch. Then she offers the joint to Kamel, who reaches a hand out into space. It isn't long before the bones in her skull seem to soften slightly; she feels herself lifted several centimetres above the level that gravity normally holds her to. Your friend's cool. Momo has interrupted the heroine of the TV serial. She hasn't the slightest desire to discuss Ange's qualities with him. She prefers Kamel's attitude and imitates his impassive shrug. Her mind has gone blank; she is floating somewhere between her body and the screen.

The television is off. That's the first thing she notices on opening her eyes. Next to her, Kamel is asleep. The room is plunged into semi-darkness, night has fallen. She gets up and goes to inspect the tiny kitchen. By the sink, a yogourt container has tipped over under the weight of the spoon left inside it. Momo has vanished. Perfect: she'll at last be able to slip away without having to invent an excuse. She grabs her bag, which is sitting by the couch, and heads for the door, only to find it locked. It takes several seconds for it to dawn on her: she is locked inside an apartment with a total stranger and doesn't even know who lives there. She reflects on the chain of events that led her to this place, on the moments when she could have made a different choice and avoided being trapped. She could have gone on walking when Momo first approached her, she could have left him after the first coffee, she could have followed Ange's example and gone home, she could have refused the joint, she could have smoked it but left straight afterwards, she could have stayed awake. But she had done the opposite, never suspecting that the sum total of these tiny decisions would lead her to this spot. She hasn't the slightest idea how to leave an apartment other than by the front door. She returns to the living room as quietly as she can so as not to wake Kamel. Slipping through the gap in the curtains, she carefully eases open the French doors that lead on to a small stone balcony with wrought-iron railings. She is surprised to discover that the apartment is on the top floor. Down below, two men are in motion, one of them trailing the flattened form of a dog. All she can hear is muffled music and the noise of a distant engine. Gusts of strong wind rattle the shutters attached to the wall by metal hooks. Tightening her grip on the guardrail, she imagines herself floating down, following the swirling currents of air, as light as a dead leaf, until she reaches the ground and regains her freedom. Given her current physical state, she can't hope to pull off such an exploit: she is well and truly locked in. How long can she wait for Momo to return? More than that, she's not even sure that he's coming back. Call for help. She could phone him, at the risk of waking up Ange. Only she doesn't know the address of the apartment; nor did she pay attention to the route Momo took to get here. And besides, he would probably want to contact the police. She would have to explain her reasons for being there, and the police would notice they had been smoking pot. They might even search the apartment and discover a quantity of cannabis far in excess of what three people would have on hand for their personal use. She would be charged with trafficking in illicit substances and wouldn't have enough money to afford bail. Too risky. She is starting to feel cold on this strip of balcony suspended over a void. No way is she going to stay in this apartment; she wouldn't last long. She remembers a film about the Second World War. In it, a Jewish man was hiding out in an apartment. Following the disappearance of his perverse caretaker, the place turned into his prison. It was the middle of winter. After eating every bit of food down to the last crumb, he took to his bed, where he stayed under the blankets, motionless. Watching the scene, she wondered what goes through the mind of a man who can no longer feed himself, who has nothing left to do except wait for an unexpected rescuer: how would his thoughts change as the hours ticked by and his body ate away at itself from inside? She thought about the stench of her own decomposing body, how it would alert the neighbours, and how, as usual, turnout at her funeral would be low. Stories every bit as sordid were heard the previous summer, when old people died in their own homes from heat exhaustion without anyone noticing. The government was held responsible, not the old people's children. But she is not ancient enough for this particular situation to get the better of her. There is only one solution: to wake up Kamel and ask him for the keys. The guy seems a bit of a lump, but harmless enough. Encouraged by this idea, she decides to put her plan into action. But when she goes back inside the room, Kamel is no longer on the sofa. Stunned, she stares at the crumpled place where he had been sprawled out a short while earlier. She looks around the room. How could he have vanished? She hasn't even heard the front door, which is still locked. She checks the kitchen. No sign of Momo or Kamel. All that remains for her to do now is to sit down on the couch and wait for someone to come and save her.

She thinks back to her afternoon. She was walking towards Place Carrée when Momo approached her. She remembers that when she heard the voice call out, miss, she was looking up at the top of a tree, where a strange bird, a cross between a pigeon and a sparrow, was perched. She didn't have time to get close enough to examine it carefully. Again, she sees the subtle changes that took place in Momo's eyes as she gradually relented. What gives the impression that the look in someone's eyes is changing? She has the beginnings of an answer but always comes back to the same vague conclusion: the shape. But the shape of what exactly? The skin around it? The pupil? The iris? She doesn't know. She thinks back to the firm pressure of his hand on her shoulder, as if he had known she was about to get up and wanted to stop her. His eyes, which carefully avoided her, while wandering suspiciously over Momo. The phrase she had uttered in a single breath. She doesn't remember the exact words she used, only the sense of relief she experienced afterwards. Whether he replied yes or no by then hardly mattered: she had dared to take a step she never would have thought herself capable of. Then he said, I'll call you, he didn't say when. He didn't say yes or no. Mentally she weighs the effect either word would have had on her. In fact, she's not sure that she wants to go to the theatre with him any more. She fears being alone with him, even though in the past she has invented numerous permutations of precisely that situation. It has taken her too long to make it happen, and she has grown used to drawing on that well of possibilities. It would be better if he refused so that things between them can carry on the way she wants them to, in an imaginary realm where confrontation and disappointment can be avoided. Isn't it more exciting to mould reality in one's own private laboratory the way one chooses to? For if he accepts, the mechanisms of seduction will be set in motion. She will have to behave as she would in any other romantic adventure: resist her desire then give in to it. As always, the beginning would lead to the end. She will have to love him and suffer for it. She promises herself that she will do everything in her power to not wait for his phone call.

Her stomach rumbles with the sound of an emptying pipe. She realizes she hasn't eaten a thing since morning. They have finished the carton of orange juice. The cupboards in the kitchen contain only a salt shaker and a bottle of oil. There are the filter papers and the small packet of weed on the table, but smoking would make her appetite keener. She lies down on the sofa. She has no idea how much time has passed since she realized Momo and Kamel had disappeared. Closing her eyes, she tries to empty her mind, but anxiety prevents her from falling asleep. Her heartbeat doesn't slow; at a dizzying rate her brain continues to produce bits of ideas, pieces of thought, unrecognizable images, which she feels powerless to stop. Her chest tightens; she has just remembered that tomorrow is Monday. If she is not out of here by then, she'll miss the start of her shift; disciplinary measures will be taken against her. The thought of being reprimanded, or even fired, by a boss she can't stand adds to her distress. She wants to believe that between now and the early morning Kamel or Momo will be back. If they stay out all night they'll still have to come home in the morning, even if only to grab a few hours' sleep. Feeling cold, she covers herself as best she can with her jacket. He must be peacefully asleep, in a warm, comfortable bed, while here she is freezing. She pictures Ange snuggled up against him, sleeping the sleep of the righteous. She feels certain that woman never has nightmares. Ange is protected by her honesty and her directness, which undo the traps before she even reaches them. With her rectitude and her principles, Ange would never find herself locked in by two strangers, in an apartment whose precise address she didn't know. Any more than she would let herself be paid 250 euros for not having sex with a diplomat! *She* would. Ange knows how to be pleasant and cheerful with everyone, yet she never lets herself get caught out by unforeseen events. Anyway, there are no such things as unforeseen events in her life, just plans put into operation. Her power lies in her ability to strike up conversations with just about anyone, while at the same time maintaining a prudent distance so that nothing untoward can happen to her. For example, Momo said more to Ange than he did to her, despite her being the one he initially tried to pick up. Yet Momo made no attempt to seduce Ange, and it is not Ange who now finds herself shivering on a couch-shaped raft that no wind is coming to push. For her part, she would have been only too delighted to settle for a friendly, civilized chat with Momo, before calmly setting off for home. So what is it? Perhaps it's because Ange gives the impression of being in control of whatever she does, whereas she acts without thinking. For Ange lives things the way she planned to live them and draws satisfaction and strength from having followed her plan to the letter. It probably has to do with willpower. Ange looks happy, Momo had said. What about her? What does *she* look like? No one ever tells her. She is not like Ange, it's as simple as that. I will never be like Ange, get that through your thick skull. She admits her fate is not as enviable, but it is hers. What happens to her could never happen to Ange. Which could also mean that she will never live with him.

The rumbling of a motorbike in the street. She opens her eyes, she has slept. It takes her several seconds to get her bearings from the slit of bright light between the curtains. No one has come, and she is still on the same couch, no warmer, her stomach tense. She closes her eyes again. She has run out of patience, doesn't want to stay inside this cage a moment longer. By banging loudly on the door she might manage to alert the neighbours. Except they are also likely to call the police. To escape the room's sense of confinement, she takes refuge on the balcony. Beyond the rooftops and the pointed hats of the chimneys, the sky is starting to brighten. For the moment it is only an indistinct halo of pale light, the tips of the sun's rays sliding the length of the planet, sweeping the night from their path. Several vehicles are gliding below. The city will soon be coming to life. She decides to call him as soon as the sun is up. To hell with it. Too bad about Ange, too bad about what she thinks, too bad if he blames her for letting herself get lured in like a little kid, too bad if he loses all respect for her. She will ask him not to call the police, and they'll try to find another solution. He won't refuse to help her. Perhaps his first thought will be that she is lying, the way she lied about being a prostitute, but she'll know how to convince him. In any case, she won't have a choice. So there is no point panicking. One way or another, she'll get out of here. Besides, any minute now Momo and Kamel could turn up with a bag of warm croissants. Everything is possible, after all.

Despite the cold, she stays out on the balcony to watch the sunrise: the sky turning from a pale blue to gold, the warming of the stone facades, the garbage truck trundling by, the birds singing, the steady rise of sounds and voices. Privileged moments. The day looks set to be fine. As the sun rises over the apartment buildings, she goes back inside. She spends a long time searching for the phone, at first all excited at the prospect of her imminent release, then more and more alarmed at not being able to locate it. Eventually she is forced to admit that there is no telephone in the apartment, and she is convinced that she has lost her final chance of escape. She sits back down on the couch. She is exhausted.

There's a sharp cracking sound above her head. The noise is coming from the loft. She has no idea what to expect. On top of everything else, she may also have to share the premises with a mouse. There's no limit to how low a person can sink. Heart pounding, she climbs the few rungs of the ladder leading up to the bed. And there before her appears Momo's puffy face. You been crying? he mutters in a sleepy voice, but she is unable to speak.

She asked Momo for the keys. After locking up the night before, he had fallen asleep with them in his hand. He didn't want to wake her. She doesn't listen to his explanations. Insults or kisses, either would do to celebrate her release. But she doesn't have time: she wants to go. Momo watches in disbelief as she rushes out, not even bothering to close the door behind her. At least give me your number. She smiles, pictures Momo adding the words *it's my birthday.* Without replying, she charges down the stairs.

She is now walking in the street that she had so yearned for all night. What she saw from high above she now sees up close. Everything seems immense, but at last within reach. With every step, she exults at the sensation of the firm ground beneath her feet. Before turning the corner, she looks up, tries to spot her nighttime perch. She never would have thought that the sight of a balcony could be so moving. She feels like someone released from prison after being wrongfully convicted. After a few bad turns, she finds the Châtelet métro station. Twenty minutes later, she will be at home. She will eat an entire packet of LU biscuits, take a shower, get changed, leave again; get to the station slightly out of breath, relieved, read 7:53 on a clock. Crossing the station concourse, she will, as she often does, imagine herself boarding a train. But at eight o'clock she'll be sitting at her desk, ready to announce the 8:15 a.m. TGV to Lille, as she does every Monday morning.

I 'll call you. I'll call you soon. A subtle nuance. How should she interpret it? The shift from a vague future to an immediate future – is it just a way of talking or does it suggest the start of something serious? A need to get closer to the anticipated action? A code to be deciphered?

For four days, the telephone has been silent. She has hardly spoken a word. The usual questions and comments to colleagues reduced to an absolute minimum. How are you? Good weekend? Awful weather! Not a peep about her misadventures. She has no intention of stoking rumours with an account of the past twenty-four hours. She knows full well that whether she boasted about it or complained, it would do her no good. More than a year ago, she overheard a conversation in the women's toilet at her office. The voices of two women, each in her respective cubicle, who thought they were alone. She had come in; the women had carried on, no more able to see her than she was able to see them, each from behind her closed door, skirt pulled up, arse exposed, chatting away as calmly as though they were sitting over a cup of tea. They had tried out several adjectives for her – quiet, cold, withdrawn – until they finally settled on the vaguest and broadest of them all: strange.

She wonders if he is going to call. The question punctuates her days, crops up at any moment, at work, during meals, while she's asleep, and as soon as it starts to slip her mind, returns with even greater urgency. Each time, the question seems to overpower yet another portion of her brain. No longer is it just one question, but ten, a hundred, a thousand identical questions, which wind up occupying nearly all the space available. Leaving her with just enough for what is strictly necessary. In the meantime, she functions. And so it goes, until Thursday evening.

On the news, she is watching images of an enormous blackout in New York. People are sleeping outdoors on pavements and in parks, unable to get home, the correspondent explains. She's not sure that one should feel sorry for them. Sleeping outdoors is a hundred times better than being locked in! Have millions been affected by the absence of electricity? asks the presenter, who already knows the answer. She has never been to New York; it's a city she views with some suspicion. Every accident, incident, attack seems to happen on a scale not comparable to events in Paris. As she is nevertheless trying to take an interest in the displaced New Yorkers, who have been plunged into darkness, the telephone rings. One hand pounces on the remote control as the other swoops down on the handset. No doubt about it, the call is from him. She doesn't feel ready for the verdict. Waiting at least had the benefit of prolonging the yes or the no. She picks up. He begins with his usual, how's it going? As if they had seen each other the day before; as if, for the two of them, time passed at a different rate. She makes herself repeat okay with the same apparent detachment. Then, for several seconds, all that stirs on the line is the sound of their breathing. He says, about tomorrow, she feels her heart tighten, it won't be possible; she stops listening. The rest, the reason, the excuse, the pretext, whatever can be called what he is now setting forth to her in detail, it no longer matters. Once again, it has to do with Ange. She is relieved and disappointed; something between the two, shuttling from one to the other so rapidly that the two merge. She attempts to console herself, at least she tried. Except now she is certain she would have preferred him to say yes; she won't dare ask him for anything again. Leaving aside the invitation to the theatre, being alone with her is what he has wanted to avoid. She realizes that he is still speaking. She holds the receiver away from her ear, then hangs up.

She doesn't want him to reassure her about what he no doubt intended to refer to as their bond of friendship. She detests these empty words, which people apply like so many sticking plasters wherever they detect emotional leakage. She doesn't want to witness the perverse transformation in him brought on by guilt. Had she stayed on the line, he would have levelled the high points of their story armed with his premeditated good intentions, would have opened up an area of common ground between them through which he could circulate without suffering any emotional shocks. He would have taken the opportunity to put his own house in order as well; he would have confidently declared what he doesn't really believe but would hope, by trying to convince her, to convince himself. And she would have been forced to take this pummelling without flinching. If he had given her a blunt no, the message would have been unambiguous, clear, precise, clinical. Bye, thanks, we'll forget it ever happened. The opportunity was there, we didn't take it, too bad. The story would come to an end; she would have battened down the hatches and would at last have been able to act as if this man didn't exist. But he spoke at length, more talkative than ever before, justifying his decision with all sorts of clauses and subclauses. He's thought about it, hesitated, and refused. She understands that his words had only one aim: to make sure that he wasn't losing her despite his refusal.

She lets the phone ring. Five rings, and the answering machine picks up the call. Listen, I don't know why you're taking it like this. Then he stops talking. The miniature cassette records his silence. Her eyes are riveted on the phone. She is not taking it like this. It's not easy to explain, but he ought to be able to understand. A long beep marks the end of the call. He has hung up.

Sometimes in the métro she has the impression that she is disintegrating. She's sitting in the company of other silent passengers, not thinking about anything in particular, swayed by the motion of the carriage progressing through the tunnels. She isn't asleep, but it is only at the final brake that she realizes the train has entered a station. It then takes her several long seconds before she knows if she has to get out at that stop or not. She has to review the preceding hours in her mind, follow the trail of cause and effect to work out why she is here at this precise moment, sitting in that métro, and decide to stay. The métro sets off again. And in the course of the journey to the next station, she again loses all notion of time and space. As the train comes to a halt once more, she has to perform the same mental calculation so that this time she can struggle to her feet and slip through the doors, which are about to close.

She retrieves a bottle of whisky from the disarray of a kitchen cupboard. Fifteen centimetres of golden liquid. She swallows the first gulp with a slight wince. The taste gives her goosebumps. Alcohol dissolves most troubles, penetrates the mucous membranes, slows the nerve impulses, relaxes obsessive thoughts – the fragile, drunk heroine is condemned to eternal sadness. A fairy tale in reverse. Total flop. No one cares any more about the ravages of passion; our age has stopped believing in them. And yet people cry out for drama more than ever, ready to pay a high price in exchange for it. There has to be action, upheaval, constant change. Thrills are required to distract and impress the customer. The abrupt halt of their telephone conversation appears to signify a rupture, but not one she can take seriously. Whisky number two. She feels as if they have set out to explore a region where the climate is harsher. Heavy showers, bundle up, bursts of sunlight early in the morning. She pictures the two of them in long oilskins by a stormy sea, hunched over to shield themselves from the gusting wind. How to talk in such conditions? The first thing to do is to seek shelter. She feels certain that each of them knows where to find the other. She knows the place where he has gone to hide. She actually should be congratulating herself: she's rescued them from one hell of a tight corner. Raising her glass, she toasts the empty room. For now, it's bound to be a bit painful. There are moments, she explains to her green plant, when radical measures are required if the worst is to be avoided. If their conversation had got out of hand, they would have ended up throwing their raw feelings in each other's faces. Full-blown carnage and no one to wipe up the mess afterwards. She now has to wait for calm to return. It will take time. She can't imagine what he might be doing now, still less what might be going through his mind. Chances are he is with Ange. In which case, he's having a beer in the living room or eating with her in the kitchen. If she were a fly, better still an ant, stationed on the edge of the sink with antennae out, she would listen until Ange chased her away with a swipe of her sponge. What a revelation it would be! In her human form, she has never overheard even a snippet of private conversation between them. The odd words required for the smooth functioning of their life together – shall we go, can you take my bag, yes, I'll have some – but nothing resembling a discussion or a row. She therefore lacks the material with which to reconstruct their conversations. Perhaps they are watching a film on TV, he very intent, Ange distracted, announcing the solution to the mystery in advance, he complaining, she apologizing. It's not my fault, it just slipped out; anyway, you guessed as much. Or else they are making love. The image of a dark room filled with sighs, then more sighs. Mustn't switch on the light: what his naked body is plotting against Ange's would appear in full view. She doesn't want to know, which is understandable. She finishes the bottle. Is he upset? Angry? Offended? Riddled with remorse? Or perhaps pleased? Glad to be rid of her? Can he see her, a blot of yellow oilskin in the midst of a damp fog, hidden in some far corner of his mind? She juggles the various options but can't manage to sort them out. She lacks key data. Even for herself, the storm has brought down a number of certainties she felt were solidly anchored. Such as, there could never be any misunderstandings between them. How does one define a misunderstanding, though? The magazines on the shelf don't deign to reply. Between them there had previously been an understanding, which has mutated into a misunderstanding. What is the difference? She has had too much to drink; she is unsure about the next steps. Good and evil are both an arbitrary distinction and an infernal dichotomy. The main thing is to understand each other. She doesn't have the strength to carry on talking to the furniture. She dozes off.

The ringing of the phone pulls her from the depths of sleep. She is stretched out on the sofa between two pairs of stone arms and stone legs. With much difficulty, she extends her hand to catch hold of the receiver and stop the noise in her ears. She doesn't say hello, doesn't have a single drop of saliva left in her mouth. How are you? For the first time, he has said it with feeling. No longer is it mere politeness or a verbal tic: he wants to know how she is. The expression is no longer a screen, it conveys genuine intent. For the first time, she doesn't parrot back like a fool, okay. She gives a real answer to his real question. I have a terrible headache. Even as it sinks in that he is there, at the other end of the line, that he has called her back. She is surprised, but she tells herself it couldn't have been any other way. The storm has passed, their bond has held. The forgiveness is tacit, the hard feelings have never been explicit or implicit, there never were any. It's the start of intimacy. Two people who know the same thing, without having to put it into words. The conversation that follows is the one they haven't had yet: What time is it? Seven o'clock. I'm going to be late. Did I wake you up? I'm glad you did, I didn't think I'd slept for so long. You needed it. And you, did you get some sleep? Not much. He must have faced facts. What has happened between them isn't trivial. He hurt her, and it has affected him more than he could have imagined. Despite all his past efforts, he can no longer delude himself about the essence of what exists between them. Ignoring it is now more awkward than acknowledging it. And he acknowledges it, as she just understood from their conversation. I'll call you, he says. The words are the same, the intent has changed: she believes him. As she puts down the phone, her whole body is electrified. Tonight she will go to the theatre alone, but that doesn't matter anymore.

She is at the microphone. She reads out: *The TER 47433 service, bound for Beauvais, departing at 11:22, will leave from platform number 7. The TGV 7040 from Lille will arrive at platform J. Attention please, attention please, please note the change of platform. This regional service will be stopping at Amiens, Lamotte–Brebière, Daours, Corbie, Heilly, and Méricourt–Ribemont.* Her voice fills the entire station, soaring over the platforms, the halls, sailing into corners, crashing into glass walls. She is present everywhere, and yet no one recognizes her. There is a little trick she does to avoid stumbling over her words: she focuses on what she is saying without focusing on the fact that she is saying it. Never fails. The travellers soak up the information she sends them through the invisible loudspeakers. She is perfectly anonymous, talking to everyone and yet addressing no one. Occasionally she dreams that one of them won't head straight for the taxi rank, won't rush down the stairs into the métro, won't revert quite so quickly to his habitual self the moment he steps off the train, and that instead he'll stop and tell her about what he saw during the course of his trip. All she knows about the towns and villages to which they travel are their names and positions on the map. That is all she has to picture them. Her own journey goes only so far as announcing destinations, navigating between syllables of names, pronouncing numbers and letters correctly. On the rare occasions when she has taken a train, she has experienced the same sense of misgiving as would a doctor who has to undergo medical treatment. And then, in order to get away, you need to know where to go; you need a destination. A motive is what tears through the protective layer of the everyday. Departure is an upheaval, which can only be calmed by the pleasure of experiencing the desired place. She would have liked to travel everywhere; in other words, nowhere. But while she may never have had a valid reason to leave, she now has a good excuse to stay.

After walking out of the station, she stops in at a café. She wants to celebrate their reunion. The waiter is surly, but in her current state she could put up with insults and still be smiling. Hot chocolate, its sweet taste, comfort, a childhood treat. To prolong the pleasure, she drinks it with a small spoon. Everything has yet to start; all is held in suspense. Full of promise. In bud. The horizon is clear, the best can be imagined. He has just offered her the place she has been trying to occupy for a long time, by her own crude and ineffectual means, without ever daring to demand it. She knows that everything will be more complicated later. But for now, what happens next is nothing compared to the present, which overwhelms all else, encompassing both past and future. A happy anticipation of what she now has no more reason to fear. Behind the window, pedestrians are walking by in waves. She passes the time following several of them with her eyes, testing the force of her gaze. The challenge: to pierce through the layers of thoughts and preoccupations that cut them off from the world around them. The rules: to use only her eyes. The purpose of the experiment: to determine the time it takes for them to turn their heads in her direction. The findings: first of all, there are those who are impossible to reach, who forge ahead without noticing anything. Wasted effort, they're the sort who will never respond. Then there are those who react at once and yet seem to be the most absent. Their heads jerk round suddenly, as if their skulls were attached to a wire on which she'd given a sharp tug. They gaze straight at her, forcing her to withdraw into herself as if she'd been bitten. Lastly, there are the ones she has to make an effort with and who make her feel as if she's fishing. At the last minute, just as they're about to disappear from sight, they turn their heads, slowly, as though thinking someone had called their name. They don't always see her, but they look in the right direction. They are her favourites because they belong to the same category she does. Now that she has finished warming up, she turns her attention to the people inside the café. Easier because no one is moving, more risky because she is in the same room. Around her, the tables are empty. The customers are crowded up at the bar, cigarette in mouth, glass in hand, words on lips. The waiter, resting one elbow on the zinc counter, is searching for wondrous worlds in the cracks of the ceiling. She starts with the hunched backs. No luck. A woman did move her head, even almost saw her, but midway let herself get distracted by something out in the street. And then, all of a sudden, a bite. She had barely begun to stare at him when the man spotted her.

He climbs laboriously down from his high stool and walks towards her. She feels embarrassed, hasn't the least idea what his intentions are. She stirs what remains of the cold chocolate at the bottom of her cup. He looks like a tramp, bushy beard, dishevelled oily grey hair, multiple layers of clothing, and yet is carrying Chanel, Longchamp, and Armani shopping bags, lots of them. She signals to the waiter, who has just discovered a cache of hidden treasure under his thumbnail. The legs of the chair in front of her scrape over the tiled floor. May I, asks a deep voice. Without waiting for a reply, the man sits down and arranges his fancy stuff on a second chair. I did some shopping, they're having sales this week. The man studies her face. He doesn't strike her as aggressive; he awakens her curiosity, and so she lets him talk. I'm not what you think. Odd introduction. Neither is she what he thinks, but in her case it is far less obvious. He explains to her that he is not what he seems. You know, a tramp, a homeless person. But he prefers people to assume that he is; it helps him with his investigations. As he talks he holds her gaze, his eyes serious, to dispel her doubts. The object of his investigations? Human nature; he's been studying it for several years. Compiling data about people's behaviour in the face of poverty. His appearance suggests one thing, his bags another; his words attempt to make it all coherent. She can't decide whether he is lying or telling the truth. A bit of both. He is lying, but thinks he is telling the truth; or else telling the truth to justify his deception. You don't come here often, I've never seen you before. True, but for once she felt like dropping by after work. She is not about to start telling him her life story; after all, she has to remain on her guard, she promised herself. He's found a lovely little scarf, pure wool; he'll show it to her. He thrusts his hands into the Armani bag and brings out a hirsute piece of cloth, which he displays proudly without unfolding it. Not bad, eh? I haven't tried it on, but the colour should be fine. Tell him that he's off his rocker . . . She prefers to answer that yes, the colour goes well with his skin tone. Visibly the man wasn't expecting that; he seems pleased. She wouldn't work at the station by any chance? Surprise. Yes, she works at the station; as she says the words she blushes, without knowing why, as if she had been caught doing something red-handed. She wonders how he could have guessed that she . . . Her voice? That would be a first. No one has ever recognized her like that before. A person would need to have spent a hell of a long time listening to announcements over the loudspeakers to be able to make the connection. But if he spends the night asleep in some corner of the station, then perhaps it is her voice that wakes him every morning. And she thought she was talking into thin air. There might be someone without a train to catch who listens to her reciting times and destinations. She doesn't dare ask him if he lives in the station; that would cast doubt on the truthfulness of what he has said. He has started talking again. Do you like theatre? She doesn't know; it depends. The timing of the question couldn't be better. Funny you should ask. That's where I'm going tonight, though usually . . . He smiles as if to reassure her. She'll like it, he's sure she will. However much she tries to tell herself he is raving, the impression persists that he already knows her. He is following her every reaction. She succumbs to the fascination of small details: the strip of red skin fringing his lower eyelids; the way the hairs of his beard poke through his skin; the sudden, slight dilations of his nostrils as though, from time to time, they had to make way for more voluminous particles of air. It's better to go to the theatre alone. He says it while continuing to stare intently at her. No way can the man know. He could just as easily have remarked that it's better to carry an umbrella when it rains. But no, he had to mention the theatre, precisely on the day when . . . He found her sitting in a café on her own; he drew his conclusions from that. The wonders of logic, psychological decryption, a gift for observation. Absolute knowledge allows the future to be foretold. You don't agree it's better to go alone. Oh it is. It is.

Whatever the extent of the oddball's divinatory powers, she is no longer in the mood for guessing games. A small gesture to the waiter, who is now studying them closely, not missing a crumb of their weird tête-à-tête, a perfect distraction for a rather dull late afternoon. She pays, gets up. The man's voice for the last time. You're right to go alone, trust me. She shrugs but is happy to hear those words. No one has ever proved that guardian angels don't exist. Not angels who have wings, like the ones she saw the other night on Ange's back, but angels who protect you, the real guardians.

The rooflines of the apartment buildings appear distinct, their symmetrical placement down the length of the avenue far more striking than usual. The declining light bathes the buildings in its orange hues. She has passed this way dozens of times, but this evening the sight of these stationary buildings does her good. Lit as they are just now, the walls are no longer barriers but mirrors, filtering moods so that only the best ones remain. One day she was given a pair of tinted orange sunglasses. They made the world more beautiful. She wore them at every opportunity, dreading the moment when she would have to take them off. After several delicious weeks, she lost them. Where or how, she had no idea. She has had other pairs since then, of course, but has never found the desired effect again. Which has led her to conclude that for every pair of eyes there exists a specific tint. Colour is absorption, what remains of light deprived of certain wavelengths. Orange equals light minus blue, simple arithmetic. All the colours mixed together gives white. Maximum superposition, absolute density. What she needs is to filter out a certain blue wavelength that makes the world a little too cold for her. Yet she also knows that losing those glasses was not a bad thing. If they had stayed with her, she would have grown accustomed to them. Repetition would have diminished the effect.

It's eight o'clock. She is outside the theatre, which looks the way she imagined it would. A small, finely crafted building that resembles a palace. Unique architecture for a special place. The few times she has been to the theatre, it felt as if she were stepping into a sanctuary meant for an initiated few. The solemnity such places exude makes her uneasy. The artifice of the sets and the costumes prevents her from letting go of herself. If it were up to her, all plays would start out on the pavement. No calls for silence, no spotlights, no tiers of raised seats. The actors would mingle with the crowd and suddenly launch into their roles. At the foot of the stairs, people dressed for the occasion have started to gather. She feels rather drab by comparison. They are waiting as well, but not the way she is: they are out for the evening, want to have fun, whereas she is on a mission and came to find the actress who bears her name. She collects her ticket and stations herself slightly off to the side of the stream of new arrivals. The muffled buzz of conversations, the clusters of lights on the walls and ceiling, the faces, made-up, freshly shaven, cleansed of worry in anticipation of what they are about to see, give her the impression that she is inside a cocoon. The notion of time has been abolished. The people are the same ones who gathered here a hundred years earlier, all they have done is change their clothes to keep up with current fashions. She seems to be the only one to have doubts about her role. What she lacks is an escort, someone she could imitate. No one is paying attention to her, she reflects, which must mean that she really does stand out. If she were a ghost, she would roam the foyer at every performance in the hope of finally being seen. If he had been there, he would have acted as a buffer between her and them.

An usherette in a black suit is asking her if she is looking for someone. She hesitates. Yes, her husband, he's been delayed. The young woman shows no sign of surprise; swallows the lie as painlessly as a gulp of saliva. The fingers with their manicured nails twist her ticket apart while the eyes take in her shoes. If your husband has his ticket, I'll take you to your seat. One of the usherette's tights has a run behind the ankle. She considers mentioning it but doesn't, for fear of upsetting her. She edges her way between knees and the backs of seats towards the place the usherette indicates with a disproportionately large gesture. Strained smiles, heavy sighs, people shift their legs to one side, rise to their feet, as the entire row takes note of her arrival. She settles into her seat, relieved. A few seconds of required immobility to make them forget about her.

A young couple is sitting to her left. Their joined hands placed on the centre armrest, as if they were on a plane about to take off. They're having an energetic conversation, of which she catches only every other sentence. In the Solitude of Cotton Fields is much better . . . How can you say that when you haven't read it . . . you have to read it, otherwise you'll never be able to understand Bernard-Marie Koltès's other work. She doesn't know who Cortès is. It sounds like the name of an explorer, a conquistador. If she had been an explorer she would have set out alone for distant places, by land and on foot. Perhaps he would have known about Cortès; it would have given them a topic of conversation. Not that silence between them would be embarrassing, but places of public entertainment oblige you to talk. Another couple has sat down to her right. Two generations older. Siamese lives: the past starts from the moment they met. They have ended up looking similar, in the ever more dizzying rush of time their movements have slowed at an equal pace. After undoing their coats, folding them carefully, lowering the seat with trembling hand, sitting down and arranging their things on their laps, they stare at the red velvet curtain. All she can hear is their slow, sonorous breathing. She tries to breathe like the woman, imposing on her lungs the same intakes and exhalations of air. It's always Shakespeare with you, I've had it with Shakespeare. The young man has raised his voice. Startled out of her daze, the elderly lady sits up in her seat and adjusts the dial of her watch. They're late, she remarks to her husband. The man looks at his watch. They're not late, it's eight-thirty. A bell rings. The lights go down.

The set remains the same throughout the play. The offices of a small PR company at the start of the twenty-first century. Six metal-and-plastic desks, six chairs with adjustable height and backs, six computers; some shelves and filing cabinets; a whiteboard on the wall; a coffee machine. Laid out on each desk are pots of pencils, note-pads, Post-its, staplers, along with a few of the occupant's personal effects – a cuddly toy, a postcard, a framed pho-tograph, a packet of sweets. The action takes place in an unnamed town in the United States. The play opens on a Monday morning as the six employees – five women and a man – arrive at their desks and pick up where they left off the previous Friday evening. There is one final character, who comes on later, the boss, whose adjacent office shares a door with the stage. The first, fairly ordinary, lines of dialogue serve to establish the atmosphere of the office and the role of each employee within it. Weekend activities are discussed, someone complains about a machine that's not working or about a missing file; there's banter to show most of the six employees know one another well. It's mainly the women who expose themselves in these small brushstrokes; in anecdotes that reveal the key aspects of their lives, the main traits of their personalities, their everyday worries but also their recurrent obsessions. As for the man, he is rather worn out. Not much of a talker, he nevertheless makes an effort to take part in the women's running jokes. Naturally, the boss is a tyrant; coarse, but not nasty. He likes having all these women under his command. Finally, there is one employee who distinguishes herself from the rest, the new one, Noémie. She talks less than the others; not that she ignores the conversations, but she keeps a vigilant eye on her work. She has the absent air of a person absorbed by a single ongoing thought. Noémie resists becoming part of the group, who do everything to draw her in with their questions, their teasing and provocations. Noémie doesn't play the game; she wants to be left alone; she lets no one get close. But the more she holds back, the more the others are intrigued. Her secret is like a splinter, painful but invisible, except when very close. Prodded by her colleagues, who ultimately mean well, she finally opens up: her husband was in one of the twin towers of the World Trade Center during the September 11 attacks. All the women immediately assume that he didn't survive, but Noémie can't bring herself to admit it, for she has received no tangible proof of her husband's death. To her colleagues, her hopes appear groundless and unhealthy. Yet none of them has the courage to talk about it. According to them, the best remedy is to forget, and the women encourage her to look for a new partner. But Noémie sustains herself on illusions and can do no more than haunt the margins of normal life. For her to fit in, she would have to think as the others did and give up the only thing that allows her to go on: the conviction that her husband is alive, somewhere. In the end, the male employee, normally silent, reveals to her that he was a volunteer in the Ground Zero rescue operations. From what he saw, her husband could only be dead. After hearing these declarations, Noémie does not return to work the next day, nor in the days that follow.

Right from the start, she feels certain that the actress playing Noémie is the one with the same name as hers. Her performance is so perfect, it seems to her that the actress has become Noémie, who from now on can only have this actress's voice, postures, and expressions. After a certain point, all she sees on stage is another version of herself, who is the actress living the role of Noémie.

In the middle of the play, she turned around. Dozens of faces, illuminated by the diffuse light of the projectors, had their immense eyes trained on the same spot; not moving, intent. She found it fascinating.

The lights come back up. Eyes blink. To her left, the hands are apart, each one now resting on its respective thigh. The young couple has resumed their discussion with the same intransigent passion as before – the plot's hard to swallow; the main actress, a bit weak – and get up from their seats as soon as the applause has died down. The elderly couple to her right, by contrast, is quite motionless, their fingers entwined. The play has abruptly propelled them into a place to which only they have access. Their immobility is no longer a sign of their age; they are still in their seats because they have yet to return to themselves. She feels intrigued and gives in to her curiosity. Are you all right? A kindly, apologetic smile from the old lady, who shows no surprise at the question and is quick to reply that the play has brought back memories for her and her husband. From the war, you know. She doesn't, but would like to know, only the husband then says, let's go, thereby bringing to an end the conversation which has barely begun. No point insisting. Which of the two of them disappeared, which of the two of them thought the other one was dead, which of the two of them found the other years later, the mystery remains intact. And because of their sense of discretion, the hunched, grey-haired couple takes their story away with them.

Someone told her it was the third door at the end of the corridor. Hanging from the walls are posters of past productions at the theatre, testimony to the short-lived glory of the actors who appeared in them. She reads some of the now-forgotten names as she passes. Fame has never tempted her. She has never sought to do anything at all that could earn her the recognition of others. Nothing in her life strikes her as worthy either of praise or exposure. Her job consists of talking into a microphone and enunciating pieces of information as succinctly as she can. She produces sounds. Practically anyone could do it. In any case, she has never wanted to be indispensable. Seeing her name printed in a newspaper, being recognized and fawned over by people who have an idealized, distorted picture of who she is would embarrass her. She would believe she was a fraud. The last poster in the corridor is the one for the evening's play. She sees her name, the actress's, their name in fact. Like everyone else, yes, she would feel flattered to be admired. She would know lots of people, who would know her in return. Her telephone would ring, she would be invited to dinners in imposing mansions, where she would be served not smoked salmon but caviar. Her eccentricities would be indulged, might even add to her reputation. Lots of men would want to sleep and stay with her. As for him, he would like her more; Ange would no longer make the grade. But at the height of her glory, some meddling journalist would discover the switch. It would be too much for her to bear: suicide, and the end to the promising career of the SNCF train announcer-turned-celebrity. Her ex-colleagues would be interviewed: she was a wonderful person, we were all so close.

Draft of fresh air. A man has come out of the dressing room and strides straight past her without a glance, even though there are just the two of them in the corridor. She can't believe her eyes, she knows him. But by the time she finally decides to say we've met, Maxime is already too far away. The door has remained ajar. Someone is humming; a woman's voice. She knows the piece, which consists of only a few notes, one tone up, one tone down, again and again. She used to play it on the piano; she remembers the tune but not the name. She gently pushes the door and steps into the room. In the mirror covering one of the walls, she sees the actress examining herself in a piece of another mirror laid flat on a table. *Noémie* is the first word that comes to mind. But before she has time to say anything, the actress wheels around and the two of them are looking at each other. The actress belongs to the second category, the ones who immediately sense the presence of someone's eyes upon them. As tense as an archer's bow, sophisticated, a milky way of tiny freckles on her upper chest. What are you doing here? The actress expects an explanation. Find the words before the surprise turns to annoyance. I've come on account of our name, we have the same one. The actress raises her eyebrows in displeasure. What ridiculous undertaking has she launched into? She is no longer sure what she wants.

We have the same name. She has nothing further to say; it's what she came for. The reaction of the person in front of her that must now give her presence meaning. Caught off guard, the actress replies that, yes, that does happen, more often than one might think; a lot of people share the same surname. She is trying hard to come across as accommodating, despite having only one wish: to get rid of this odd intruder. Yet another star-struck fan, who will have seen in the similarity of their names a pretext to meet her. She is aware of the unease she is causing but is still convinced that she can't just leave, that beyond the small talk and the apparent incongruity of her visit, something else needs to happen. The actress has stopped spouting platitudes. There could now be the slam of a door, the hum of ventilation, the meow of a cat, even perhaps an explosion, but instead there is a kind of grey silence made up of the remnants of distant sounds, which neither one of them bothers to identify. Eventually, the actress invites her to sit down in an armchair whose back touches the mirror. Listen, I don't understand what you want. She doesn't know what she wants either. She saw her name on the poster in the métro just before she found the dead man and thought there might be a reason. A reason? The actress knows that public figures receive attention from every kind of maniac, that she shouldn't complain, but there has to be a limit to how much time she can give them. And then Maxime had been in the corridor. She knows Maxime? Touché. Curiosity is aroused. She has gone up a notch; the actress has started to wonder, to have doubts, to worry. And what are you doing here?

Maxime doesn't give the actress money; he tells her that he's in love. More noble, no trace, no responsibility in the eyes of the law. He makes love to her in the dressing room after her performances. She doesn't even have the time to get out of character; she's still immersed in Noémie's denial, still has her voice, her mannerisms. She is tracking her phantom husband, and that phantom takes the form of Maxime. And as she passes from one body to the other, an imperceptible transition, the beating heart that slows after the race, she could not be more vulnerable. Their love-making prolongs the experience onstage. When pleasure finally brings her back to herself, he is already putting on his trousers. The time to ask questions has passed.

She knows all that; there is no need for the actress to tell her. The bearers of secrets are condemned to wander on the periphery, plunging into the world around them to create an illusion, regularly excluding themselves so as to let nothing show. They are tempted to confess but are gagged by their own guilt at having kept silent for so long. A single judge has handed down their sentence, a judge all the crueller for being none other than themselves. And the only ones who can recognize them are those going through the same penance, those able to signal them without giving themselves away. The actress, on the defensive, refuses to let her in. And so she finally plucks up the courage to say it to her. If you're so upset when he leaves, maybe you don't trust him, maybe you sense that he's lying to you about his feelings. A tightening, a closing down, why is this woman mixing herself up in all this? Quick, stop her from disrupting what the actress spends her evenings putting in order. But because the other woman has the same name, because her tone of voice attests to her honesty, because what she says makes sense, the actress doesn't reply and sits down in the armchair opposite her. And suddenly it strikes her that the mirror no longer divides the space but multiplies it. They are not two any more but four, they and their reflections, the perfect image of their lives split in two. Four sides of a single person who doesn't exist. They are no longer moving. No one can tell how long this lasts, not even they. And for a few seconds or several minutes, nothing happens in the dressing room. Until the realization comes that she is ready to talk. Ready as she has never been before; without apparent reason or motive. For the first time since she was thirteen, she begins to tell the story of the rite of passage. She talks about the pink room, about the piano, the bed with the spring mattress, about the pink bedspread, the piano in the room. She is not emotional but focused on making her account as precise as possible, as if this were her only chance to consign what happened to the invisible pages of another's memory. She doesn't say I, but she.

She's done. The actress has covered her mouth with her hand. She doesn't feel anything in particular, only the satisfaction of having said exactly what she wanted to say at the moment when she wanted to say it. She stands up. There is nothing to add. To continue would be superfluous. They shake hands. They won't see each other again.

She has never considered the rite of passage as something traumatic because no one has ever been shocked by it. Lonely people have no misfortunes, only stories that are never told. But this time she has told something that she had kept to herself for over fifteen years, since the days when she and Marion would sit together every afternoon on a bench at the lycée, not doing anything in particular. While speaking, she had had no sense of removing a weight from her shoulders. The rite of passage is not a memory that could be hidden away in some distant corner of her brain because of neuronal deterioration. It is a physical imprint, practically a substance that has leaked into her bones, muscles, and blood. Like DNA, whose coded helixes determine our individual characteristics, it is part of every cell in her body. She can talk about it, but she will never be able to get rid of it.

When she returns home, she has the impression that the apartment has grown larger. The objects have not moved, but their arrangement appears to have been altered, as if each one had been turned several degrees to the left or the right. The smell seems different too. Perhaps something happened here while she was gone; an event that left olfactory traces too diffuse for her to detect where they came from. Stretched out on her bed, she closes her eyes and imagines that the city has ceased to function. The city is still on the other side of her windows, but nothing is happening, not a breath of wind, not the slightest movement. True silence. The sort you can only taste in the deepest countryside in the dead of night. What to long for now? It has taken one day for the thing to happen that only twenty-four hours ago had seemed impossible. What she accomplished – confiding in the actress – took place without the least premeditation. Years spent in the same mental groove, and then, all of a sudden, a chance to move on, a chance that perhaps had always been there or that had been created by a particular set of circumstances. She has already adjusted to her new dimensions, and so naturally that even she is surprised.

Final thought before falling asleep. Above and beyond all else, the good fortune she has at last been given.

He'll call her soon; she no longer has any doubts about that. This certainty should dispel her concerns, she ought to be reassured. They have come to a turning point, the most delicate and hazardous moment of all: he has proved that he is not indifferent to her. Before this, everything could have broken apart without deeply altering their lives. Now waiting has been transformed into an idea of what might blossom between them. It feels exactly as if someone were permanently trying to scare her, except no one is ever around. She is entirely consumed by the thought of what is to come; she sifts through facts, imagines possibilities. She wants to explore all avenues, to guard against making a wrong move when the time comes. Her feelings at this point are so absolute that they can only lead to perfection. By sheer faith, she thinks she can defy the unpredictable. What she overlooks in all her forecasts is that the intersection of their respective desires will never produce the expected result.

Towards the end of the morning, she returns to the street market. She walks the whole length of it without paying attention to the goods on display and blindly charts her course to the accompaniment of the merchants' arias. Two euros, two euros a kilo, last peaches of the season, beans, beans, ladies, the best beans in town. Buying nothing, present in this atmosphere of harangue and transaction, engulfed, borne along by two opposing currents. She allows herself to be pushed by the movement of the crowd, the sudden eddies, the halts, the momentary gaps. To be there like everyone else, but without a reason, without resisting. She is expelled at the other end of the long tunnel of tarpaulins and trestles, opposite a flower stall. As those around her walk off, she stops in front of the buckets and the bouquets. The florist in a long dark-blue apron is cutting the tips off the stems with a pair of clippers. To make them wilt more slowly, now that they've been torn away from the plant they grew from. Amputation to prolong life – she's never quite understood it. Something is tugging at the bottom of her trousers. A small fist at the end of a small arm, the crown of a child's head, a child who hasn't realized yet that he's clinging to the wrong leg. He thinks he's safe, even as he holds on to a stranger. At her mercy, boundless trust. She doesn't dare move, in case he panics. The child is captivated by the flower seller's gestures. If she gently slipped her hand into his, would he notice that it was an unfamiliar hand that was holding him? She feels tempted to find out. To see how far she could get before he looked up and, in terror, caught sight of her face. He would start to cry; she reconsiders and drops the experiment. A woman with her back to her is buying a bunch of roses. The mother. She'll stand there without moving until the woman sees him and smiles at her son's mistake, so the terror will pass quickly. But when the woman turns around, it is not her son that her eyes fix on but her, incredulous.

Because of the sunglasses she doesn't recognize Marion right away. But Marion recognizes her. The dark glasses lend her the air of a Hollywood star who has slipped into a market for a taste of local colour. She wonders if those brown lenses are the ones through which Marion sees the world best. Marion calls the boy, who realizes his mistake. Without taking his eyes off her, he lets go of the trouser leg and moves away with little steps, his head screwing round as he goes. No trace of fear; only a kind of intrigued curiosity, as if he had just discovered a new species of animal, which he was surprised to have been able to approach without danger. On one side, there is the little boy and Marion, who is looking her up and down; on the other side, she stands there wondering what would be the best attitude to adopt. Between them, the flower seller, who has resumed cutting the tips off the stems. Do something, move, dispel the awkwardness, break the tension of this unexpected encounter. She could head back the way she came. Pretend not to have seen or recognized her old friend. She'd be swallowed up by the crowd. There'd be no one to hold it against her, no explanation to give. Before, she would have avoided the confrontation; she would have done it without hesitating. But just now, something stops her from turning away and propels her forward. She takes a step. Emotion and reproach alternate in Marion's eyes. She lowers her gaze and forces herself to smile at the child, who has shoved a thumb into his mouth and is sucking it with abandon. Either of them could or should have called the other, but the one who thinks she's

the victim turns the other one into the culprit. At the court
of broken friendships, she would be taken before the judge
in handcuffs, without the right to a lawyer. In her defence,
Your Honour, she was powerless. No clemency. Sentence
is handed down: to write ten thousand times *To be loved is
a responsibility*. She wouldn't dare say that she hadn't
known. She is now only a metre away from Marion. The
child has lost interest in her, he's rubbing the soft petal of
a flower between his fingers, the tranquilizing effect of
touch. For a few seconds, she would like to be in his place.
She imagines taking Marion's hand and being engulfed by
a wave of serenity. But the situation is urgent, usual words
must be found. Why not rewind the film, start again from
scratch as if it were the first time? Don't even think about
it. If they hadn't already known each other, they would
never meet. Marion is asking the child not to play with the
flowers. They don't belong to you. The child looks up at
his mother to gauge the seriousness of the order, then
retracts his hand. She is about to say that the flowers don't
mind, but realizes that is hardly an ideal way to begin
under the present circumstances. She can feel Marion hes-
itate between acting spontaneously or taking refuge
behind the resentments of the past. It then strikes her that
every story is determined by its opening lines. Which is
why such sentences are so hard to pronounce. He's pretty
well-behaved usually. The signal. Marion is talking to her
at one remove. The child is the intermediary in a hesitant
attempt at communication. She has no choice but to follow
the lead. He's cute. She already knows they won't get very

far like that. If there were a dozen or more kids, that might keep them going longer. She watches the child hopping from one foot to the other as he plots his next expedition. She finds it fascinating that Marion could have given birth to him. To have that strength, to have the determination to take on that particular role. And for the rest of her life to protect, to worry, to manage to keep the threats at bay. To believe in the miracle, whether from ignorance or conviction. She looks for resemblances, traces of the mother's personality in the child. But the little boy's bearing seems quite distinct from Marion's. A little person in his own right. It is only over time that the mother will put her stamp on him. For now, the degree of kinship can be seen in the degree of obedience. She knows that it is customary to compliment parents on their children. She'd like to tell Marion how impressed she is and to sound sincere. For she is impressed, even if it seems that the existence of the child makes the rupture of their friendship even more final. She'd like to do the right thing, play by the rules for once. No missteps; to use the opportunity to show that she means well. Even if there can be no follow-up, she would like Marion to feel that she doesn't disown their past. Things turned out the way they turned out, that's it, like the wind, the pressure of actions and reactions. She can't explain, it's too tricky, she'd get tangled up and only make the situation worse. By going through the child, she can no doubt show Marion that she still cares. She softens her voice. Do you like the market? For a few seconds the child stares back at her without blinking, then, brusquely, buries his head in his silent mother's coat. Silly kid. She represses an urge to pull an extremely ugly face. Have you left Montpellier? Of course she's left Montpellier, you idiot, she's right there in front of you. Awkwardness makes you say the most ridiculous things. Marion moved two years ago, her husband works in Paris. She is about to say you should have let me know, but she catches herself in time. She's not used to asking questions; it makes her feel like a private detective who's found her client's girlfriend and is checking her identity. And you, are you working? Marion motions her chin at the child, who is again sucking his thumb. I look after him; it's a full-time job. A smile flits over Marion's lips, and without looking at him she runs her hand through the child's hair. Suddenly, she feels, how to put it, inappropriate, extraterrestrial, entirely unsuited to her gender and species. One day, a man had confessed to her that he envied women solely for their ability to have children. She had called him a misogynist, he hadn't understood. She wants to ask Marion at what moment did it become impossible for her to hold back, but the question wouldn't sound right. At best, Marion would say, it comes, it gets to you in the end, it even becomes an obsession. She hears Marion calling to the child. Timothé! Immediately it reminds her of the jingle in the advert for Timothei shampoo. Timothé! The child puts back the large red apple he was about to make off with and returns, dragging his heels. A successful display of authority. And you, how are you doing? Marion must be saying to herself that things haven't changed, that the passage of time has been no help, that she's still on her own and struggling, husbandless, childless, haunted by bad luck. In addition, she doesn't have much to tell, she's bound to disappoint. And soon it will be that Montpellier look again, that sorry helpless stare which means, I understand, but which can't understand, and which, in its deliberate sympathy, chains her to the past. When she replies, fine, Marion thinks about it, and even if Marion didn't think about it, she'd think that *she* was thinking about it, which comes to the same thing. She can say whatever she wants, argue that time has gone by, but the changes Marion perceives in her will pass through the filter of the incident confessed to years earlier, and it still stands between them, even after a marriage and a child, and perhaps for these two reasons even more so than before. She'd like to say to Marion forget it. But she would still have to manage to answer the question, and her head is spinning and she has an increasing desire to throw up. She must have turned pale, for Marion has let down her guard somewhat, she addresses her by her first name. Soothing familiarity. She could talk about him; Marion would no doubt see it as a positive element in her life. But what to say? That there is a man who . . . who what? Kissed her by mistake at a party and hasn't laid a finger on her since. Who lives with an angel but spends his evenings bored stiff in front of the television, this last fact as yet unproven. Who refused to go to the theatre with her but managed to speak to her on the telephone for almost five minutes, his words making her feel that her life has changed. She puts herself in Marion's shoes: at best, she'll find it amusing, at worst it will confirm what she already thought. Wait a second. Marion rushes after the child, who has trotted off in pursuit of some pigeons. She watches her go, sees her catch up to him just as he reaches the curb. She is left standing there alone, looking off in the direction of her vanished friend. The flower seller asks her if she needs any help. She shakes her head but can't move from the spot. This is the moment, the longed-for opportunity. To escape. A few strides would be enough for her to disappear into the crowd of market-goers. And so bring an end to their pathetic and disturbing encounter. She turns her head. Marion is busy talking to the child, pulling him by the arm. She makes a run for it. Stiff limbed, intent, one step at a time, she reaches the central alley of market stalls. Marion has perhaps seen her by now, but her decision was made a long time ago; there's no turning back. One more metre and she is swallowed up by the crowd. She's safe. When she's sure that she is well hidden from view, she looks back. By standing on tiptoes, she can just make out Marion turning round and round, eyes on the lookout. If she waved to her now, if she walked back, it would be easy to invent an excuse. She'd pretend that she had never meant to leave. I went to have a look at something. But she doesn't have the strength for that. She watches Marion hoist the child into her arms, then walks away from the market. How long did Marion spend looking for her? A minute at the very most. Is that how she should measure what she meant to her friend? She imagines Marion recounting the incident to her husband. I suppose it's too late to do anything. And Marion won't have any reason to hold her tongue, the rite of passage will come spilling out, beyond her control and without her permission. She feels her stomach tighten at the thought of it. By now, Marion and her son are two specks in the distance.

There's a message on her answering machine. He wants to get together with her. Anywhere will do. She'll go. They'll see each other. Alone at last. They'll talk. She'll have to find a topic of conversation. She can tell him about Noémie. She'll ask him what he would do if Ange disappeared. No, let's see. She'll ask him what he would do if she disappeared. Too dramatic. She won't ask him anything. She'll just say, it's strange not knowing if someone is alive or dead. Too heavy as a starter. She'll talk to him about the weather. Too banal. She'll talk to him about the place where they are. They'll comment on the look of the people they see going by. She could teach him the staring game. No. He'll find it childish. Or else he'll kiss her and there won't be any need for them to talk. No. He won't dare, not in public, not at the risk of running into someone who might know him, or Ange.

She presses the play button. A woman's voice. Panic. Ange has discovered everything and is challenging her to a duel. Marion has got hold of her number and wants an explanation because she doesn't understand why she treated her like that. But the voice says neither Ange nor Marion; it says her name. For a few seconds, she thinks that she has left herself a message but has forgotten all about it. She is suffering from a split personality. *Schizophrenia* is the medical term for it, if memory serves her right; so that could be the problem. But as she listens, she realizes that it's not her voice. I got your number from Maxime, I'm sorry to disturb you like this, I wanted to tell you . . . The voice stops. I wanted to tell you that I've left him, I wanted to say thank you. The actress then takes several seconds to hang up. The red light stops blinking. She could almost cry. Not from sadness or joy. Something else, but she doesn't know exactly what. It's not every day that someone says thank you to her. For the duration of the message, the roles were reversed. She became another person's guardian angel. Despite the fact that she never thought she could protect anyone from anything, least of all without knowing about it.

The next day, in the middle of the afternoon, she is outside the entrance to the Parc Monceau. She spent all morning thinking about the actress, about Maxime, about their break, about the remark of hers that led to it. She feels as if she has rescued the actress, and since the previous day a sensation of lightness hasn't left her. Hence the desire for green open spaces. She has chosen the Parc Monceau because she has never been there before. Entering the park, she reflects how one person can change the life of another, without meaning to, by a sentence or a gesture. A gesture or a sentence that someone else could repeat dozens of times without having any effect. Without ever realizing it, a person can change another's life. Couples are lounging on the grass and children are roughhousing with their parents. Lone men and women are reading or getting bored on the benches. Whenever she is in a park, she is always faced with the same dilemma. All those orderly paths overwhelm her. A park should be explored instinctively, without markers. But the walkways impose their fixed itineraries and lead to artificial crossings, which force one to choose different sections of the park over others. The only way to get to know the place is to follow the layout of paths, to explore them all without exception. At each fork, however, one of the paths has to be abandoned and might never be found again.

Near the pond, she notices a man sitting with his back against the trunk of a willow tree. His legs are stretched out in front of him and he uses them to support the notebook he is writing in. Through sheer concentration, he keeps the world at a distance. Farther along, she sits down by the water's edge but continues to spy on him. He doesn't look up; he is galloping forward without moving a muscle. She imagines herself doing the same thing: emptying her head onto one page after another. But what would she write about? Her days at the offices of the SNCF! The man has lifted his head and is looking out at the surface of the water. She has never met a writer before. Do you write? For a moment she thinks she is hearing her own thoughts. But then she spots a pair of black feet in sandals just beside her. He is there every day, a man's voice announces from on high. The new arrival has settled onto the grass thirty centimetres away from her. She tells herself that maybe she knows him, but no, she has never seen his face before. No doubt she is not the sort of woman who needs to be asked permission. She should perhaps stand up, tell him that she's taken, married, but she can't bring herself to lie. The man has turned his attention to the surface of the water, perhaps looking for inspiration as well. Do you write? She shrugs. At least he's someone who tries to be funny. She can pass herself off as a prostitute, but not as a writer, an authoress, she isn't sure what term she should use. You could be. Well, he must take her for an idiot, unless it's the best compliment he can come up with. Actually, no, she couldn't be. And so what does she do, apart from spying on poets? The question takes her by surprise. She doesn't spy on poets. She doesn't know any. In fact, he's the first one . . . she's seen . . . in her life probably . . . she's never come here before. He was joking. She at once wishes she could take back her dumb reply. It must be some deep-rooted need of hers to justify herself to strangers. Especially since he doesn't even seem to be trying to pick her up. His name is Atoki, and he insists on knowing what she does for a living. She hasn't the faintest idea why he's so curious. She thinks of a whole list of professions: accordion player, tiger tamer, Sunday school teacher, champion jockey, chimney sweep, striptease artist, lunar astronaut. She has no end of choices to become something she is not for him. Tell me the truth. This Atoki person is really starting to get on her nerves. She's an SNCF train announcer, there, that's all, happy now? Atoki stares at her as if he hasn't understood. He wants to know what SNCF stands for. She may be naive, but either this guy is pulling her leg or he was born on another planet. SNCF, the railway company. Atoki seems impressed: he has never met anyone with that profession before. It sounds like a good job to him. You're not from around here? Atoki is a refugee, he was born in the Democratic Republic of Congo. His words sound like the opening lines of an advert for an NGO or an adoption agency. She doesn't know where the Democratic Republic of Congo is in Africa; she prefers not to ask. Which is just as well because Atoki seems none too keen to talk about his native country. He wants to ask questions. He tells her that it must be quite something to talk into a microphone and address hundreds of people at the same time. Actually, once you get used to it . . . He wants to know if she ever feels like saying the first thing that comes into her head. Changing a departure time or the number of a platform, for example. If you want to get fired, that's a good way of going about it. Of course the idea has some appeal, but she has never thought about it. Over time, certain prohibitions have the power to merge into what is normal and violating them becomes inconceivable. It's hardly in her interest, in any case, to defy the unwritten rules of what is pompously referred to as professional behaviour. Atoki's full attention is on her; she tries to understand the reasons for this blatant interest. A foreigner, slightly disoriented, tries to fit in, to form ties, to understand through its inhabitants the place where he has been assigned to live. Because he will probably spend the rest of his days here. The distance this man has travelled to end up sitting next to her in the Parc Monceau in Paris must be the equivalent of five years' of métro rides for her. She has never been to another country, not even Switzerland or Belgium. She has never been a refugee or a foreigner. And yet she thinks she can guess: no points of reference, a permanent sense of incomprehension, of rejection, of being stigmatized. And so foreigners of all sorts find themselves in parks because all parks are similar. Parks don't reflect the tastes of a society as much as buildings do; in a park an immigrant can feel a little at home. Atoki is still not satisfied. He now wants to know what aspect of her work has astonished her the most. She makes a face. Atoki waits, as if unaware of the incongruity of his question. It feels as if she is taking part in a television quiz. What kind of thing? Anything. She is about to say nothing, that her work is monotonous, that she sits down behind a microphone every day to read out stoically whatever she is asked to read, that the words are always the same, that the trains are rarely ever late, that everything is timed down to the last minute, that unforeseen events are kept to a minimum, that she produces nothing, invents nothing, that the only people she has contact with are her colleagues, who avoid her and whom she avoids, that many travellers are convinced that what they are hearing is a synthetic voice and not a real person. If she were born in the Democratic Republic of Congo, then, yes, there would be astonishing things to relate, but in her case, honestly. Poor refugee. To have travelled all those kilometres and to stumble across her, who can't even come up with a single original anecdote to tell him. Oh, but actually, there is something. Atoki waits with baited breath. Recently she met a strange man in a café who was pretending to be a tramp. Although she had never seen him before, the tramp knew her. The tramp had never taken a train but he slept in the station and heard her announcing the departures and arrivals. And it was from her voice that he recognized her.

The poet is no longer under the tree, and Atoki has fallen silent. He observes her for several seconds, then lowers his eyes. Whether he is lost in thought or embarrassed, she can't tell from his expression. She doesn't tell stories usually, but the words came, lured out of her by Atoki's interest. That's an odd story. Atoki's face looks serious. Perhaps she has shocked him. Or he must have remembered something painful. In his case, the word *refugee* says a lot. She imagines a war – young black men armed with Kalashnikovs astride military trucks, a famine – a skeletal child in the stick-thin arms of its young mother. What I don't understand is why there are people sleeping in train stations in a country as rich as yours. Atoki addresses her as if, as a Frenchwoman, she were personally responsible for this state of affairs. Yes, well, it's not very logical, but she doesn't see how it will change. She has always seen people sleeping outdoors in Paris. There are many explanations for homelessness, but no one has ever managed to eliminate it. Atoki has gone back to contemplating the surface of the water, its crests now taking on a reddish tint. She doesn't reply. She doesn't like talking about that kind of thing, it never leads anywhere. She has no opinion on the matter, any more than she has a solution to the problem. On her SNCF salary, she isn't the person who is going to improve the lot of the poor. And yet she can't help feeling guilty. In the métro, after finding the dead homeless man, she ran off. She could tell Atoki about that incident as well, only she fears it will make him even less talkative. He would take her for a coward, he who must have witnessed horrors in his own country. She has pins and needles in her legs. Time for her to be off. Atoki turns his head as if he had forgotten that she was there. What is the name of the station where you work? Gare du Nord. He is only asking because, who knows, if he ever finds himself without a place to sleep, he'll go in and listen to her. A smile, a handshake. Following one of the walkways, she heads straight back to the exit of the park.

At the third stop, two teenage girls have entered the carriage and sit down opposite her. They don't say a word, and look so different that she wonders if they are together or not. The one on the right seems unable to cope with what has happened to her body, whose proportions have changed without her having any say in the matter. The girl on the left looks like one of those young models who appear in women's magazines. Her hair is long, straight, and layered. Shiny lips and eyeshadow. A real Barbie, with headphones on her ears and a CD Walkman in her

hand, ignoring everyone and yet attracting the stares of
the male passengers around her. The news report about
young American girls comes to mind. Has this adolescent
ever had a man's penis in her mouth? She wonders if the
girl is aware of the sexual attraction she incites. It isn't
because of her makeup or haughty expression – it's her
fragility, which is so badly concealed. And she realizes
that at the same age, when she felt apart from the world of
adults, she too must have been this walking temptation.
There's a bed with a spring mattress and a piano. Before
her is the pink room. She screws her eyes shut to erase the
image, then opens them again. It doesn't help. The enormous, polished-wood wardrobe by the front door, the
shelves stacked with perfect piles of dishcloths, towels,
packets of lavender in the folds, the bed with the spring
mattress, the metal bedposts she would grip as she
invented storms that billowed up the ocean of carpet, the
bed, the golden spheres at the end of the bedposts which
became crystal balls whenever she played at being a
fortune teller, the night table with its marble top, the
lampshade with the tassels she used to braid when she was
bored. She sees herself in that room at thirteen, sitting on
the wicker chair practising Mozart's first piano sonata.
She still knows the notes by heart, the rhythm and the
melody, the look of the score on which stave, minims,
crotchets, quavers, dots, and bar lines made up a code she
was proud to be able to decipher. And suddenly, it is no
longer herself that she sees playing, but the teenage girl
opposite her, sitting in her chair at the keyboard. She finds

her so charming, so vulnerable, and all the more desirable for being unaware of her seductive power. It dawns on her that this was how she was seen even as she thought she was someone else. At the time, she didn't know. A cruel injustice, a trap of ignorance. She has clenched her hands, and she notices that her nails have left small white-rimmed indentations on her skin.

The second teenager has let out a sigh. She is wearing jeans and a huge anorak. Her thick thighs stretch the material of her trousers and the anorak hangs loosely about her torso. Her hair is tied back with an elastic band. Her prescription glasses have slipped down her nose. Her entire body, right down to her pupils, is motionless. Except for her thumbs, which are frenetically working the buttons of a miniature electronic game. She hasn't the slightest idea what is flitting across the girl's screen, but she thinks she knows what the teenager is using it to escape from.

No message. She counts two and a half days. A reasonable amount of time. She doesn't allow herself to doubt. Perhaps Ange has gagged him and locked him in a closet. Or he hasn't had a chance to free himself for the meeting he will be arranging with her. She's dying to call him. In fact, imagining it has become a daily mental exercise: picking up the handset, hearing the dial tone, dialling the number; the rings, the click, Ange's hello, hanging up at once. The chances that he will pick up the phone are too slim. And besides, he said, I'll call you, not call me. She'll have to be patient, that's all there is to it. Having made up her mind, she prepares herself a quick dish of pasta shells with grated Gruyère cheese and settles down with her meal in front of the television. A man in a suit and tie is being interviewed as part of a televised debate. His name is given at the bottom of the screen: Yves Métayer, Terrorism Expert and Professor at the Institute of Political Science. The man earnestly explains that we have to stop deluding ourselves, that in five or ten years we will witness an actual Third World War. Not a conflict between nation-states but a full-blown religious war, Christians against Muslims! The journalist smiles into the camera. Aren't you being a bit too pessimistic? That's precisely the kind of blinkered judgement that will make this war impossible to contain, replies the professor, growing increasingly agitated. This conflict will be extremely bloody, you'll see. The journalist thanks Yves Métayer and announces a commercial break. The pasta shells have slipped from her fork; she is left open-mouthed. She doesn't watch the news very often, she hadn't known there was already talk of a Third World War. She doesn't really believe it, but if it were actually to come about, where would she be in five years' time? Here. The first target in a war is always the capital. Would she leave? She swallows a few more mouthfuls of pasta, and when she's finished, her mind is made up: she'll stay.

Walking through the station to her office, she thinks about going somewhere. With him, for the first time. She has stayed because of him and will only go away because of him. It's no longer just a vague idea, as it was in the past, of wanting to leave without having the will to do so. To her surprise, she finds herself imagining the various steps necessary to organize such a trip. They would choose a place. They could talk for hours about it without growing bored, reeling off the names of unknown cities and countries until they found the right one. She'd take care of the tickets. She wouldn't buy them at a ticket window, but from one of those automatic dispensers, which remind her of the casino slot machines she has always dreamt of using. She would choose the time of departure, very early in the morning, at an hour when Paris was still rousing itself from sleep. Out of bed and straight to the station, nothing to interfere with the anticipation of departure. Time of return: late evening, so as to arrive in the dark, coming back to a city already half asleep, to seek refuge at home, with memories of the trip as bed companions. She would take the seat by the window; first she would ask him what he wanted. She would check the information printed on the thick paper and carefully put the tickets away unfolded. They would arrange to meet at the far end of the platform. She would be carrying an overnight bag with two or three changes of clothes. Toothbrush, toothpaste, hairbrush, the minimum. Hand in hand, they would walk the length of the purring train until they reached their carriage. Their carriage. They would sit down. She would inspect everything: the materials of the seats, the luggage racks, the windows. She would take a good deep breath of compartment air. And inside that train, with him by her side, she would feel safe, ready to circumnavigate the globe without ever stopping.

He called her on Wednesday at 6:27 p.m. She had just glanced at the kitchen clock. He arranged to meet her the next day at six-thirty, in front of city hall. Ange had a dance class. For the next twenty-four hours, she accomplishes everything she does with incredible ease. The thought of getting together is a kind of balancing pole. Her body feels the effects: she holds herself straighter, is no longer tired. It's as if she has been chosen. She is no longer adapting herself to life. Life suddenly seems to be adapting itself to her.

She doesn't sit down on the stone benches for fear that he might not see her. She adjusts her hair and tries to act as naturally as she can. Her head jerks round intermittently, as though she felt him watching her, as though he were continually stepping out from some unsuspected corner. She would like to see him so she can pretend not to have seen him. For a moment, she is distracted by the tumultuous stream of pedestrians on the square, wind-up figurines marching in a precise direction, but whose straight-line trajectories seem random. A collision has just been narrowly avoided; barely glancing up, the man and woman continue on their way. The sound of their footsteps is lost amid the din of engines and car horns. A voice rises above the commotion. He is there, behind her, scarcely a metre away. She walks over the moment she recognizes him; she doesn't dare look him in the eyes. She sees the sides of his jacket flutter. He has just left work. She doesn't move, leaving him to take the initiative. She feels the coolness of his lips on both her cheeks. He suggests they go for a walk.

Until the Île Saint-Louis, not a word is spoken. She'd like to take advantage of this silence but can't. Everything is mixed up in her. She thinks she has to talk. To justify their unusual presence in this place, at this hour of the day, the fact that they are together for the first time. To prove to him that he wasn't wrong to invite her. To keep him there, give him reasons to stay. Because she is worried that he could change his mind at any second and walk off after realizing his mistake. She has never been very talkative, but right now her whole brain is refusing to co-operate. It feels as if she is playing Scrabble with herself. Bits of words, the beginnings of phrases form in her head, but she can't manage to string them together. Her only consolation is to think that perhaps a similar pandemonium is whirling inside him. She doesn't dare look at him to check. And then, as they turn a street corner, he places a hand on her back. A brief caress, as if to reassure her, as if he had sensed her panic. The contact calms her fears. She knows only one thing now: she is walking by his side.

They have sat down on the banks of the Seine, by the Pont Marie. Not the side where the students show up in the afternoons and where people come to smoke and have fun on summer nights. But the other side, which is quieter. They sit close to each other. She lets her legs dangle over the water, her eyes wandering randomly over the golden buildings in front of her. He sits cross-legged; stealing glances at her out of the corner of his eye. This goes on for an indeterminate length of time. Then he says, how are things? His voice sounds new, as if he had never used this voice before. But the ensuing silence worries her slightly. A giant sightseeing boat is advancing along the river; a mass of tiny tourists are waving their hands. The boatload, drowning under the didactic onslaught of a nasal voice, holds their attention for a moment before getting sucked into the shadow of the bridge. She leaves her eyes trained on the exact spot where the boat has vanished; he keeps his eyes on her. Then he asks. What are you thinking about? The passage of the boat has given her a little time. She shrugs. Nothing. She doesn't know. About so many things that she doesn't say. I've never seen you look so pretty.

She then has the certainty, the troubling, flattering certainty, that he is about to kiss her. She is dying to let him. Hasn't she imagined it dozens of times, this kiss that is in no way accidental? And yet something tightens inside her. She is on the edge of a cliff and can't go any farther. After this kiss, there will be no turning back, she will no longer be able to love him in her own little corner without triggering strange defence mechanisms over which she has no control. She has looked forward to this scene for so long, has wanted it more than anything else. But now she puts off doing what she has yearned for all these months. His wanting to kiss her turns into a threat, and his desire feels like a weapon that could only wound her. A frightening reflex that she is powerless to stop. She feels ridiculous, at a loss. The spell is broken. Taking hold of her hand, he gives it a squeeze; she squeezes his back. She wishes she could stay like that, but she can't stop herself from erecting a barrier of words between them. We should be going. Another tourist boat is passing along the river, in the wake of the one before it. At first glance, its passengers look the same as the ones before.

They walk back over the Pont Marie. He must be telling himself that he made a mistake, that her behaving like a jumpy teenager doesn't make any sense. He must not understand what she wants from him any more and must be thinking about Ange. He'll be able to tell her the truth: nothing happened, I held her hand, she wasn't feeling well, you know, she tends to be fairly unpredictable. And yet the story about the prostitute had made an impression on him. For the first time, he had realized that she wasn't the bland woman he had taken her to be. In front of city hall, he must have watched her for a few minutes before calling her name. Her hidden, darting looks, her hesitations, her air of being present and yet absent, as if her body were translucent. People find it annoying, she knows that. And yet he had seemed to put up with it, at least until now. He can't ever have met anyone like her, surely that is what attracts him. In her awkwardness and abrupt way of asserting herself, he must recognize something of himself. And afterwards? How could he deal with her spontaneous reactions? How could he even consider getting involved with her? And risk upsetting a life that, when all is said and done, must suit him just fine. Keep Ange at a distance, risk hurting her or living with a guilty conscience. And all that for a woman who recoils before he has even offered her his lips. If kissing is already such a trial, no wonder he loses heart and doesn't want to imagine anything further between them! I'll walk you back. He spoke in a flat voice. An immense traffic jam has brought the rue de Rivoli to a halt.

He steps away, and she doesn't have it in her to hold on to him. Too little time, too little intimacy. In less than an hour, she has ruined everything. First prize for disappointment, the clear winner. She should have known that she wouldn't be up to the task. And yet she thought she had prepared herself. Tell him that there are good reasons to justify her behaviour but that she doesn't know how to explain them. A whole string of insults come to mind – opportunist, nasty coward, cheap asshole, pickup artist. But using them against him wouldn't help her case. If he thinks he's easy to get close to, if only he knew how much patience she's needed. He must be comparing her to Ange, and, it goes without saying, she doesn't stand a chance. She would like to tell him that he shouldn't think like that. Ange is Ange; she has her wings, she knows how to fly, light and charming. She, on the other hand, has no wings.

She has a voice that she uses correctly only when addressing strangers. She has never asked to take Ange's place.
She has never asked for anything. Besides, it was he who
phoned her. She isn't even sure what she wants. If only she
could be certain that he is like the others, she would know
how to back off and leave him alone. But she thinks of him
in a way that she has never thought of anyone else before.

They walk down into the métro. Music is coming up
from below. You hear it? He nods. At the bottom of the
steps, a roly-poly little man is sitting at a miniature keyboard. His thick fingers pound the keys of the instrument,
which emits more or less harmonious metallic squeaks.
They pause to watch the unusual spectacle. She recognizes
the piece: *Für Elise*. E – D – E – D – E – B – D – C – A –
C – E – A – B, with a rock beat. She used to play it and
always detested it. Just then, he takes hold of her arm and
turns her towards him. She senses that he wants to say
something serious to her. But the sight of him standing in
front of her like that, embarrassed, with that awful music
in the background as the little man presses on, improvising
some grotesque tune, gives her a fit of giggles. Taken
aback, he lets go of her. His arms drop to his sides. Again
an unexpected turn. Do I make you laugh? She shakes her
head, as if trying to get rid of the silly idea that has
wormed its way into her. Explain before he takes offence
and gives up on her for good. It's the piano, I used to play
it when I was little. He doesn't understand. He looks at the
little man, who is more pathetic than funny. He no longer
feels desire for her, she can sense it; he no longer knows the

reasons that prompted him to come for her. You ought to go, Ange will be waiting. She spoke without hostility or bitterness, with an assurance that stood in stark contrast to her retreat just moments earlier. Soon, they will have put an end to this shaky adventure, which they wrongly believed they had wanted to embark on. And suddenly she thinks she knows what he wants to say to her: Ange is the one I love. Ange's beauty, her assurance, her straightfor-wardness – and he would compromise his relationship with such a woman! All she can ever be for him is a fantasy, a solitary, bewildered creature who arouses his curiosity. It was out of pity that he arranged to meet her, at once flattered and sensing a responsibility for the interest she showed in him. He confused his willingness to do some-thing for her with some amorous feeling.

She doesn't dare touch him. The energy that flowed between them has been cut, replaced by a mass of isolating air that their hands can no longer penetrate. It feels as if she has been dropped into a void, without warning. She sees him turning things over in his mind, searching for the right reasons. Now, yes, she is ready to kiss him, but she doesn't dare. She thinks about rolling around on the floor, faking an epileptic fit or a faint. Then he would have no choice but to stay and look after her. The ground is right there; all she has to do is throw herself down. Whether she faints for real or not hardly matters, he could never be certain that she faked it. Truth or lie: in moments of urgency, you no longer make the distinction. As soon as he turns his back on her, she will be overcome by despair, and

yet another disappointment will be added to her collection.
She has to stand up for herself. Why should she allow him
to leave her like that, as if she had the plague, just because
she wouldn't let him plant his lips on hers? She isn't quite
sure what the symptoms of an epileptic fit are. Better the
faint, then. She just has to let the muscles in her knees and
neck go limp and collapse in a heap. She will probably get
hurt a little if he doesn't catch her in time. Too bad about
the bruises. She closes her eyes, he opens his mouth. But he
doesn't have the courage to tell her; nor she to let herself
fall. See you later, they finally intone in unison. His face
tense, he strides off towards the turnstiles. She remains
where she is, both hands clutching the hem of her jacket.

Then come two weeks of forced daily grind. Without her
knowledge, a piece of lead has been inserted into her chest.
At times she looks for the operation scars on her upper
torso, but the skin is taut, unblemished. Her outer layer is
intact; the damage is on the inside. Every gesture is an
ordeal, a conscious effort to convince herself that eating,
going out, working, sleeping are in fact necessary for her
to go on living. She doesn't want anything. She'd like to
stay on her couch staring out the window, like old people
in a rest home who have nothing but their past to mull
over. Her existence is a succession of moments at home
and moments at the office, interspersed with brief trips
outside, a cycle that goes on and on for the simple reason
that she doesn't know what to replace it with. She spends

the weekend in pyjamas, listening non-stop to "A Lucky Guy" by Rickie Lee Jones and gulping down cornflakes straight from the packet. Two evenings in a row, she forgets to switch on the light before sitting down on the sofa. The telephone doesn't ring. But she no longer pays attention to that either. She doesn't talk much any more. She just moves her head a little when her co-workers say hello; not even their disapproving looks bother her. There is only one thing she forbids herself to do: to foul up when announcing the trains. Her voice remains constant, a limpid stream that betrays none of her anxieties. During those brief moments when she is speaking into the microphone, she is leaving her leaden body behind and merging with the vibrating air that emanates from her throat.

Later on, she can't remember any of her thoughts from this period.

After a week of this dry routine, she wakes up one morning with the sensation that the lead inside her has broken up into several pieces and migrated to different parts of her body. The heaviness is still there, but it seems more evenly distributed now. To make this new state last, she knows that she has to keep herself busy. Reorganize her clothes in the wardrobe, put the magazines in order on the shelves, rearrange the bottles of cleaning products in the cupboard under the sink. She makes sure that she always has something to do, scrupulously makes her bed and does the dishes, scrubs the bathtub twice a day, tidies up, washes herself meticulously, reads the posters in the métro. Whenever she inadvertently gets bogged down, she replays the scene on the Île Saint-Louis. Pinpoints the exact instant when they began to draw apart. She goes back to a second or two before the fatal moment, when she wasn't able to let herself be kissed. The sequence is always the same: there is that incredible, almost palpable tension between them. She realizes what is coming, panics, talks, the tourist boat goes by, then it's over. She would like to erase what happened next. The shame of it! Even twelve-year-old girls know how to stick their tongue into a boy's mouth and move it around while breathing through their nose. Nestor Karma had warned her: details count. The kiss had to be precisely that. She blames herself for her behaviour until eventually she convinces herself that it couldn't have been any other way. She writes *It wasn't my fault* on a piece of paper, which she tapes to the back of the toilet door.

Every time she thinks about him, the pieces of lead shift, crushing her insides.

One evening after she has eaten her dinner, rinsed her plate and cutlery, and wiped up the crumbs with a sponge, she finds it hard to sit still on the sofa. She switches on the television, but instead of soothing her, the programmes accentuate her disquiet. The two-dimensional beings gesticulating onscreen look like sad puppets, as if life had been reduced to a limited number of preordained gestures. She switches off the set, stands up, and wanders around the apartment searching for something to do. But no sooner does she take hold of something than she loses all interest in it. Using it becomes an empty gesture, bringing neither distraction nor relief. She has only herself for company; the lead is starting to exert its grip once more. She should go out, meet someone, in the hope of feeling something other than her own physical limits.

The street is empty. She wonders what day it is and has to make an effort to remember. Monday. Rain has darkened the pavement, patches of damp stand out on the walls, the air smells of vegetation, as if man-made odours no longer existed. She walks along suspended above her regular footsteps, fascinated by the ease of her movements. And so it goes until the combined effects of the wind and the rain begin to wear off, until her surroundings become oppressive, as though everything around her were gradually drying up. Ill at ease once again, she goes into a bar. The only customer seated at a table is a young man on his own, writing. Three men are laughing in chorus with the barman at the counter. Some music playing in the background lends the place a vague romantic charm. She has stepped into one of those realms where external events are transformed into words and stripped of their consequences. They let her sit down without paying attention to her. A few minutes later, the barman comes over with a dishcloth over his shoulder and the hint of an amused smile still playing on his lips, the last trace of the story told by the men at the bar. But he vanishes the moment he takes her order, leaving her alone, still craving company. For a few seconds, she turns her attention to the young man, who is contemplating the loose sheets of paper that have barely been touched by ink, but he doesn't look her way once. A newspaper has been left on the seat next to her. *L'Inédit*. She has never seen any copies of it except in this place. She opens it at random and begins to read.

Religious communities, political communities, ethnic communities, minority communities, a place where we find others who resemble us. In all societies, a need to conform. Innovation is a risk machine, use it cautiously, it isn't included in insurance contracts. You will be covered for refusing to respect the prevailing way of life. Go out of your way to run yourself aground! What's the point, death lurks in the wings. Without surprises, no bad surprises; stay perched on the branch where your predecessors made their nest. Be careful: any shifting around could lead to a fall. Do as you please, but stay within the norms; you are being watched. Enemies of the unusual are united, but there are no half-measures for the ones who have escaped conventional thinking. Every day, hundreds of people avoid one another. Because of modesty, of cowardice, of incomprehension, of laziness, of fear, of pride. There is no button to push that would slow them down, for what is left behind must be, in theory, found ahead. Waste, the evil wrongs of a consumer society in which infinite choice is permitted and, once attained, bears the misleading designation of freedom. We glance at others as though they were shop windows. Man adores ease. He battles on to prove, wrongly, that he is right; he revels in empty words, loyalty, integrity, trust. Trust vanished a long time ago. People want things to run well, but things have no legs, they exist or they don't. People shut themselves away in ugly, rickety dwellings. At least they hold together, just don't get too close to the edge. Never has the cult of the goddess Security had such a following. If the agreement of tenses is a basic rule of language, agreement among human beings is as rare as a solar eclipse. Don't miss it. Assuming your senses have not been numbed. Most of the time, circumstances dictate everything else. There are no truths, only points of view. It is always the next note that reveals the accuracy of the one before it. You have to listen to a piece all the way to the end in order to appreciate its beauty. It's true that boundaries shift, ways of thinking evolve, but power relations continue to impose their laws. Today, in the West, women who wear the veil are a symbol of the absence of choice. The innocent pupil raises his hand: Sir, is television a form of submission? You've got it all mixed up. Human rights advocates will howl: *You* have the choice. In a word, explain the difference between choice and freedom. Subtlety is the enemy of power. Stir up the concepts in a single pot, fodder to be served to the masses to fatten them up and keep them quiet. Choicefreedom – capitalism's hi-tech weapon. The mission of the saviour of the globe is to spread democracy in order to stimulate markets. Money does not guarantee happiness, but it helps. Make a note of that, it will come in handy later on. In the year 3000, statues of the kings of petrol, father and son, will be erected at the entrance to the capital of the world. All advertising posters will read: ORGANIZE YOUR CAPITAL, PLAN AHEAD. This is the quest for the Holy Grail of our time. Man will never be cured of his mortality.

The article is by someone named Gaëtane Lonrice. She isn't sure she has understood what the writer is trying to demonstrate. She swallows a gulp of red wine, looking at the wall opposite her. A large painting hangs there showing about thirty nude women sitting, kneeling, or lying on their sides in a swarm. They have been painted in such a way that their eyes converge on a single point – the viewer, who sees only their faces, their necks and shoulders, sections of their arms and legs. In the foreground, however, there is a woman whose breasts and pubic hair are visible. What the composition seems to suggest to her is that the intimate parts of the other models are not worth showing because they are the same as the first's. Only their faces make them different.

No one has stirred. She tries to recognize the music that is playing. She looks around for the name of the bar and sees "The Three Tadpoles" printed at the top of a menu on the next table. Odd name for a bar. She is trying to imagine the anecdote that might have been responsible for it, when she hears the door close. A man has come in. He raises a hand to the barman, casts a quick glance at the imperturbable young man, and then gives her a hard stare. She looks down at the few centimetres of wine left in her glass. She hears him order a beer. She knows what's going through his head: a woman on her own, drinking alcohol, on a Monday night no less. Just then, it occurs to her that what she needs isn't company but the company of the man she hadn't been able to kiss – Ange is in his arms on the sofa, they are watching a film. But it is too late. The man has put down his beer against her glass of wine and is settling into the chair opposite her. His name is Ivan.

Ivan is a psychiatric intern. He lives in a small studio flat on the top floor. By standing on a chair, Ivan can catch a glimpse of the Eiffel Tower through the fanlight. Which is in fact the first thing he invites her to do after taking her back to his place. To climb up on a chair. Pretty, isn't it, he says, standing right by her legs, encouraging her to look. Then he helps her back down and serves her a glass of red wine while asking her what she does for a living. She tells him that she is an SNCF announcer. By choice or necessity? he shoots back, shoving his glasses up the bridge of his nose with his index finger. Both, she says, because she has never thought about it before. Next, Ivan points out five drawings in coloured crayon pinned to the wallpaper. He strikes her as a bit young to have children; but she asks all the same. No, he doesn't have children, the drawings were done by his patients. He seems annoyed at her for not having guessed. He explains to her how the shapes on the paper reveal certain aspects of the psychological disorders these people suffer from: suicidal tendencies, mythomania, anorexia. She considers telling him about the lead – he's a doctor after all, he'll know what remedy to prescribe – but he has gone back to commenting on the drawings, which are all very beautiful, he finds. Has she heard of Antonin Artaud? She has to admit that she hasn't. Ivan extracts a tome from a pile of books on the carpet. On the cover is a black-and-white photograph of a man with enormous eyes. That's him, he says, and a few seconds later he puts the book away. She doesn't dare ask for more details. For a long while he tells her about his taste in music, about the ardent passion felt for him by one of his female patients, about his wanting to convert to Buddhism. Eventually, he sits down next to her. He runs his fingers over her cheeks and tells her that she has an interesting face. His erudite chatter has left her rather dazed. She lets him kiss her, then caress her thighs, her breasts. She ends up with her jumper and bra dangling from her arms and her knickers down round her ankles. At which point he says, just a second, and starts rummaging around in the closet. He brings out a length of climbing rope.

She hasn't moved, even though she is starting to feel cold. Ivan's hands fiddle dexterously with the yellow-and-purple cord, which he folds, coils, and tugs on hard to form two slip-knots. She asks him what he's doing. His lips curl into a smile; his eyes brim with tentacles. He is only going to tie her up. Without hurting you, of course. He hopes that she doesn't mind. She scans the room in search of a clue that would explain his behaviour. Until he got hold of the rope, Ivan hadn't seemed to exhibit bad intentions; he had kissed her tenderly. She tries to reassure herself. Perhaps she is going to serve as guinea pig in a medical experiment, probably all perfectly harmless: reactions and behaviour of the bound woman. After slipping the rope over her wrists, he'll sit beside her with a notepad and run through a whole series of questions with her, like any other psychiatrist worthy of the name. But as Ivan approaches with a thrilled look on his face, all set to ensnare one of her wrists with his homemade lasso, she panics. She thrusts both hands down between her thighs and tells him, without animosity, that she's not really in the mood for getting tied up. And as he seems puzzled by the sincerity of her declaration, she takes the opportunity to pull up her knickers. With a theatrical sigh, Ivan sets the rope down on the couch, kneels in front of her, and rubs her bare calves with his fingers. But why is she taking it like this? His voice is measured, his eyes attentive. Is she frightened? Does he look that mean to her? As he asks the question, he removes his glasses to show her the kindness in his eyes. A black eyelash has dropped onto his upper cheek, waiting for the wish he will never make. She shakes her head. It's a bit odd; she's not used to it. He starts to get up and, as if operated by some spring mechanism, his limbs straighten to their full extent. He starts waving his arms about, clapping his palms against his thighs. Lots of people use ropes; come on, lots do. Lots of people tie themselves up, she must know about that. Maybe so, but it's never happened to her. She's not sure why she's still there, justifying herself, listening to a psychiatric intern trying to persuade her to do something she doesn't want to do. Ivan has swept the rope on to the floor and returned to the sofa. Okay then, no rope, and he dives back on to her for a kiss. She forces herself to match the spasmodic, circular movements of his tongue. She is just starting to relax when a rough material brushes her fingers. Sitting back, she sees that Ivan has managed to slide on one of the slipknots. He displays a wicked grin: that wasn't so painful, was it? She looks down at the small, flexible tube wrapped around her wrist. She should rip it off in fury, screaming how she can do perfectly well without lunatics like him, thank you very much. Only she can't muster the appropriate insolence, the combative energy that would allow her to impose her will on him. Instead, she feels ashamed. And so she takes the middle path, the only escape route open to her. Can't we do it the normal way? She closes her eyes. The last words have stung Ivan to the quick. Normal way? What the hell does that mean? He thought she was more open, more adventurous. Again, always following conventions, does she at least know why she is refusing? Well then, he'll tell her: it's because she obviously has a real problem. Silence in the room while the city emits its nocturnal sounds outside. The lead has solidified inside her chest. Here he is shouting about a problem after spending just a few hours in her company. He's a psychiatrist, he must know if she has a problem, but can she trust him? Like some corrosive agent, the rope-lover's verbal assault has invaded her. Perhaps her opinion of herself has been atrociously wrong, wrong for a long time. She could have been mistaken about everything. Ivan's jaw shifts back and forth, and she notes the tips of his upper jawbone under his skin. She wonders what kind of drawing Ivan would make. She removes the rope from her wrist. Ivan doesn't protest. He rubs his forehead as if to erase the lines that have formed there without his having noticed. His eyes are empty of all desire. She can put her clothes on again.

She spends the following days in the same lethargic state as before the incident at The Three Tadpoles. And when it finally rings, it takes her a while to locate the phone. It's Ange. She doesn't recognize the energetic voice that is forcefully trying to drag her out of her torpor. Who? Ange. A sightseeing boat floats by on the river under her feet. He wanted to know what she was thinking about; she'd been unable to tell him. She feels the lead liquefying again and flowing back into her limbs. Ange has never called her before. An acquaintance might have seen them sitting on the banks of the Seine. Yes, yes, I'm sure; it was two weeks ago, a Thursday, in the late afternoon. The scandal of their clandestine escapade, the confession of the guilty party. She has become the enemy to be eliminated. Hence the phone call, to arrange a time and place for the duel. Last resort: confess. Nothing happened, not even a kiss, just a squeeze of the hands to feel the warmth of the other person's body. In any case, Ange has already won. She'll tell her that she's giving up. She doesn't have much to lose any more. But Ange goes on. We're going out for a drink with some friends tomorrow; we wanted to invite you. Who is we? Is he included? She may have a problem, but she's not that naive. After her stunning performance, she finds it hard to believe she could get the benefit of a second chance with him. She doesn't know what he could have told Ange, but if he has left out the essential part, Ange may have got it into her head to play the benefactor and generously arrange a reconciliation. Do you want to go? She is finding it harder and harder to think. She feels like going back to the couch, switching off all the lights, and not moving. When? Tomorrow. Ange asks her if everything is all right. She's a bit tired, on account of the lead. Silence on the line. She hears Ange sighing. You should come. I don't know, she replies, and jots down the address of the bar on a France Télécom envelope lying next to the phone. Before hanging up, Ange advises her to get some rest.

She tells herself, yes. Then afterwards, no. But why not. No, she can't. And so the entire next day is spent making the same decision and then changing her mind. On leaving her office, she instinctively goes back home to change. Casual clothes to inform the people who see her that she attaches no importance to the evening. Just as she is in the doorway about to leave, France Télécom envelope in hand, she reflects that it is weak of her to have accepted, that she is putting herself at his mercy. But it is impossible for her to stay at home thinking that she could have gone.

A waiter appears before her. He intones an over-articulated good evening. The place is filled with smoke. Bursts of conversation and splinters of music shower down on to the immunized, voluble crowd. She is coming out of hibernation and the excited hubbub leaves her stunned at first. It takes her a few moments to adjust. She hears the offended waiter repeat his good evening. She has just caught sight of Ange's profile at the back of the room, and she explains to the overly courteous waiter that she is meeting friends. She barely has time to count five people seated at the round table before she recognizes him from behind. The line of hair across his neck forms a little point that deviates to the right. His shoulders are not quite symmetrical. She feels that her legs are ready to turn around. She has nothing to say to these people, they're from a different tribe. In a few seconds, he is going to look at her and she is going to lose whatever social skills she has left. She wishes she could call back to base, have herself dematerialized, and be sent back immediately to her own planet. Hello. Ange has spotted her. It feels as if a thousand eyes are glued to her. She can no longer see a thing, she doesn't even know if he has turned towards her as well. It seems that they are expecting something extraordinary from her: to start dancing or to get down on all fours, to amuse them until she is admitted into the club. He stubbornly keeps his back turned. He can't find anything better to do than ignore her. The lead starts circulating at high speed through her veins. Ange shifts back her chair slightly and offers her a cheek. Finally, he turns his head, gives her a brief, neutral look, and says that he has to go for a pee. She could strangle him on the spot and it would take three of them to subdue her. Have you met Maxime and Sylvie? It is indeed the same Maxime who is there, with his wife, the one with a penchant for Iranian head scarves. He gives her an official diplomatic smile, calibrated to dispel all suspicions. Ange introduces the man next to her, whose first name she forgets. The only seat available is between him and Maxime.

She sits down just as he is getting up; their chests nearly touch, they avoid looking at each other. Because she has to announce that she is not staying, she keeps her jacket on. Her voice is trapped inside her lungs and she hasn't been able to dig it out yet to say what she wants to say. Pointing to Sylvie's cup, she orders an espresso from the waiter. You're not drinking? Ever alert, Ange misses nothing. She shakes her head as the others look on, eager for distraction. She pretends not to be aware of their tacit wishes. They don't insist. Maxime lights a cigarette, Sylvie stifles a yawn in the palm of her hand, and Ange goes into raptures over the elegance of the place. The fifth guest is picking at his fingernails. The chair next to her is still empty. He is taking his time on purpose. Perhaps there's a queue for the toilet.

Or else his zip is stuck. The thought makes her smile, a smile that Ange is quick to spot. What are you laughing about? No aggression, just an irrepressible need to be everywhere at once. She tells herself that Ange would go inside people's heads if she could. She imagines a tiny little Ange traipsing down the labyrinthine corridors of her brain, criticizing the poor state of her synapses in the same way she would criticize the installation of pipes in a factory. Just then, the chair on her right is pulled back. He has returned. He kisses Ange on the cheek, sits down, and declares that the toilet flush is broken. At which point, Ange and Sylvie start discussing the recent exhibition of paintings they saw at the Grand Palais. She then dares to look at him, and the lead metamorphoses into a kind of viscous rubber. In profile, she finds him a touch more severe than usual, a touch more agitated. He is asking the man at the other end of the table about his search for a job. The man has just received a very tempting offer from Renault, but he's hesitant to accept because something better might still come his way. If only he would turn his head in her direction – just once – and take note of her presence, she could excuse herself and promise to leave him alone. But he is still questioning the future Twingo-manufacturer, and she can see only a quarter of his face. She is convinced that he is doing it on purpose, and for the first time she is gripped by a terrible desire to hurt him. She turns to Maxime, who is taking another cigarette from his packet, his eyes bleary with boredom or else from plotting

anti-American manoeuvres. I met a friend of yours.
Maxime looks up, reluctantly obliged to recall the identity
of the woman who has spoken to him. A friend of his? He
adopts the expression of someone preparing to hear a good
joke. A friend of his, yes, she's an actress. Maxime thinks,
sits up, checks to see that his wife is still enumerating to
Ange the gifts of the young woman who does their cleaning, then adopts a courteous attitude. He offers her a cigarette, which she accepts. Really, she must be mistaken, he
doesn't know any actresses. She glances to her right to
check: he is still talking with the fifth guest. She raises her
voice a little. Is he certain? Surely you wouldn't doubt the
word of a diplomat? Maxime frowns, as if begging her to
calm down. And what is the name of this actress? The
same as mine. A pinched little smile plays on Maxime's
lips. You're out of your mind. There is no need for her to
continue, but she feels she can't stop herself. Once again,
she sees the moist banknotes she shoved into the taxi
driver's hand. She has immense power now, and the relief
she feels at using it is both divine and unfamiliar. She
could swear that she saw him backstage in the dressing
rooms at the theatre where this actress is performing, she
can even remember the day if he likes. Maxime turns red.
Do I ask what you're up to at the Hotel Lutétia? The
words spurted from the diplomat's mouth. The others
turn their heads; so does he. At last she meets his eyes and
understands. That he has been struggling to ignore her
and that he almost succeeded. Around her, no one quite
knows how to react. Sylvie studies her husband's face,

while Ange gives her a reproving stare. She stands up and leaves without a word.

On exiting the bar, she heads off at random, going wherever her footsteps take her. She turns corners, not with any destination in mind, but because certain streets are more deserted or darker than others. It's no longer a question of lead or rubber, but of an electric current that's shaking her entire body. She'd like to keep walking until her legs start to hurt and wind up buckling under her weight. Then she would sit down at the edge of the pavement, her soles in the gutter, and try hard to keep as still as possible. She would manage to lose consciousness or, worse, would doze off until dawn, until a street-sweeper came to shoo her away from her curb. She would have lost her memory and would wind up at the Salvation Army, with a bowl of disgusting soup for dinner. She would have forgotten who she was and from then on would be completely anonymous, with no other ambition than to maintain her bodily functions. Again that childish desire to disappear out of spite, to obliterate herself in order to have the effect on others she never had while alive, to feast on the reactions of the few people who would be informed of her death. Maxime would claim to be saddened, which wouldn't stop him from feeling disdain for that poor girl who wasn't very bright. Ange wouldn't understand how a person could let herself go like that; she would be scandalized, saddened, as she would be by the death of any small creature, such as a hamster or a cat. As for him, he would feel guilty, would regret his behaviour, then eventually would think about her from time to time as he would think about a friend who moved abroad, one of those people you like to hear from but don't go out of your way to stay in touch with.

She recognizes the Place des Halles. Her improvised walk has brought her back to within a few hundred metres of where she set out. She's smack in the middle of the place he had advised her to avoid at night because of that friend of his who got mugged. Too bad for him, just now she's going to cross the square because she has no reason to listen to his warnings any more. Between the trees, she makes out human forms, in groups, hardly moving. The same groups that loaf around here during the day, their faces cloaked in darkness now, more menacing. She senses them watching her. She quickens her pace, eyes fixed on the tips of her shoes. As she nears them, she stares far into the distance ahead. Above all, she mustn't let them enter her field of vision. At her approach, one of the silhouettes starts to move and heads straight for her. Hey, miss, where're ya going? She can't help herself, she shoots him a furtive glance. Twenty at the most, head full of dread-locks. Miss, I'll walk ya home. His mates look on. And then, she feels her body loosen up completely; the muscles along the back of her neck relax, her head swivels. She is talking, responding, no thanks, and even manages to add, in a light-hearted voice, have a good evening. The man stays where he is. She feels relieved and yet at the same time almost regrets not having accepted. She notices that she is still holding Maxime's cigarette.

She eventually finds some matches in her bag. Her hands tremble slightly, the wind keeps blowing out the matches, and she has to make several attempts. The taste of the tobacco makes her feel sick, her head spins, and yet smoking seems the most sensible thing she can do. She walks around the giant head slumbering in the palm of a stone hand, the only sculpture in the city she has ever liked. She wonders if a woman posed for it or if the sculptor preferred to model a face that belonged to no one. Out of the corner of her eye, a tiny shadow has appeared, growing rapidly before she has time to identify it. The man is in front of her, blocking her way. Gimme your cigarette. She observes the hulking beanpole with the scarlet face, hunched over, talking hoarsely into his chest. The tiny incandescent stick in her hand has become her sole worldly possession, the one thing she is ready to fight for. No, she replies, knowing already that she should have said yes. Gimme your cigarette, bitch. She takes a step to the right, he moves with her; a step to the left, which the scary mime is quick to match. The dwindling cigarette is starting to burn her fingers, yet she refuses to let go of it. She sees the man brandish a bottle that no longer has a label. He is going to hit her over the head or else smash the bottle and come at her with the jagged glass. A few metres away, three people are walking by, deep in conversation. Make the most of it. She moves sideways, tries to rush forward

to catch up and mingle with the group, who in the meantime have quickened their pace. The man appears before
her again, the bottle held out in front of him like a knife. A
wave of hot and cold washes over her. Fear. She sees them
in the bar, still around the table, engaged in an animated
conversation after having let her leave without going after
her. What will he think when she's found the next morning,
sprawled out at the foot of the stone face, her mouth full of
blood? Or maybe there would just be a slash across her
cheek. She and the man are frozen in place, barely breathing. The hoarse voice again, you gonna hand that butt
over? The bottle has come a few centimetres closer, a
motorbike has stopped at the corner of the street. Two
helmeted figures dismount and look up at the lit window
of a nearby apartment building. They are so close; she has
to get to them, it's now or never. She makes a run for it,
thinking that the distance must be enormous, but already,
in full flight, she is crashing into their gigantic bodies.
Taken aback, the four metal-encased eyes look her over.
Her potential saviours could decide to take it out on her.
I'm sorry, she says, trying hard to stifle the tremor in her
voice. Soften them up, don't let them sense her panic. She
has only a few seconds to win them over and make them
want to defend her. The man hasn't dared to come any
closer. He has stopped in a doorway nearby. She explains
the situation to the two bikers, gesturing with her chin at
the shadowy figure lying in wait for her. One of them takes
off his helmet, he seems harmless; no doubt he thinks
she's exaggerating. They still haven't said a word. She asks

if she can stay with them a little longer. They exchange a
look, then start watching the shadow in the doorway with
her. It shrinks back but doesn't leave. They must think
she's making a mountain out of a molehill. She isn't even
sure they believe her, and they hardly seem overjoyed to
be acting as chaperones. Lucky for me you were here, she
ends up saying, to add a little credibility to her story and
encourage them in the task she has given them. The street
is calm, nothing is happening, they're not talking, he's not
going away, she doesn't dare make any more suggestions.
The ochre cigarette filter has remained between her fingers,
crushed by her fear, almost weightless, insignificant now.
After wanting to hold on to it at any cost, she lets it fall to
the ground now, getting rid of it since it serves no purpose
any more. The two bikers are getting impatient. Where
does she live? Not far, just around the corner, up the street.
No answer. The shadow has straightened up and goes to
lean against a street lamp. She sees no sign of the bottle.
The man without the helmet turns to her; he looks her
over for a few seconds. She makes herself smile so he'll
think she's cute. She must have passed the test because he
says to the other guy, all right, you stay here, I'll take her
home. She wishes she could just leave them there, the two
idiots. He puts his helmet back on and points to the back of
the motorbike, telling her to watch out for the exhaust
pipe. She doesn't dare admit to him that she has never been
on a motorbike. Clumsily lifting her leg, she slides on to
the leather seat and straightens up. They set off at once.
Her hands are in the way. She puts them flat on her thighs,

but at the first curb she instinctively grabs hold of the leather jacket in front of her. They pass close by the man with the bottle, who doesn't bat an eyelid but gives her a look filled with hatred. What if I had said yes? The driver accelerates to avoid a red light. She feels good, rescued, out of harm's way, on that powerful speedy machine. She wishes someone would take her on a tour of Paris like this; she wishes she could press her cheek against the back of the man just a few centimetres from her face and squeeze him so tightly in her arms that this stranger would experience the same fear she had. But she is already on familiar ground. Thanks, this is it. He tells her he is just going to park the bike; it would be a shame if something happened to her now. She gets off, holding on to his arm. Thank you, really, I'll be fine. He has removed his helmet; the engine is still running. She wouldn't want to be ungrateful. He looks at her, fireworks gleaming in his eyes. If he were bolder, he would jump on top of her. Thanks again. She takes several steps, then turns. He adjusts his helmet and violently revs the engine. As soon as he has disappeared, she turns down a narrow side street. She doesn't realize straight away that someone is outside the door of her apartment building.

Her heart begins to breathe; her lungs begin to beat. She slows down, he comes towards her, they're already face to face. She thinks of logical reasons that would explain why he is outside her building. Maxime had called the police,

Sylvie had had a fit, Ange had sent him to bring her back and explain herself. I was getting worried, he says, and gives her a wink. After Maxime's confused explanation, he and Ange had gone home. He'd sat down in front of the TV; Ange had taken a shower before going to bed. When he had gone into the bedroom a quarter of an hour later, she was asleep. He had lingered on the threshold for a moment, then closed the door again, put on his shoes and coat, and left the apartment. He had taken a taxi to get here. She's surprised that he's telling her all this, as though he were expecting her to analyze his motives and give him instructions on what to do next. She just wants to say thank you, but has lost the power of speech. There is only one way she can express herself now. And when her lips touch his, she feels that she has been set free at last.

On the terrace of the café, a lone man sits hunched over a notebook. Now and then, he brings the tip of a ballpoint pen close to the page, makes a few tiny circles just above the surface without ever touching it, then puts his hands together and slides them between his knees.

She arrives slightly out of breath. She came as quickly as she could, but she's late. She feels hot. She takes off her jacket and sits down opposite him. Not bad, he says admiringly. She imagines that he's referring to her dress. A black, low-cut dress, of a kind she has never worn before, bought in a shop that sells designer clothing at factory outlet prices. She blushes, because it's the first time he has ever said anything like that. He pushes his hand forward. The waiter comes over to greet them and take their order. How are you, Christophe, he replies, as he always does, and she wonders, as she always does, if Christophe also knows Ange. He squeezes her fingers. The pressure sends an enormous charge of energy coursing through her body. Her cheeks are aflame, she could rise into the air like a helium balloon. He asks her if the espresso is good. She nods, all the while trying to maintain the most pleasant expression on her face. She's afraid of doing anything that might upset him or uncover a reality other than the one she believes she is living. From time to time he glances at his watch, casts a quick eye over the customers, then retracts his hand and lifts his cup. She shifts her knees forward to touch his, not sure if he can tell the difference. This is nice, he says, and she lowers her eyes to hide the emotion his words create in her. An hour later, he asks for the bill and refuses to let her pay. Then he kisses her out on the pavement – proof, as she sees it, that he is not afraid to show his affection in public. The texture of his tongue and the paths it likes to take inside her mouth have become familiar to her. Each one of his kisses gives her a sensation of intense sweetness, something she has never known before. As he climbs into the taxi, he gives her a little wave. She responds with an enthusiastic wave of her own.

For two months they have been seeing each other like this, in the same place, in the late afternoon, once or twice a week, depending on when he is free. He calls her in the morning before she leaves the apartment and arranges to meet her after work, at a time that varies according to his schedule. Occasionally, she has to ask her office for permission to leave early. As she has always been punctual and is rarely absent, permission is granted, along with a knowing look that aims to get her to talk about the reasons for her early departure. But little more is given than a cordial thank you. At the café, they order two espressos and two glasses of water. They spend the time available to them searching each other out with their fingertips or knees, laughing at their timorous adolescent behaviour. Sometimes they discuss the weather forecast, or the film on television they watched separately at home, or the places they have never been to, or the odd look of a passerby. He tells her the stories of novels she has never read, describes the house he'd like to buy near the sea, somewhere between La Rochelle and Royan, makes fun of his bosses whom he can no longer stand, extols the beauty of his favourite sport, horseback riding. She finds him wilful, admires his marked taste for very particular things. Never has a man told her so much about himself, and she has trouble taking it all in. But she likes listening to him; his confidences show that he wants to involve her in his life, even if he doesn't ask her many questions. She actually prefers it that way: to unburden herself about the past or even the present would be a dangerous undertaking, and she feels she has no talent for it. Whenever she starts to wonder why he keeps coming back to see her, her only conclusion is that she doesn't know what she expects of him either.

She has fallen into the habit of looking at the ground whenever she turns the corner of her street. She walks along staring at her shoes, trying hard not to think about him, and then, a few metres from the door to her building, she looks up, imagining that he's there, on the lookout, impatient for her return. But in spite of her efforts to stage this scene, he never appears at that moment.

Back home after their meetings, she feels that she has finally taken on the proper dimensions, that she fits in to the mass of things around her. She has no desire to go out, for time passes more quickly inside the confined space of her office and her apartment. Simple, immediate household chores consume a certain chunk of it; talking into the microphone requires enough concentration to occupy her for long stretches. The unpredictable nature of a nighttime outing, on the other hand, would be more likely to slow the passing of the hours. When she travels between her apartment and the station, she discovers that she has points in common with every person she sees. Everything, from the cellular organization of the body to the functioning of human beings, seems perfect to her. She tells herself that in others as well such a feeling must reflect their level of satisfaction. She concludes that her future will be a delicious, never-ending repetition of their meetings. As for her past, she hardly gives it a thought. When she does, the rite of passage strikes her as an anecdote from a part of her life that no longer needs to be remembered. She feels strong enough to accomplish whatever she wants. She is happy, and nothing can go against her any more.

After refusing at first, he now agrees to answer her when she asks for news of Ange. But his comments remain terse and never refer to Ange directly but rather to the state of their relationship. We had a row yesterday, she bought me a new shirt, she wants us to move, we had a pleasant evening. Afterwards, she never knows if she has the right to go on asking questions in order to find out more about a particular subject. She is curious to learn about the ups and downs that occur when a man and a woman live together, which is something she has never experienced. But the idea that she might be jealous of Ange never crosses her mind.

On the night she was almost mugged, he held her in his arms for a while and told her that he couldn't stay because there was a chance Ange might wake up. He just wanted to make sure that she was all right. I almost got my face slashed for a cigarette. He had frowned, and she had told him the story. Why hadn't she given him the cigarette? She could have, but she kept thinking that she really didn't have a choice. And besides, it was impossible to predict how the man would have reacted if she had given him what he wanted. As she talked, she was searching for a valid excuse to keep him there. In the end, she had to resign herself to going back up to her apartment and exulting in her joy alone. When he returned to his place, Ange must still have been asleep. She pictured him sitting at the kitchen table under the ceiling light, half listening to the nocturnal rumblings of the building. Coldly, staring into space, he must have tried to figure out the reasons for what he had just done. He was not unhappy with Ange, she was the woman he needed, that's what he must have thought. So what was wrong with his life? Was he bored? Were there any minor problems in their relationship that they had failed to detect? Giving in to sleep, she worried that without any clear answers he might decide to distance himself from her, to make his questions go away. Three days later, he called to see how she was doing and to ask if she wanted to meet him for a coffee.

She doesn't have a single photograph of him. One evening, feeling at loose ends, she takes a few blank sheets of paper and a pencil from a drawer and tries to draw him from memory. She was never very good at drawing. In her first sketch, he looks like a wizened old man whose eyes, nose, and mouth are in the wrong places. In the second, which she chooses to simplify, he is transformed into a fellow with vacant eyes, expressionless lips, and too much hair on his head. She thinks back to the drawings of Ivan's patients and tells herself that they were much better at it than she is. For the third drawing, she decides to close her eyes and let her hand trace the image that is forming on the inner wall of her eyelids. When she is finished, the page is covered with a jumble of lines that contains bits of face here and there, some of them spread out, others overlapping. This last portrait strikes her as the best, and that is the one she keeps.

She hesitates for a long time before making a decision. She's thinking about an article of clothing but isn't sure what he likes. She goes to several men's shops. She runs her fingers along the edges of perfectly folded shirts, piled up according to colours, like unique, precious objects. Sales assistants glide over to her in silence and show her the best-selling items of the season. With practised gestures, they ask what size she's looking for. She shrugs, embarrassed at taking on a role she suddenly realizes isn't hers, and leaves, saying she'll think it over. She considers buying a novel. She goes into bookshops, where she feels lost amongst the billions of pages set out along dozens of aisles of shelving. She doesn't remember the names of the authors he's mentioned to her. She pulls down books at random, reads in a low voice titles that ring no bells, studies their front and back covers, and returns them to the shelf, biting her lip. She looks for customers who remind her of him and sneaks a glance at what they are buying. But at the last minute, she doubts whether their selections are the correct ones.

At the café the next day, she proudly presents him with a houseplant wrapped in a large sheet of cellophane, with a length of frizzy ribbon stapled to the top. He scarcely glances at it, and she has to say to him, it's for you, so he understands that she has just given him his first gift. He stares in disbelief at the packaged greenery before him. Eventually he tells her, with an apologetic look, that he won't be able to take it home. Ange will think I bought it for her. She replies that it doesn't matter, as long as he keeps it in his apartment. He still refuses, on the pretext that offering plants to people is not his style. Reluctantly, she puts the pot down on the floor. When the meeting is over, she deliberately leaves it behind.

A few weeks ago, I went to the gare du Nord during my lunch break. My gare du Nord? Her use of the possessive seems to amuse him. Yes, he'd had a coffee in a paper cup while leaning against the counter of one of those fast-food stands. You came to the station to drink a coffee? Wait. He spent a good fifteen minutes wondering what had possessed him to come. Then he recognized her voice, amplified and projected on all sides through the loudspeakers. It was odd, I felt moved, I wasn't expecting that. She's not sure that she follows. He found her voice deep and assured, as though it belonged to a woman who was older and – at first he can't find the right word – more confident. After listening to about ten of her announcements, he tried to figure out what had led her to choose that line of work. He must say that he feels a certain pride in knowing the person who addresses that enormous crush of people, as proud as he would be if he were a close friend of someone famous.

That's going a bit far, she'll begin to think he's making fun of her. Not at all, he went there to listen to her and came away with the impression that he knew a little more about her. She now feels touched by his declarations. All the same, she can't understand why he hadn't let her know he was coming.

She looks at herself in the small mirror above the wash-basin in the café toilets. She has never asked herself too many questions about the aesthetic quality of her face. Since men are capable of desiring her, she supposes that it's not without appeal. But neither does she receive flattering comments about it. From this, she concludes that she is somewhere around average, which is fine with her. Yet that afternoon, for no particular reason, she gets a sudden urge to know what he thinks of it. After the Île Saint-Louis episode, he has never again said that he finds her beautiful or pretty; nor, for that matter, has he ever complimented her on her appearance. She doubts she should read too much into it, but for the first time she'd like him to say something to her, that her eyes have a special shape, that her lips are full, that her nose isn't too long, that her chin isn't too pointed, even if he has to lie to do so.

When she goes back upstairs, a woman in a grey suit is standing at their table. The two of them are talking. The woman's red lips pout sensuously every time she opens her mouth. She has one hand on her hip, the other curled around her neck. She doesn't dare go back to the table;

motionless, she stands there with her eyes fixed on them. A waiter carrying a tray asks her to move to one side. She uses the opportunity to conceal herself behind one of the columns in the room. They talk for a few more moments, then the woman leans down, kisses him on both cheeks and walks off with magnificence, brashly imposing her beauty on the world. She returns to her seat. Interrogating him about his opinion of her physical attributes now strikes her as futile. He asks her if everything is all right. Who was that? A friend of Ange's, she lives around the corner. She feels her heart tighten. Just as well that I wasn't with you, then. He shrugs, saying that they'll go to a different café next time.

The thought has of course crossed her mind, several times. She imagines him imagining the roundness of her breasts, the colour and size of her aureola, the colour of her pubic hair. She imagines herself naked before him. His feared and precious hands upon her. She thinks an intense physical understanding might develop between them; she thinks that she can do without his body. She thinks he doesn't want to disrupt the intimacy he shares with Ange. Then she tells herself that he doesn't really want her, that she isn't attractive enough to him, at least not as much as Ange. As long as there are no sexual relations between them, he can look Ange straight in the eye and swear to her that he has never been unfaithful. But as long as there are no sexual relations between them, he can't stop anticipating them, even idealizing them. If she had given him more clues about what she wanted, he probably would have gone along, but she fears her own reactions and believes she can protect herself by following his lead. She won't take the initiative; she won't complain if he doesn't make a move. As if testing him, she wants to give him as many reasons to make love to her as not to. But she also knows that if they go on seeing each other, they will soon have to go a step further to make or break themselves as a couple.

He licks off the traces of coffee lining his upper lip and assumes a grave expression. Sylvie has asked for a divorce, Maxime is devastated. She can't help smiling. That's hardly surprising. She said it without malice. He gives her a hard look. He obviously isn't pleased with her response to Maxime's tribulations. I really don't see what's so amusing about it. And he takes the opportunity to break off physical contact with her. Now that it is uncovered, her hand feels cold. She is about to admit that she hasn't shown much compassion, to apologize and quickly change the subject, her opinion even. But he goes on. Sometimes you really do have strange reactions. The word is like a dart, boring straight into her chest. His first chance and already he has adopted the common opinion of her. She feels like singing. A song she heard that morning on the radio, which she would have liked to dedicate to him and which she can't get out of her head. *"You're just too good to be true. Can't take my eyes off of you."* Only he might find her attitude inappropriate and use it as further evidence in support of his weirdness theory. She looks for another way out: a good argument to eject him from her life. She'll tell him that he's just like the others, even if she doesn't think so and doesn't have anyone to compare him to in any case. He'd roar back that Ange is far better and leave her to the mercy of the waiter. But instead, she makes do with biting the top of her right thumb and letting her eyes wander about, avoiding his gaze. He knocks back his coffee and shakes his head. You have to admit it's weird that you get a kick out of it, no? His tone is cutting, almost vengeful. I don't get a kick out of it, I just find it ironic. She feels the tears welling in her eyes. Then explain to me what's so ironic about my friend's wife walking out on him. She could spill the beans. The champagne at the Hotel Lutétia, the lowering of the zip in the taxi, the brightly coloured cocktails at the private club, the immaculate, palatial apartment. She has no idea how he would react, but it would serve him right. She now realizes that it's up to her to define the nature of the bond between them, either by speaking or by keeping silent. She's not used to justifying herself, nor does she have the heart of a snitch. But he is demanding an explanation.

One night as she was leaving the station, she had run into Maxime by chance. He hadn't recognized her straight off, and so she had had to remind him of the circumstances of their meeting, the famous dinner party where she had passed herself off as a prostitute. Maxime had admitted to her that he hadn't believed her story. He had invited her for a coffee, as a reward for her effort in creating such a character. Once they had found themselves a table in a local bistro, Maxime had seemed troubled. She'd asked him if he was all right, and he had explained to her the crisis his marriage was in. She'd listened, and he had ended up telling her that he was seeing another woman. He wanted to end the relationship but his mistress wouldn't let him. She'd wished Maxime luck, and that was the last they'd seen of each other until they all met up in the bar, where she had asked him if he'd broken it off, which had led to his angry outburst. That's it.

He goes on staring at her in silence, looking for an expression that might allow him to verify the truthfulness of her account. You see, she concludes, if there was someone else involved, Sylvie may have found out about it. Thanks to you! She frowns, she hadn't seen things in that light. She very much doubts that she had the slightest role in this divorce. That he should point an accusing finger at her is completely unfair. She looks down. She could stand up, tell him she's at the wrong table, and walk off without a second thought. And yet she remains glued to her chair, her mouth twitching oddly until she is able to add, I might turn out to be responsible for your splitting up with Ange, but I'm certainly not to blame for what's happened to Maxime. Her words appear to take him by surprise, to force him to reflect on what they are doing, as if he were suddenly required to look to his left and his right at the same time. But the problem with eyes is that they both move in the same direction. Maxime and Sylvie, he and Ange, it's not the same, she'd better get that straight.

He raised his voice. She's starting to despise this moment, this fit of anger pouring down on her even though she has nothing to do with it. She also has to understand that he and Maxime are different, Maxime has always had a soft spot for women, whereas he is the faithful sort . . . usually. He forces himself to finish his sentence, adding the last word in order to regain his balance. Then he stops, betrayed by his own self-description. Usually, she repeats in a quiet voice. She wants to believe that he needs time to accept what is happening.

It's night, and she is lying in bed. The city is playing softly in the background. The curtains are open, and light from her neighbours pours through the window into the room. She has always enjoyed that moment of calm when the body loosens its grip. Nothing more is asked of it. As a teenager it was at such moments, waiting for sleep to over-come her, that she would invent the perfect lover. She always met him on a beach, it was always a late afternoon in summer. She found him attractive. She never gave him any specific physical traits, but she would choose his ges-tures, always the same. The imaginary scene would reach its height at the moment he kissed her. She had never kissed a boy back then and she was curious to discover what kissing with her tongue would feel like. She could imagine nothing better than kissing the boy she called, for lack of originality, her Prince Charming. She moves her arm over the portion of empty sheet next to her. His body would be there; a mass of tender warmth would envelop her completely, the smell of another person distinct from her own but so familiar she would barely notice the difference. She would have the right to caress that body, to rub her skin against his, and to repeat the same ritual every evening. She would never tire of it. She has dreamed of this repetition with him, the assurance that he would be there the following night.

Years later, when she thinks about him again, she will recall one meeting in particular. They had met at the usual place. She arrived, her heart thumping, impatient to be with him. Once inside the café, she lost all notion of time. There was only a great bath of liquid, and she was floating in it, borne away by amnesia and euphoria. That day, after they had religiously drunk their espressos and swapped details about the minor events that had disturbed their routines since they last met, he announced that he wanted to go somewhere with her. Right now? Right now. He had a little time that day. He led her to the nearest métro station. On the train, they sat next to each other on the pull-down seats; he slipped his hand onto her back, under the layers of fabric that covered her body, touching her bare skin. They didn't talk. They smiled whenever they turned their heads at the same time to look at each other. It was then that she imagined a life for them together for the first time. They were on that métro because they were going home, as they did every evening. Home was a small apartment somewhere in Paris, on the top floor. From the living room windows, there was a view of the grey rooftops and the chimneys with their pointed hats. They were going home, and that familiar journey was becoming the symbol of a shared life, a life that struck her as more ideal than anything she had imagined for herself up till then. She was on her way back to the apartment they had chosen together; she could not ask for more.

They had got out at the Luxembourg station. Behind the railings of the park, people on metal chairs were eating, reading, breathing in the sunshine, their eyes closed. They were relaxed and unthreatening; they could be addressed without fear of being stared at with alarm. The white statues struck her as a mistake, a superfluous sophistication. He took her hand. They walked along the paths in silence, with the serene slowness of those who have nowhere to go. They no longer felt anything in particular, they felt everything. She remembers thinking that the moment should never end. That only the company of this man could make things bearable. The world seemed to be in place, in line with what she would have chosen if she had been given the choice. At the same time, nothing mattered any more. When they too sat down on the metal chairs, not far from the chess players, he rested his head on her shoulder. In her memory, they stayed in that position forever.

During the night, it seems that someone has blocked up her ears with cotton wool. On waking up, she finds it hard to breathe; she takes a stab at blowing her nose, but it's as dry as cement in there. Similarly, the back of her throat appears to have hardened, to be covered with a kind of varnish. Her forehead is hot, she has trouble moving her eyes in their sockets. The world around her, by contrast, has turned soft. The floor is made from a material that looks like wood and has the consistency of rubber. The corners of the walls are no longer perfectly straight but keep changing according to the variations in temperature. When she reaches out to take hold of an object, the thing is no longer perfectly still. Its contours vibrate, ready to change shape and elude her grasp. She tells herself that it will pass. She drinks a little tea, but the idea of a simple slice of bread and butter makes her sick to her stomach. Struggling to keep her balance, she gets dressed and gathers up her things. But once she starts walking down the stairs, she has to hold on to the banister: she finds it difficult to judge the irregular, shifting distance between the steps, as if she were inching along the pleats of a giant accordion. Outside, the light crashes down on her and sears her eyes. The ride to work on the métro seems utterly impossible. She is capable of doing just one thing now: lying down. She goes back up the stairs and flops on to the couch. Just then, the telephone rings. The handset is heavier than usual. She doesn't have enough saliva to moisten her mouth. He asks her if she's ill. I don't know. At that moment she is someone else whom she suddenly sees standing next to her with the telephone in her hand; an older, more assured, more sensual woman, who leads an exciting life, one that glimmers in the very timbre of the voice. You don't know? Her head is spinning, she might have a fever, it's probably not too serious. He asks if she's eaten anything. Some tea. He exhales into the phone. I feel quite sick, I'm not sure I can go to the station. But she immediately regrets what she has said, realizing that he must have phoned to set up a meeting. She doesn't have time to correct herself before he is already saying, in that case it would be better if she stayed at home, they can see each other another time. Something contracts inside her. She wishes she could go back, be smart enough to lie and say that she feels perfectly well. It's no good telling herself there will be next times; she has the impression that she's being punished for no reason. She would like to ask him why; because you're ill, he would answer. Little black flies are floating on the surface of the wall opposite her. She doesn't have the strength to defend herself. It's better for you; promise me you'll go see a doctor sometime this afternoon. She agrees, fearing that a refusal would encourage him to push back their next meeting still further. Look after yourself, he says, a big kiss, I'll call you later. At that instant, she is overcome by an enormous desire to confess how terribly she misses him, but he has already hung up. She would like the sofa, the chair, the table, something in the room to start talking to her and put her mind at rest.

She wakes up and realizes that she has slept. Early afternoon, the sun is no longer shining directly into the windows of her apartment. She feels rested, but her respiratory passages are still blocked, her muscles ache. To her horror she remembers that she has forgotten to call the office. She dials the number; at the other end of the line, the phone on her boss's desk rings. She remembers the title sequence of a film in which the viewer is taken inside a telephone wire, transformed into an electronic signal, and launched at great speed towards a target he can no longer avoid: the ear of the person whose number has been dialled. An authoritative male voice asks who is speaking. Monsieur Merlinter. Her boss has recognized her voice and says quickly that she has to understand. Just because an employee is given permission to leave early is no reason for said employee to assume the right to take every kind of liberty, he is well aware that she is not the sort to cause problems, but he trusts that she'll be able to provide him with an adequate explanation for her absence this morning. Thrown into a panic by this demand, she answers, my apartment was burgled, they took everything, I had to wait for the police. Too bad for him; if he had been nicer, she would have told him the truth. For a few seconds she hears nothing, then Monsieur Merlinter continues in a much calmer voice. Well, considering the circumstances, he understands. She hangs up, then dials a second number. A woman's voice answers mechanically, Dr. Hotaronian's surgery, and gives her an appointment for five o'clock that afternoon.

Three hours later, she is sitting in a wicker armchair, in a room with beige wallpaper, in front of a low table flooded with women's magazines. Hanging on one of the walls is a small notice sheathed in plastic with a list of the charges for weekday or weekend appointments for surgery visits and house calls. Classical music is playing softly through a tiny speaker. For the past twenty minutes she has been waiting her turn, like the four other people who were already there when she arrived and whom she greeted with a muffled hello, which was not met with much enthusiasm. First she had taken a look at the photographs in several magazines, not being able to read the articles because the lines kept blurring; she quickly grew tired of that. At present, she is fighting against her only real urge: to stretch out on the grey carpet at the other patients' feet and take a nap. To pass the time, she listens to an elegant woman with red puffy eyes on the sofa to her left blow her nose. Between two drainages, the woman massages her temples and sighs. Sitting on the floor between the woman's feet, a little girl is shaking and combing a doll with frizzy, over-blonde hair. From time to time, a stout woman squeezed into a woollen coat and wedged into a wicker seat asks another stout woman squeezed into a woollen coat and wedged into a wicker seat, is everything all right, mum? The glassy eyed mother doesn't stir. And then, out of the blue, a voice shouts, I've been waiting for an hour, for God's sake. It's the woman from the sofa, not addressing anyone in partic- ular but hoping to arouse everyone's compassion. She arches her eyebrows by way of approval; the two other women pretend not to have heard. I'm sick of being here, the little girl declares loudly in her turn, while her mother murmurs that it won't be long now. For a moment, nothing can be heard but the sound of traffic pierced by the shrill notes of a violin. Suddenly, the door to the room is opened by a finely decked-out brunette dressed in black, who announces a name. The younger of the two stout women climbs to her feet and helps the other to extract herself from her chair. They go out; the door shuts. No organization, the lady on the sofa pronounces after an ample sniff. Now that they're a little more alone, she considers asking the lady whether she'd mind if she stretched out on the floor. But the door has just opened. A haggard adolescent boy walks in and takes possession of one of the two wicker chairs. She thinks that he looks like a leek. Out of politeness, she tries to resist the fascination exerted by his severe acne. The woman has started blowing her nose again, and the young man has taken a comic book out of his backpack. The little girl begins to study her. And because she doesn't look away, the child gets up and comes over, brandishing the woman-shaped piece of plastic under her nose. My Barbie has a pain. She senses the mother's watchful eyes on her but doesn't know what the appropriate response would be. She's not well? Yes, she has a pain right there. And the child's finger presses the tiny chest. She could tell her that it's lucky they're at the doctor's, but the little girl seems to be expecting a slightly more intelligent response from her. Heartburn, that happens sometimes, but it will pass. The little girl smiles. So it will pass for mummy too? The mother has suddenly stopped blowing her nose. Come here and leave the lady alone. The door opens, mother and daughter go out after hearing their names. She is alone with the placid young leek, who is hunched over his album of brightly coloured pictures. If she lay down on the soft carpet, he probably wouldn't notice, but she doesn't dare. He must be getting ready to leave his office. They could be together right now if she weren't here, waiting for an appointment that isn't going to reveal anything other than the fact that she's come down with a good old dose of flu. She tries to convince herself that he was right to cancel their date. It's true that she wouldn't have been in top form. Even so, she can't help imagining the possibility that he might unexpectedly come to her place later to see how she is. She picks up a *Paris Match* with a torn front cover that now shows only the chins and chests of a man and woman side by side. The name *Paradis-Depp* appears in large letters. She leafs through several pages before putting down the magazine, unable to concentrate. The door opens, an elderly couple walks in, taking small, hesitant steps. The woman in black motions to her, shakes her hand before asking her to come this way.

The blinds in the overheated surgery are drawn; the walls are hidden by shelves crammed with files. Each one contains a record of the worries, pathologies, and sufferings of a human being. Some are slim, others far thicker, a collection of ills arranged in alphabetical order. The doctor has sat down behind her desk. She is suntanned; her black eyes express nothing in particular beyond a certain weariness. She takes a new file from a drawer and asks her to spell her first and last name, to give her date of birth, and to describe the reason for her visit. She is not unhappy to be asked questions in this way; she experiences a sense of relief, as though she were submitting to a procedure that would allow her to square herself with the authorities. So she gives precise answers to the person in front of her, whom she imagines as a fantastical being, a kind of magician immunized against pain. Undress, I'm going to examine you. The doctor points at the examining table, which she covers with a sheet of white paper. She takes off her clothes and drapes them carefully over the back of a chair. Once naked, she tries hard to act as if she were still dressed. The doctor asks her to step on to the scales, then to sit on the table so she can listen to her heartbeat. She takes deeper breaths. The cool pressure of the stethoscope against her back makes her feel as if she is being rocked by something invisible and soothing. The doctor wraps a black band around her upper arm and inflates it with a small pump. Next, she makes her open her mouth, shines a light on the back of her throat, has a good look inside, feels her neck, asks her to lie down, then slowly palpates her joints, armpits, breasts, and belly. The pressure of these hands is so calming that she already feels half-cured. She appreciates that the doctor intently going about her job does not look her in the eyes and behaves as if she were dealing with an organism just like any other, merely checking to see if it's in good working order. Finally the verdict is pronounced: you have the flu, I'm going to prescribe a light course of treatment. The doctor returns to her desk and starts writing something that she isn't entitled to see. Have you already thought about having children? For several seconds, she isn't sure if the doctor was talking to her. No one has ever asked her that question and, just then, she doesn't have the slightest idea how to respond. It feels as if the other woman has turned into a judge, and she is standing naked before her. Even worse, she will be given the maximum sentence if her answer is no. I don't know. Perhaps the doctor is full of good intentions: in the next room, she might be keeping a fine male specimen whom she orders to inseminate, free of charge, any female patient who so desires it. The doctor is still writing, as though she were now taking notes on her reactions. Time passes quickly, you know. The sentence rings out like a warning. She thinks back to the little girl in the waiting room and how clumsy she had felt while talking to her. To imagine the physical sensation of a body inside her own, the plump bulge on which she would proudly lay her hands . . . yes, she remembers having already tried to, at the market, because of Marion's child. But even with him, the thought of a child leaves her cold. Still, they say that once you find the man, having children comes naturally. She's the exception that proves the rule. It all seems unnatural to her. Intrusion rather than fusion. She isn't cut out for giving life, it's as simple as that. Too noble and too abnormal for her. I know about the time factor, but I don't think I'm cut out for it. The doctor has finally stopped writing and gives her an indulgent smile. I can assure you that you have everything you need. The situation is starting to get on her nerves. She came because of the flu, and now they want to sell her a baby. She might have everything that's needed, like other women, but she knows that she doesn't have the strength, the inner strength. She'd like to explain to the doctor that it's not her fault but she feels too shaky to talk. She realizes that she is still naked. To regain her composure, she decides to get dressed. Give it some careful thought. She has had enough. Still clutching her knickers, she looks the doctor straight in the eye. And what about you, do you have children? Once again, she gives her that small, indulgent smile. No, and that's precisely why I'm mentioning it to you. And she hands over the prescription.

In the taxi that takes her home, she replays the scene in her mind. What this woman doctor tried to get across to her was the fear of regret. Yes, time passes quickly, she knows that; she isn't arrogant enough to think that she's immortal. Though she may have felt anxious as she left the surgery, telling herself that a day would come when she would no longer be able to have children, she now knows that it makes no difference. She doesn't want children, doesn't want to replicate herself, but she doesn't know why. Any more than she knows why she is sitting in this particular taxi, watching, through this particular window, these particular buildings go by. At the first pharmacy they come to, she asks the driver to pull over. Minutes later, she is back with a small green-and-white bag containing a box of medicine. The doctor probably asks the same question to all her patients of child-bearing age, women who pounce on their partners that very night, demanding to be impregnated immediately before it's too late, or else get depressed for lack of a proper sire on hand. In the long run, what intrigues her most is how the doctor had managed to figure out that she has never given birth.

He is not outside her building when the taxi drops her off at the entrance. Throughout the journey she had clung to the hope that he would be waiting for her. As she climbs the stairs, she invents excuses for him – his bosses asked him to work late; Ange, who had also fallen ill, wanted him to go and pick her up; his wallet was stolen in the métro. On reaching her landing, she tells herself that she won't hold it against him. As she pushes open the door to her apartment, the telephone is ringing. She hurries over to answer it. I knew it was you. She says it in her new husky female voice without waiting for her caller to identify himself. She isn't wrong. He wants to know how she is and to make sure she did go to the doctor. She is proud to confirm that she has followed his instructions. I just need to have children and I'll be cured. He doesn't laugh, and she has to tell him what happened. Do you want some now? No. He suggests that they meet the following Friday.

He is usually the first to arrive at the café. But three-quarters of an hour have gone by, and she is still waiting. For a while, the hissing of the espresso machine, the clinking of the cups, the rise and fall of the conversations had kept her distracted. She no longer hears anything and doesn't take her eyes off the glass entrance door, except to survey the customers or turn suddenly whenever someone brushes past her. People are coming and going, but he is never one of those people. She has already drunk two espressos and orders a third from the waiter, who gives her a goofy smile and assures her that her date will be coming soon. Who would have the nerve to stand you up? She doesn't bother to reply. She is sitting at the same table, their table; he can't possibly miss her. Again and again, her brain spews forth this thought: one second from now, he is going to walk through that door. He is going to walk through that door, and he will be out of breath. He will look apologetic, will say that the métro had broken down, that there was too much traffic to take a taxi, he will tell her that he's sorry. She'll take hold of one of his hands, won't utter a word of reproach, delighted to be with him again. A man with his elbows on the bar has caught her attention. From the back, she thinks she recognizes the length and cut of the hair. She gets up and hurries over, steps round expecting to find him on the other side. But the person she discovers is atrociously unlike him. The man politely asks if he can be of any help. She shakes her head and rushes back to her observation post. The glass door keeps opening and closing; each time, another punch in the guts. She can feel the man at the bar eyeing her, intrigued. She avoids looking in his direction. A blonde woman comes in, then two men in suits, then a man who hasn't shaved, then another blonde woman, then . . . the whole of Paris is filing past her eyes and he'll be the last one to arrive. So be it. She decides to stay until the café closes if she has to.

The man from the bar is standing next to her; he offers to buy her a drink. Thanks, but I'm waiting for someone. She doesn't look up. Three very excited women have just entered the café. You've been waiting a while. She doesn't answer. She hates this man sticking his nose into her life without so much as a by-your-leave. A young man with a ponytail is tugging furiously at the glass door until, finally, he realizes that he has to push to open it. The time would pass more quickly if you talked to me. She wants to tell him to go back to sipping his beer and leave her the hell alone. But it seems wiser to ignore him and stick to her surveillance of the door. The man from the bar stands beside her for a few more seconds, his gaze weighing on her eyelids, which she refuses to lift, then, defeated by her hostility, he eventually walks off. She realizes that he has grey hair, invisible to her at first, and that he is in fact older than she had thought. She feels a bit guilty at not having been nicer. She does the arithmetic; she has been waiting for an hour and fifteen minutes. What on earth could have happened to him? Maybe he's left a message on her answering machine, and once she goes home she'll get a rational explanation for his absence. This thought helps her to relax a little. She takes a break from watching the door and orders a glass of white wine from the waiter, who ventures no further comments. Ten minutes later, the man from the bar is back on the offensive, standing next to her, his glass of beer in hand.

I'll leave the moment he arrives, I promise. The man is

sitting down on the seat in front of her. She is about to protest, but he doesn't give her the chance. I'm on my own, you're on your own, I just want to talk, no harm in that, is there? He looks sincere, she doesn't chase him away. After all, he might help to take her mind off things. You'll leave when . . . He agrees with an understanding smile. He has yellow, smoker's teeth, two odd lines in the middle of his forehead. To your health! She touches his glass with hers, nevertheless keeping an eye on the glass door, but everyone who walks in is a stranger. The man has noticed. So who's the happy man? She affects an air of indifference. I don't know if he's very happy. She feels the man's gaze intensify, his eyes are no longer on hers but are roaming over her chin, her cheeks, her forehead, as if he were putting her through a scanner. You should have more confidence in yourself. She lowers her eyes. The man has thick fingers, with a tiny tuft of black hair in the middle of each top joint. It has nothing to do with me; what I meant was, I'm not sure that he's very happy . . . in general. A man in a suit has rushed into the café, clutching a bouquet of flowers. For a moment she imagines, but no. Relax, he won't have any trouble seeing you when he comes in. Now that you're here, I'm not so sure. The man clenches his eyelids as if he'd been stung in the wrong place. She doesn't think she's been hurtful, just honest. But he's already expecting her to be kind to him, even if she didn't know who he was just a few minutes earlier. She finds that sort of logic hard to understand. Why should she be nice to him? Because he approached her? Of course, she's a little on the defensive. She doesn't feel very comfortable; he reminds her of someone. The glass door has opened and a woman comes in with a bundle of enraged fur on her arm. Another miss. The man is lighting a cigarette and she takes the opportunity to observe him on the sly. He must be about fifty, heavy eyelids, the skin of his face moulded by age into a rather sad expression despite the alertness in his eyes. Yes, he does remind her of someone. Residues of sensations, shadows of images flit rapidly through her mind. And suddenly she knows and bites down hard on the tip of her thumb. She tries hard not to panic. Tell him to get up, to go away, to get up herself, to go away. Impossible, he might be coming, now, immediately, in the next minute; tell him to get up and go, to leave her alone. You're very pale; are you all right? She no longer knows how to produce words. She feels hot. She focuses her attention on the flat surface of the golden liquid in her glass in an attempt to calm herself down. But she is in the pink room, sitting at the piano. Beside her, he is on the bed. She screws her eyes shut to break the image. When she opens them again, the man is holding out a glass, looking worried. She drinks down the cool water with a sense of relief. You'll feel better now. She thanks him, not knowing how else to express the wave of affection that has swept through her. She feels rather foolish. Let's hope he doesn't ask her for an explanation. He sits down again and talks to her as if nothing had happened and they were starting over from the beginning.

It's past ten o'clock: she has been in the café since six.

The man has bought her three, perhaps four more glasses of white wine, she has lost count. He never came. She can't remember exactly when she stopped watching the glass door. But when it occurs to her to look around again, all the faces appear to have changed, without her noticing the bodies those faces belong to come or go. Whether he is in Ange's arms or lying injured in hospital, she no longer cares. The man has talked a lot about French politics, about globalization, and capitalism in the United States, she can't remember all the details. He has talked about the younger, very pretty woman he lives with, who has gone away on a trip for a week. She needed to shove off for a while. The expression struck her; she imagines a woman with very long black hair rowing alone in a boat, rowing herself through the water. He has talked about his work as a photographer, about the subjects he prefers to shoot, about his financial problems. Now he asks her if she would agree to pose for him. She starts to giggle; she's drunk, she knows her face has turned scarlet. I might as well tell you, I'm not going to bed with you. The man bursts out laughing. Men, she reflects, always burst out laughing whenever they are caught out. Nothing could be further from my mind. But she sees that his cheeks have gone red. You have an unusual face. She grimaces. I'm not sure what I see when I look in the mirror, but I think you're lying. The man smiles, and in that instant she senses that he is happier than he has been in a long time. And what about you, do you lie? That's my speciality. Everything is a bit blurry around her. She feels rather content to be there. You can't say no.

She is finding it difficult to focus on the man. She should go home. He tells her that he'll help her find a taxi. Think about it, at least take my card. He pulls out a small cardboard rectangle from one of his pockets and pushes it across the table. At first, she has a twinge of doubt. She reaches down to the floor, rummages in her bag, and finally extracts a business card, which she lays alongside the other. Identical. The man frowns. He picks the second one up to examine it more closely, looking perturbed. You have my card? I found it in a taxi, Olivier Chedubarum.

She had climbed the stairs and battled to get her key into the lock of the door. The answering machine is flashing. Not bothering to switch on the light, she presses randomly on the machine until the cassette clicks into motion. I'm sorry, I hope you didn't wait too long for me, something urgent came up at the office, I'm going away for a week, I'll call you when I get back, I send you kisses. Going away for a week? Where to? Who with? Why? She listens to the message a second time. After the brief explanation he has taken the trouble to give her, she ought to feel reassured. Instead, she feels like throwing up. Rushing to the toilet, she lifts the seat and leans her head over the bowl. She stays like that for one long minute, coughs, spits saliva, sticks her index finger down her throat and waits for a liberating contraction, which doesn't come. Can't even bloody puke. The floor tiles are hurting her knees. Good for nothing, that's what she is. A salty taste of tears reaches the corners of her mouth. She doesn't know what to do now. Go on waiting, not just for an evening, but for an entire week. She begs God, who doesn't exist, to make sure that he never comes back.

Out of bed, métro, office, métro, dinner, into bed. Seven times in a row, each one virtually identical. A week spent waiting for him to return, reliving in her head her favourite moments at the café, going through the motions just to keep up a good front.

Sunday. She gets the idea to draw seven lines on one of the walls in the kitchen so she can cross one off at the end of every day, just as she saw it done in an American film. But she can't find a pencil and worries that if she uses a pen the owner of the apartment will hold back part of her deposit. Afterwards, she forgets to buy the necessary equipment to begin her accounting project.

Monday. Nothing.

Tuesday. At the office, one of her co-workers makes a personal remark to her. It comes from the woman who has been there the longest, the one whose conversation she overhead in the toilets. The day before, Régine was given a gold-mounted diamond from her husband for their twentieth wedding anniversary. Although the two of them never speak, the party in question comes over to show off her jewel and, while she's at it, enquires about her. No date tonight? The answer flies out of her mouth without a second thought. The diamond would look nicer with the price tag on it. The other woman gives her a withering look, tells her that such bitterness is painful to watch.

Wednesday. She is lying naked on her bed. She looks at her pubic hair and finds it ridiculous to have that much hair in that particular spot.

Thursday. The telephone rings early in the evening. Wrong number. The man wants to speak to Audrey.

Friday. The telephone remains silent. He has now been gone for a week.

She should call Ange. Ask her if anything has happened, if he's back, if he's safe and sound. But she has the feeling that trying to get in touch with him would violate an unspoken rule, one inherent to their relationship. In addition, she would run the risk of losing him if Ange found out what was going on. What *is* going on? They meet in a café, kiss and touch; they make no plans except to keep doing it, they promise each other nothing. Not much to get excited about. She can't imagine that Ange, to whom he always returns, the ravishing and divine Ange, could ever become jealous. Would he leave Ange for her? Now and then she tells herself that he might want to, but most of the time she avoids asking herself the question.

She is sitting on the couch with the telephone on her lap. From time to time, she pretends to dial the number, moving her fingers over the buttons but not pressing down on them. She could always give a false name. She leans down to grab the phone book from under the coffee table, opens it at random, and plants her index finger in the middle of the page. Marie Masson. A petite brunette, sporty, bubbly, early thirties. She grew up in a rather modest family with her brother and sister in the suburbs of Paris. She was an attentive eldest child whose parents continually praised her. Full of determination, she passed her law exams with high honours. She then chose to defend people seeking political asylum in France. She loves her job, would like to have children but is waiting for the right man. Hello, my name's Marie Masson. Ugh. She shuts the phone book and opens it again at another page. Alice Tournelle. Blonde, tall, and slim, dynamic and ambitious. The only daughter of two Parisian intellectuals, the mother is an anthropologist, the father a journalist. From an early age she showed a genuine talent for the sciences. At twenty-two, she graduated from the École Polytechnique and was immediately hired by the Alcatel Corporation. Within a few years, she was promoted to a position with considerable responsibilities. She earns a good living, goes out a lot, denies herself nothing, has an occasional romantic adventure with one of the dynamic young executives she meets at her business conferences. She has the respect of her subordinates, who consider her kind but firm. Alice Tournelle speaking. The role suits her, but she wouldn't last five seconds. Last try. Isabelle Léonier. A redhead, obviously, curves in all the right places, gentle features. Married very young to a boy her own age, she was divorced five years later and finished her studies. She is currently working on her philosophy thesis at the Sorbonne. She has many friends, does volunteer work for an NGO, and is mad about rock climbing. It's Isabelle, Isabelle Léonier.

She pushes the directory to one side and goes back to staring at the phone. Ange is too perceptive. She'll recognize her voice or else start asking all sorts of questions, finding it suspicious that a woman she has never heard of is calling them at home. If he were back, he would have been in touch, there's no question about it. Which means that he's still out of town, in a place where the telephone hasn't been invented. His trip has been extended, he is up to his eyeballs in work, he lost his address book with her number in it, it's been stolen along with the rest of his papers. Wait, have confidence, convince yourself that nothing is gained by worrying about nothing, remember that life has a nasty habit of eluding whatever predictions you try to impose on it. Wait, but what to do while waiting? She has to find someone to talk to in order to stop brooding. She goes to fetch the two business cards from her bag.

Olivier Chedubarum remembers her at once. I'm delighted that you haven't forgotten. The session will be fun, he tells her. She doubts that she is very photogenic. Photogenic is a word invented by bad photographers as an excuse to justify their bad pictures. He invites her to stop by his place in the afternoon. She writes down the address on the back of one of his business cards. It's easy to find, you'll see.

The stairway is dim. She couldn't find the timer switch. A faint white light drips down from a window on the first floor, emphasizing the horizontal edges of the stone steps.

The silence here is clean and cold. She slides her hand up the polished-wood banister to find her way. The building once belonged to Madame de Staël. The deep voice resonates down the stairwell. Looking up, she catches sight of Olivier Chedubarum's head trapped in the perspective of the spiralling stairs. She doesn't know who Madame de Staël is, even though the name sounds familiar. She leans on the banister to say that she didn't know, but Olivier Chedubarum's head has disappeared. She begins climbing again. This building would be a perfect place for Alice Tournelle; he's probably trying to call her right now; she's forgotten to put on makeup, which isn't going to help the photo. The door is ajar. She knocks gently and, an instant later, Olivier Chedubarum materializes before her, cigarette balanced on his lower lip, his hair a mess, his eyes alert beneath his swollen eyelids. How are you, come on in, this is my studio.

Olivier Chedubarum has headed over to a table strewn with unpacked boxes of film, rolls, negatives, papers, magnifying glasses, pencils, screwdrivers, lenses, cameras, which he starts to move about efficiently but in an order that seems arbitrary to her. Hanging on one of the studio walls are twelve colour photographs arranged in two rows, one above the other. It takes her a few seconds to comprehend what she's looking at. Kiwis and breasts, kiwi hearts and nipples. The cross-sections of six kiwis and the nipples of six women have been photographed close up. Inlaid into the emerald flesh, the black seeds ring the pale green core, its outline always different, unique, similar to the outline of the nipple encircled by its brown aureole, whose diameter and colouring always vary. Do you like them? She says yes, in the same way she could have said no, for she isn't sure what effect these photos have on her, other than that of looking at familiar things she has never paid much attention to. When she turns around, Olivier Chedubarum is busy positioning two large floor lamps that are directed at a stool, behind which hangs a large sheet of black cloth.

Someone is watching her. On the threshold of what until then had been a closed door, there is a long woman in a dressing gown. Only expanses of white space are visible between the door frame and the contours of her body, as if the room behind her contained no furniture, no limits. Who is she? the woman asks. Olivier Chedubarum straightens, surprised by the sudden apparition as well. He says to her, my darling. The woman hardly reacts. My darling. The woman's eyes are still trained on her, as if to push her back. She says her name, but it sounds false, it doesn't belong to her any more. The woman hears it, ponders it for a moment, shoots an outraged glance at the photographer, and closes the door again. Don't worry, she's a bit jealous, she's, how shall I put it, sensitive. With that, Olivier Chedubarum disappears to the back of the studio. She hears water running from a tap. He returns holding a branch of tiny tomatoes pearled with droplets of water, which he sets down delicately on the table. He locks the front door and his wife's door, then places black screens over the two studio windows. He screws a lens on to a camera body, which he screws on to a tripod. She doesn't dare move. Olivier Chedubarum's index finger straightens, indicating to her the stool in the middle of the setup. She sits down without a word. He points at the curvature of her neck, that soft intimate hollow, receptacle of kisses, tears, and sighs. I need to see all the skin in that spot. He goes to fetch his mounted camera, which he positions within a metre of her. She hesitates, takes hold of her T-shirt with both hands. Her two breasts, cupped in her bra, suddenly occupy the centre of the room. There is no visible reaction from Olivier Chedubarum, who holds out a blanket to her without further instruction. He dips his head behind the camera, she then furtively slips off her bra and drapes herself in the rough material, which she holds in place with one hand. He brings over the bunch of tomatoes. Tilt your head. He deposits the fresh, light fruit on her neck. Now don't move. She can no longer see anything but Olivier Chedubarum's fingers dancing around the camera, which hides his face. A drop of water runs over her chest. The intense light from the lamps forces her to blink. There is no more studio around her; Olivier Chedubarum has been absorbed into the light. Only his shadow continues to shift on the ceiling. She feels as if she's floating in space. She tightens her grip on the blanket. She hears the shutter clicking repeatedly in the absolute stillness of the room. The heat from the lamps slowly warms her up, she relaxes, alert but almost released from consciousness.

The lamps have been switched off. She doesn't want to believe the session is over. Her neck is stiff from having remained in the same position for so long. Olivier Chedubarum has become one with his body again. He retrieves the tomatoes, which have magically stayed in place. You're very patient. It was easy, even pleasant. He offers to make her tea. She then notices the way he walks, somewhat hesitantly, as if he were advancing down a too-narrow corridor and continually knocking into the walls. She uses the opportunity to get dressed, wondering what part of her he shot. She runs her fingers over the base of her neck: the skin is still damp, smooth. She would never have believed that piece of her could be of interest. Afraid of committing a blunder, she doesn't dare move around much, still less to put her hands on one of those enigmatic devices, which could go off at the merest provocation. Olivier Chedubarum returns with a tray bearing a pot of steaming tea and two cups. He sets it down at the foot of two chairs next to the windows, then removes the screens in front of them. She has no idea what time it is. He probably has called. And she realizes that for the first time in a week, she has been granted a respite: she hasn't thought about him once.

The doors are still locked, the woman hasn't reappeared. All that can be seen through the window is sky. She feels assuaged by the simplicity of the moment and the solid presence of the photographer. She is no longer fully certain that she is in the world she left behind when she went up Madame Thingamajig's staircase. A move into the fourth dimension, a detail has changed, but it takes a chance event for it to become apparent. That man you were waiting for, did you find him? Olivier Chedubarum is filling the cups. In his massive hands the teapot resembles a toy. I'm not sure I want to talk about it. The herbal scent of the tea reminds her of a medicine. She imagines that Olivier Chedubarum intends to cure her of an undiagnosed illness that only he has noticed. She sucks in a mouthful of hot liquid. In any case, she shouldn't stay too long. He seems to mean a lot to you. He says it in a kind, responsive voice, the one used on children to get them to tell their secrets. You remind me of someone. Olivier Chedubarum sits up, flattered. Someone nice, I hope. No, not really, someone who stepped over the limits. Olivier Chedubarum sits back in his chair, smiling tenderly. You're a strange girl. Yes, that's what they usually say. They drink their tea in silence, as if it were a ritual that belonged to an old friendship. You'll send me one of the photographs? Come and collect it. She sets her cup down on the tray and writes her number in the Clairefontaine notebook he holds out to her. It was nice. She gets to her feet. Olivier Chedubarum doesn't take his eyes off her.

In the métro, a little girl of about ten is fluttering around a man who is undoubtedly her father. She hops about, straddles his knees, strokes his cheeks with dramatic ostentation, before jumping down and immediately starting all over again. Her eyes shine, a sprig of a woman unconsciously flirting with the prince of her dreams, who lets her romp as she pleases and does little more than hold her by the waist to prevent her from falling backwards. She observes this innocent seductive dance, hypnotized but also worried that at any moment it could descend into something sordid and unspeakable. She feels as if she's watching two similar scenes taking place at once. The first tender, that of a little girl expressing her affection for her father, the second that of a father, turned into a man again, holding his prey down on his knees.

He has been gone for ten days now. She doesn't have the courage to wait any longer. When she dials the number, her fingers tremble. Too bad if Ange answers, she'll hang up. Hello? His voice, at last she has him on the other end of the line. Her heart starts pumping faster, reacting to the abnormal volume of blood that suddenly surges into her chest. Have you been back long? It takes a while for him to answer. I was going to call you, I wanted to think things over. His voice is heavy, as if he had rehearsed the phrase dozens of times. Above all, no reproaches, she seems to remember reading somewhere that men don't like that. Even so, make him understand that his long silence hasn't left her unscathed. I've waited, you know. And as she says it, she reflects on how cruel it is to let someone wallow in the hope of a future life together when the subject is too fraught even to be discussed. I've been thinking about you. What exactly could he have been thinking? About the concentrated way she listens to him, about the rush of emotions his intense look provokes in her, about the overwhelming affection she's unable to hide? Or has he never noticed these things that always seem so blatant to her? Ange has gone off to see a friend and she won't be back until tomorrow, we can see each other at my brother's place, he's away on holiday. At the café, at his brother's — she would meet him anywhere. The only thing that counts is that she not have to wait any longer. His brother lives near the Place-Monge métro station. She hangs up, climbs to her feet and launches into an impromptu dance, waving her arms about, hopping from one foot to the other, following a rhythm she alone can hear, until, sweating and breathless, she collapses on to the sofa.

She has knocked, the door opens. He has a rather wobbly smile on his face and has yet to speak. She wonders if she is destined to spend her entire life knocking at apartment doors, waiting for a man to let her in, or if these are simply accidental repetitions. She is wearing her low-cut black dress, the one that earned her the compliment. She doesn't feel very comfortable in it but wants to make an impression. They walk down a long hallway, so long that she can't see the end of it, and reach the living room, which is a mess and has very little furniture, a coach, a lamp, a piano, as if the occupants were in the process of moving. Littering the floor are copies of *Le Monde*, a decorative carpet patterned with detailed accounts of the agonies and sufferings of distant peoples. My brother and his wife work long hours. The life of a modern couple chasing success: hurried mornings, exhausted evenings, the rest of the day apart. At bottom, not so much worse than her own. They've gone to the Balearic Islands. She doesn't know where the Balearic Islands are, couldn't care less. Why is he waiting to come over and kiss her? Why is she waiting to sit down or talk about her day or ask to use the bathroom to redo her makeup, in other words, to behave like any normal woman who shows up for a tryst with her lover? Too hesitant to touch each other, they go on standing there, mute, alone together for the first time.

He has just remembered the piano. The parquet floor groans under his shoeless feet. He lifts the lid and presses one of the white, ivory keys with his finger. D. Without thinking, she has said the name of the note, he has looked up. Surprised, pleased. She is about to go over to him, but he stops her by raising his hand. His index finger shifts over, presses down on a different key. A. A nod of the head, an admiring look. The index finger hovers over the keyboard and strikes once more. E. The questioner wins. No, it's the black one before E, you nearly got it. She stands a few steps away from him, stiff as an "I," on the alert, abnormally attentive to his slightest gesture. You wouldn't by any chance be a bit obsessive? She hasn't a clue what prompted his remark. She is ready to defend herself, to charge back with unimpeachable arguments, when he brings a finger to his lips, commanding silence. Play something. Not now. The tune the fat little bloke was playing in the métro, remember that? It was pretty awful. Something else then. It's been a long time, I've forgotten how. He takes hold of her hand and leads her over to the velvet stool. She puts up no resistance. Have a go. She knows she won't be able to, and time has nothing to do with it. But it's not yet possible to make him understand. She slides on to the rectangular stool and positions her hands, ten fingers out, ready to crease the ribbon of keys and make the chords of the instrument sing. Behind her, his breathing, his anticipation. She feels her arms seizing up. It's the same with horseback riding, he ought to know that. Anyone who doesn't climb back into the saddle right after a fall will never jump over obstacles again. Because of intractable fear. I can't. He has no reason to insist, but he probably thinks he has found a weak spot, the beginning of an answer, the key to her identity and the reason for his own attachment. Make an effort. He places his two hands over hers and pushes them down hard on the keyboard. The jumbled notes fill the room with an unholy dissonance. A symphony for the handicapped, our first composition. Their cheeks are practically touching. She shuts her eyes; her whole face is tense, as if in pain. She knows that he can see her out of the corner of his eye. You won't be able to do it like that. He wraps his arms around her and rocks her until her eyes finally open again.

I didn't go away on a trip. She stood up without a word, shutting the lid of the piano. That day Ange had called him just before he left the office. She had been crying, she felt he'd been distant towards her lately; she couldn't stop thinking about it. He had tensed up in his chair, his stomach had cramped, but he had tried to reassure her. It was nothing, really; nothing at all, he had a lot of work at the moment, maybe he was a little distracted, but it was nothing to worry about. This was how he had got out of it. I told her as best I could that I loved her, I'm not even sure that I was lying, you know. She is standing in front of the balcony window, her profile impassive, gazing out at the city. When he turned the corner into the street that led to the café where she was waiting, he was twenty minutes late. Even before he reached the entrance, he spotted her behind the window. Her eyes were glued to the door, she didn't see him. Her head was resting on a hand with a small spoon in it. All he could see was her profile, her patient mouth, her watchful eye. He was about to cross those few metres between him and the glass door, he was going to walk in and sit down in front of her. I was going to tell you that it's over, Ange is the one I love. But it did him no good to rehearse the scene in his mind, his feet refused to budge. Through the space between two curtains, she sees a woman sitting on a sofa, smoking pensively, a telephone positioned on her lap. She too is waiting for some poor disembodied voice to tell her that her turn has come; she too is hoping that this voice will give some illusory significance to all that has happened to her previously. On the other side of the café windows, he'd watched her slip her hands between her knees. It struck him that he was observing a well-behaved child intent on pleasing an absent adult. Yes, he felt something for her, but was it enough? What was he doing there, unable to go either forward or backward? A man who could make decisions, that was how he had always thought of himself. But now, he never would have believed . . . He has slid down beside her, avoiding contact. Out on the street, he had thought back to his conversation with Ange, who senses everything, who misses nothing, who probably knows him better than he thinks. On no account hurt that woman, that was the principle he had to follow. And so he'd turned back from the café and retraced his steps. She recalls the stock scene of the prison visit, where two characters separated by a glass panel can't touch and press their hands to the same place, on either side of the glass barrier. I don't know what I should do, you understand. She doesn't want to listen to another word, she doesn't care about explanations that brush against reality without managing to contain it. It's complicated, I can't leave Ange. She has never asked him to do anything of the sort. She's not even sure that if she were in his place she would leave Ange for herself. It makes no difference, since she is already with him in her own way. She feels the delicious weight of his hand on her shoulder. I'm not comparing the two of you. Yes you are, and deep down you think that Ange can make you happier than I can. He isn't sure he has ever thought of the problem in those terms. It's more a matter of what already exists, of not having the energy to start all over again, with no guarantee of reaching a better result. Our past holds us together.

She can't help letting out a sigh. True, but what a sad platitude masquerading as an escape hatch. Despite all the books he's read, he's the one who's hesitating as if he hasn't learned a thing. She feels that she knows so much more about the nature of his feelings. You're the only one, you understand, there won't be anybody else. She has driven her words straight into his heart. He tightens his fingers around her arm and pulls her towards him.

The blinds in the bedroom are drawn, the bed has not been made. He lays her down on the rumpled mounds of the duvet. To give herself up to the inevitable, without hesitation. He lifts her black dress and helps her take it off. Her legs are bare, several brown hairs are sticking out from under the edges of her panties. He takes off his shirt and trousers, lies down beside her, squeezes one of her breasts, his mouth pressed against her cheek. He is there, he wants her. She runs her hands through his hair, kisses his forehead, yet her body holds back, her insides petrified. All these weeks, and now, when all she has to do is to let herself go, this stupid resistance. She hates herself. Stop the commotion in her head, chase away the irrational anger. He isn't the other one, he's himself. She feels his hand move down over her stomach, his fingers slipping in under her knickers to stroke her crotch. Not to think, not to think about the pink room. He finishes undressing her, there's the sound of a packet being torn open, she feels his soft hot skin everywhere against hers. She wants him, she has to want him. His lips press against hers, his erect penis is between her legs. He penetrates her. Clasp him to her, push him off, give in to his rhythm, refuse, enjoy, scream. She grits her teeth, struggling not to struggle. He moves gently; a wave of desire rises up in her, from the bottom to the top, as though towards the surface of the sea. Follow the current, leave her brain behind on the shore, plunge, with her bones, her muscles, her flesh, her blood, deep into the other person. No longer to be millions of little selves lost in all the painful minutes of the past; to be one now, at one with oblivion and him. Long moans simultaneously escape from their bodies, one embedded in the other. A terrible weight crushes her chest; she can't hold back her tears.

He is stroking her hair; watching her intently with anxious eyes. She sniffles, tries to swallow whatever is stuck in her throat. She wants to shrink from shame. He is waiting for the explanation. This time, she is going to have to talk.

He had been her favourite adult. Ever since she was a child, ever since they all used to go to the country house on weekends. He took the trouble to ask her questions; the others preferred to let her play quietly with the objects they gave her as presents every year. Perhaps she was not an easy child to talk to. She was not cute or cheeky, she possessed no particular talent likely to amuse them. But he would talk to her and, unlike the others, he would listen so as to engage only with her. At first, she had been suspicious of these attentions, which were in such contrast to those of the rest of the clan, then she had come to appreciate them, to seek them out. At meals, she did all she could to be seated next to him. When he went for a stroll in the park with his walking stick, she would skip along beside him. She adored being with him. One day, early in adolescence, she had begun to wish that the first boy who kissed her would look a little like him. After that, the thought never left her. Her first love would be a younger version of this man, since it obviously couldn't be him because of their family ties. That was what she thought, without anyone ever having explained things to her. The others seemed unaware of the growing affection she felt for him. They went on making sure that she ate properly, that her bowels were regular, without worrying about where her newly pubescent heart was leading her. At a certain point, he started coming up to her bedroom, or at least that was what she supposed, since she couldn't remember an earlier period when he didn't come to her bedroom while she was there. He would come to the pink room, the one with the piano, when she went up there to practise her music. He would come when she had already started to play. She would turn her head without stopping, would smile at him, delighted to have an audience at last and that the audience consisted only of him. He would motion for her to keep playing and then close the door behind him. The others would be around, busy, in the kitchen, in the living room, in the garden, but never in the room with her when she was playing. Perhaps the music wasn't to their taste or she didn't play well enough, they had never said. He must have liked music. She enjoyed thinking that it was above all her way of playing that he liked. He would sit down on the bed.

He'd say, that's lovely, carry on, lowering his voice so that it wouldn't disturb the bubbling notes that flowed out from under her fingers. She would put her whole self into it; she never played better than when he was there.

The window was open that day. She could hear their indistinct chatter from the garden where they were finishing lunch. They had given her permission to leave the table, their conversations bored her. She had gone up to the pink room, eager to feel the docile, tightly sprung keys under her fingers again. She began warming up with a series of arpeggios. He would be there soon, she was expecting him. When he came in, she noticed red blotches on his cheeks. She assumed they were because of the wine he'd been drinking out in the sun with the others. Without knowing quite why, she blushed when their eyes met. Midway through a Beethoven waltz she had been working on for several weeks, as he was sitting on the bed as usual, she heard the bedsprings groan. She didn't look in his direction at that moment, but she knew that he had stood up. She sensed him approaching, and that set off a rush of nerves in her, which increased her fear of making a mistake. She didn't want to stop, though, because she was sure that he wanted to look at her hands more closely, to appreciate her dexterity. She was proud of the interest he took in her.

And then, she felt his lips on her neck. Her entire body quivered. She stopped at once, not daring to move. She wasn't sure what to make of it; she had never been kissed like that before. Thrown so abruptly, shocked, her mind struggled to regain its balance. He wanted to show his affection; it was a game. He took hold of her shoulders and made her stand up. She let him guide her, unable to grasp what he was expecting from her. When he turned her around to face him, what she saw in his shining eyes both pleased and terrified her. He told her that she was very pretty. She knew he wasn't supposed to say that, and it frightened her. She tried to laugh, to pretend that what was happening wasn't happening. But instead, she only let out a brief moan, a ridiculous sound of protest. That was when she saw him place a hand on one of her small, growing breasts. She wanted to tell him that he shouldn't do that, but she was afraid to go against him. He would laugh at her, consider that she was no longer worthy of his affections. She could have stepped back. Making a noise was out of the question, the window was open, she would have risked being noticed. What they were doing was forbidden. If the others had come in, they wouldn't have believed her and she would have been punished. She could have left the room and escaped. Only she hadn't. Her guts had contracted so much, she couldn't move. She was no longer able to act on her own.

He guided her over to the bed and told her to lie down. The bedsprings creaked again. She closed her eyes. Foolishly she told herself that at last she was going to find out what sex was. She felt his hands on various parts of her body. Later, she heard him groan. Something wet ran over her belly.

The room is dark and hushed. She realizes that she has told it all in one go, as if her voice had been the instrument of a consciousness much freer than her own. She wonders if she'll have the strength to lift her body when the moment comes. Then again, perhaps the brother will refuse to leave the Balearic Islands and she will be allowed to remain lying on this bed for the rest of her days. People will come and care for her, like a sick patient, they will feed her and wash her, they will be far more concerned about her fate than back when she was willing to walk on her own two feet without any help. She won't have to go anywhere, she won't have to make any more decisions, a horizontal existence in which her eyes will always be able to rest on the same white ceiling or close whenever she chooses, without her having to get ready for bed at fixed times or to twist and turn in search of a comfortable position, which she would have to abandon reluctantly on waking. When she turns her head, she is surprised not to detect in him a calm similar to her own. Tight lipped and frowning, he studies her face, then shakes his head and pulls up the duvet to cover her nakedness, a mirror of her exploited vulnerability. He slips his boxer shorts and shirt back on, then lies down beside her. She feels like telling him it doesn't matter, that it's all water under the bridge. His look of pained compassion is starting to worry her. Perhaps he has seen in her account something she could have missed after all these years. Or worse, he could be undergoing the same transformation that Marion went through after the confession on the school bench. And then he'd never be able to separate her from what she has just confided in him; his every look would bear the trace of what he had experienced through her words and her words alone. Forget what I said. He stares back at her as if she's just gone beyond the limits that each person sets to reach an understanding of the world around him. Forget? How can anyone forget something like that, you mustn't feel guilty. Between anger and pity, he hadn't noticed guilt. She grabs the edge of the duvet and pushes it aside, comfortable in her nakedness. Don't you find it strange that we have hair down here? He doesn't seem to want to think about it. He puts his hands on her arm as if he's about to shake her, you don't seem to realize how perverse . . . He doesn't finish his sentence and hugs her as tightly as he can. Let's go away; I'll take you somewhere. She's not sure she follows. Somewhere? I don't know, London, have you ever been there? She shakes her head. Well then, London it is. London. The name bounces around in her head, sparking small jets of joy. At last her turn has come. Like all the others she has seen so often getting on trains, she is the one who will be going away with him. And not just anywhere, but abroad, to the place where she imagines the gare du Nord's longest rails come to an end.

They'll leave the following weekend. When he announces it to her the next evening, there is no mistaking his change of heart. His voice is firmer, more cheerful than usual. Making up his mind to go away with her appears to have temporarily settled the matter for him, whereas previously his only response was to avoid her. Your ticket will come through the post. He arranges to meet her by the entrance to Customs on Saturday morning at eight-thirty, half an hour before departure. Will that be okay? I don't have a passport. He reminds her that she only needs her identity card, because of the EU. She knew about the existence of the European Union, but she hadn't been aware of the passport thing. The free movement of goods and people, young lady; but that doesn't mean you can forget your card. He tells her that it's going to be good, really good, she'll see. She gets a sudden, overwhelming urge to touch him through the receiver. See you Saturday, then.

She didn't dare ask him what he's going to tell Ange to justify his absence. Probably a lie similar to the one he told her. A business trip. But Ange won't be waiting, at least not in the way she had, because when all is said and done Ange is the one he'll go back to. Or maybe not. She smiles to herself. There is a mirror next to her, and she sees herself in it. Not quite the same face, at least different from the one she saw that day in the toilets at the bar. A somewhat troubling discovery. Not that she finds herself more beautiful or younger, feature by feature her face hasn't change at all. Yet she is more herself, closer to the ideal image of who she thinks she is. She shuts her eyes, opens them again, the impression persists. She wants to say hello, as if she were meeting herself for the first time, a bit nervous but fully intent on getting to know this new version of herself in the mirror. It didn't occur to her to ask him how long they will be gone. To play it safe, she'll ask for four days off.

She finds a nylon sports bag buried in a back corner of the hallway closet. With broad red and white stripes, a single zip, an adjustable strap, and tiny fluff-balls of dust clinging to its edges. She doesn't remember buying it. Or receiving it as a present. Or having put it away there, or ever having used it. It probably belonged to the previous tenant, who mislaid it or just left it there to get rid of it, too lazy or too guilty to throw it away. The presence of an abandoned bag in her apartment strikes her as an excellent omen. A bit on the small side maybe, yet without any visible defects. But if they are only going away for two days, which seems likely given the circumstances, she doesn't need to take too much. And if by luck they are to prolong the adventure, she considers it equally sensible not to overburden herself.

She has laid out two piles of clothes on her bed. The essentials and the optionals. Knickers, bras, and socks are separate. In the pile of essential items is her talismanic black dress, worn the previous day at the brother's apartment. She looks over the two mounds, trying to imagine herself in the streets of London wearing each outfit, like a model at an open-air fashion show. She would walk confidently, smiling as if she loved strutting about, and the delirious spectators would be applauding. She wonders if the English sulk as much as the French. She seems to remember that they have a reputation for being quite pale, because of the bad climate, that the men are blond and the women aren't admired for any special physical traits. She decides to remove the red dress from the pile of optionals and stuffs it into a drawer. No point in carrying the memory of Maxime all the way to another country. She still has to eliminate a jumper and a pair of trousers before her travel wardrobe can fit inside the orphaned bag, which she has trouble calling her own. One hour later, the bag is ready. There was no need, of course, to get her things ready so soon. But this way she doesn't run the risk of leaving something behind in the rush, which she would later regret. She makes sure that her identity card is in her handbag. She puts the sports bag on the floor in the hallway so that she can say to herself every evening on returning home from work, this is the proof that we're going away. Two days later, the tickets are in her mailbox, satin-smooth, stiff, flawless. One Paris–London ticket, one London–Paris ticket. She reads everything that is printed on them, from the top left to the bottom right. There's her name, the name of the two cities, the departure and arrival times, her carriage and seat number, the price, and all those figures whose meaning she has never understood. She counts on her fingers, happily realizing that she was right: they aren't going away for two days but four. She carefully puts the tickets in her bag for safekeeping.

Outside the door to the men's toilets, Monsieur Merlinter is standing in front of her. You want to go away? He observes her with impatient eyes, which blink repeatedly as though he wanted to change the image on his retina that obstinately remains the same, in spite of his obvious efforts. This morning she happened to pass him in the hall and rather than going to see him in his office, which would have felt like an official visit and forced her boss to adopt an attitude appropriate to his rank, that is to say, busy and unbending, she preferred to approach him before he disappeared into the toilets, thereby offering the lovely possibility of keeping their talk short. Even though he isn't supposed to involve himself in the private lives of his subordinates, Monsieur Merlinter has not been able to resist the temptation. Feigning an air of detachment, he had to enquire just what she was intending to do with herself during the time off he might or might not give her. I need a holiday. She used the magic word on purpose. All the girls in her office say they need a holiday. Impossible therefore for him to fault her for the uniqueness of her request or the abnormality of her behaviour. As well as blinking, Monsieur Merlinter's eyes are now darting back and forth between her and the toilet door handle. How many days? Four. She said the right number. The day before, after packing the previous tenant's red and white bag, she had rehearsed her speech, so as not to be tempted to reduce it when confronted by her boss's inquisitive look. Four . . . Monsieur Merlinter half opens the door as if to confer with the people who might be inside. Mustn't flinch now. Monsieur Merlinter has one foot on the tiled floor. Four is fine, but even so, check into whether you have that much time coming to you. Of course, she says. The door has already closed behind him.

She hesitates. Then, on the day before the trip, she decides to ask one of her co-workers, a fairly calm and courteous woman who sits to her right, if she has ever been to London. The woman ponders for a few seconds, surprised to be consulted on the matter or perhaps surprised that she is being consulted at all. It's nice if you like to walk, there are monuments, but the people aren't much fun and it rains all the time. No matter, they'll stay indoors. In bars, which won't be much of a change for them, or at the hotel, if in fact he's planning for them to stay at a hotel. There must be plenty of museums, he'll certainly want to go to them. She won't refuse, even if she always ends up feeling painfully bored in such places, burdened by a sense of obligation to admire all the works on display. As for monuments, she's not too keen on those either. Big Ben, that's the name that comes up whenever London is mentioned. She imagines that it must be more or less what the Eiffel Tower is to Paris. She makes a mental note to slip her umbrella into the sports bag. One of the ribs has come loose, but it still keeps the rain off pretty well. They'll just have to huddle together. He'll put his arm around her neck, she'll slip hers around his waist. A fine and beautiful cliché, worthy of the best romances of her age, which she will be all too happy to imitate.

That same evening, she checks the contents of the sports bag for the fifth and final time, and adds the umbrella. She is lifting her leg to step into a special London-departure bath, and just like that the telephone starts to ring. She rushes forward with little steps, holding one hand over her crotch, supporting her breast with an arm, stark naked in the middle of the living room. Yes, hello, it's Olivier Chedubarum. Talkative, in high spirits. She eventually understands that the photographs are ready and that he wants to show them to her. I'm off to London tomorrow. How she has adored saying those words, with a hint of weariness in her voice, as if it were all one to her, as if it were no more than a dull, routine occurrence that she was obliged to mention. It's her revenge, a way of lifting her nose at the entire world, which continues to play its tricks, uncaring, and which has now delegated a single spokesman to her in the person of Olivier Chedubarum. With him? Yes, with him. She's said it, she's in heaven. Now someone will know they're going away, alone, the two of them together. Olivier Chedubarum suggests meeting up that very evening so he can give her copies of the best photos. She hesitates, she has to get up early the next morning. But at that moment everything seems so perfect that she has no desire to deny herself anything or to act for purely rational reasons. A last little outing to mark the occasion, to celebrate her departure. The water in the bath is untouched and cold when she approaches Le Père Pinard, a café on the Place des Halles, at seven o'clock.

She recognizes the phrase. *It's my birthday, I'm forty*

today. She imagines . . . the idea delights her; she's about to say to him, look, I know you, realizing that he said it on purpose to pull her leg, to make a joke about the past, to invite her along to the café. She turns around: Momo isn't talking to her but to a tall, fine-looking girl who is firmly shaking her head. And when his eyes sweep over the place where she is standing, he doesn't stop, doesn't notice her. Point taken. That day, Momo had stumbled on to her by chance, because she had been the one to turn around, not because of who she was. She doesn't dare go over; she keeps on walking in the direction of the café, trying hard not to think about it any more.

A cardboard folder is on the table. Olivier Chedubarum stands up, she sits, the waiter sets down two glasses of wine in front of them, the file is opened. What Olivier Chedubarum then shows her causes her to gape. She sees a sister, a cousin, a likeness, but it's not her, not fully. The look in the eyes is hers, but not the expression, which is fierce, severe, and doesn't correspond to anything in herself. Perhaps others have always seen her like this and she simply hasn't known it. She picks up one of the photos to study it more closely. There is a small luminous dot, slightly out of focus, the drop of water that had landed on her upper chest and left a trace on the film before it fell. The tomatoes are the tomatoes she had seen in Olivier Chedubarum's hands. And yet her face is not the face she thought she had presented to the photographer. Gone is the sense of well-being she had experienced in the glow of the enormous lamps. Nevertheless, it had seemed to last for a long time, long enough to be captured on film. You don't like them? It doesn't seem to be me. Olivier Chedubarum bursts out laughing. You look good, though. A nice way to say the image flatters her, that she looks better in it than in real life. That's not what I mean. But how to explain it to him? She wonders if the result would have been the same if the pictures had been taken by a different photographer. It might be Olivier Chedubarum's eye that has trans- formed her, but how can she be sure? Actually, you can keep them. Olivier Chedubarum shakes his head. I'll end up believing you think I'm a bad photographer. She doesn't know a thing about photography, she's in no posi- tion to judge, it's not that, it's just. Take them anyway, stick them in a drawer, one day you'll wind up liking them. She shrugs. After all, she's off to London tomorrow, that's what counts, the photographs are of no importance. To please Olivier Chedubarum, she tucks the folder away in her bag. He then orders another round and starts telling her about how he covered the student riots in May '68 and managed to have his first photographs published in the national press.

She has lost track of how long she's been listening to Olivier Chedubarum. Yawns twist her mouth out of shape, but she is unable to control them. She has had several glasses of wine, or maybe only one, which she is finishing off now. She has to go home. Her legs are dragging her down. She is in a taxi. She has said goodbye to Olivier

Chedubarum, she no longer remembers what he said to her. This time tomorrow she'll also be in a taxi, but in London, with him. As she lies down on her bed, she thinks of a bushy haired puppet called Big Ben.

She opens her eyes. Remembers. Sticks the face of the alarm clock up against her bleary eyes. Several long seconds go by before she can focus on the slender hands. When she finally makes them out, the world around her suddenly shrinks, leaving only the narrowest slit through which to escape the inevitable. 8:10, ten past eight in the morning. Horrible horror. How could she have let it happen? If she had the time, she'd punish herself by giving her head a good bang against her bedroom wall, but she has only twenty minutes to get to the station. She puts on the clothes she finds on the floor, then her coat, slings the sports bag and her handbag over her shoulder, looks for her keys, hears objects dropping to the floor without knowing what they are, finds her keys on the kitchen table, battles with her feet and shoes to get the former into the latter, glimpses 8:15 somewhere, opens the door, locks the door, rushes down the stairs into the street, quick glance to the right, to the left, hesitates, searches her mind for the shortest route to the station, begins to run. The bags hit against her sides, she does her best to hold them in place, but the tighter her grip the harder it is to run. She brushes up against several passersby, who give her long stares, she would like to shout insults at them, she sprints at the crossings to avoid red lights. Her heart is knocking around in her chest. Fire spreads across her forehead, temples, cheeks. A stitch is stabbing her in the belly, she breathes out forcefully to soften the pain. Her legs are weighed down by the alcohol still circulating in her blood, her stomach is begging for food, her brain distracts her by churning out thoughts. Don't miss that train, no matter what, don't stop, get as far as Customs, want it enough to make it, even if you have no more breath, keep running until the end, until the meeting place, run, don't stop, find him, go faster, faster still, get there, don't miss that train. Her métro pass isn't in her bag, her métro pass is in her bag. She feeds her ticket into the machine and starts running again. People are in front of her, they don't get out of the way, they're stupid and slow, wrapped up in themselves, wearing Walkmans, deep in conversation, they all want to stop her from getting there. Excuse me. She calls out the words from a distance so they'll reach their target before she does and she can run past the obstacles without slowing down. She has to stop on the platform to wait for the métro. The tracks go all the way to the station. She'd climb down into the tunnel and start running in the dark and the damp to get there on time. The beating of her heart resounds in her eardrums, every fold of her skin is brimming with sweat. The whoosh of the train, the approaching headlights. She gets on. She would like to do something to make the ride go faster. She forces herself to catch her breath, she's bright red. Several passengers watch her as she bends over, hands on her knees. Finally the letters spelling Gare du Nord glide past through the windows. The doors open. She runs out on to the platform, up the escalator, along the corridors, spots the signs marked Eurostar, she knows the way, she's on home ground, she's been here hundreds of times, she's about to collapse. She enters the station concourse. People, too many people, people everywhere. She threads her way, avoiding the groups that come streaming towards her, the kids lounging around on the floor. Don't miss the train, so close. She looks up. The clock shows 8:55. Impossible, that can't be right, she keeps going, staggers up the last steps, barely ten metres to go before Customs. The platform is empty. No one, not a passenger in sight, he's nowhere to be seen, he isn't there, no one but the customs people in their glass cages. She goes over. As if from thin air, a woman in a blue uniform rises up in front of her. Boarding is over, miss. She has no more breath, no more saliva, no more words. She puts out her hand, her head is spinning, her ears abuzz. You can't go through, boarding is over. Do you hear me?

She has sat down on the ground. Her heart is threatening to pop through her chest. Everything is turmoil inside her. From emotion, exhaustion, anger, disgust. It feels as if her hair is standing on end, her body is a solid mass, racked by shudderings that keep changing its shape. She wishes she had the power to turn back the clock, to start again. Barely half an hour, a mere half hour and she would have been all right. Where is he now? If he had stayed here, he would have waited in front of Customs to tell her they weren't leaving any more. The fact that he's not here means he took the train. And on that train he is brooding over his resentment, while she has no way of explaining to him what really happened. He must think she changed her mind and missed the train on purpose, out of cowardice. That thought is more than she can bear; because he's gone, she has to leave and find him. She struggles to her feet. She heads over to the Eurostar counters. She'll take the next train. With a bit of luck, he'll still have enough confidence in her to guess what happened and wait at the other end. She manages to get a seat on the 10 a.m. Eurostar. At a fast-food stand, she has a coffee and in quick succession wolfs down two warm pains au chocolat. She is so exhausted she can hardly think ahead. Now and then a recurrent, fleeting image, always the same one, flashes through her mind, her mad dash, her feet pounding on the concrete, step after step. Most of the time, though, all the while keeping an eye on the clock, she distractedly observes two pigeons circling around each other, small automatons oscillating under the weight of their heads and tails.

After the French customs officer there is a British customs officer, a stiff and expressionless woman who compares her identity card photo against the living duplicate it represents. He came through this gate earlier, and the official probably looked at him in the same way, with that air of professional detachment. She could describe him to her and be assured that he was here before. Excuse me, I'm looking for someone, I was wondering if you saw him pass through, he took the nine o'clock train. The customs woman slowly lifts her eyes to meet hers and frowns, visibly surprised that the subject under examination possesses the power of speech. He's tall, or at least taller than she is, a bit taller, well, that's not to say that she's very tall, she's average, he's got brown hair too, not very dark but not very light either, the kind of brown that people with brownish brown hair have, his eyes match his hair, a little greener, not that he has any green in his hair but there's something luminous about his eyes, which she associates with a hazelnut brownish sort of green, a good-looking guy basically, though perhaps not in the strictest sense of the word, it's more that he's to her liking, it's hard to explain what she likes, anyway he can't be too bad-looking, on account of Ange, who wouldn't like a man whose looks didn't go well with hers, he often wears a suit, but probably not today, since he's not on a business trip, although, yes, he's meant to be on a business trip so he's bound to be wearing one to look the part or perhaps he slipped it into his bag to feel more comfortable, but on that point she can't say for certain. Several syllables come out of the customs officer's mouth, coagulate into a mass of sounds that approximates a real but incomprehensible sentence. Eventually the official raises her eyes in exasperation. En-glish. English, oh yes, she'd forgotten, the English speak English, that's only logical. She knows a few basic words of English. Let's see, some polite phrases, the numbers up to ten, how to say her name, how to say I don't understand. He must speak the language, that's what matters, he'll translate. The customs official motions for her to step aside and make way for the people behind. She joins a group of passengers moving forwards with determination, then waits with them in front of a glass wall through which railway tracks and empty platforms can be seen.

Where is he? Right now, still on the train, if he has taken the train, he has taken the train. Where else would he be if not? He would never have gone home without letting her know first, he wouldn't be nasty enough to punish her like that for being late. Of course, he could have waited for her so they could have taken the next train together. But he must have thought they might have trouble getting two new seats or that changing the tickets would cost too much. He must have hesitated, then decided not to change the plan, thinking she would have the presence of mind to do the same.

The doors open, the travellers surge forward, the platform fills with a chaotic flow of humanity, the train is taken by storm. She is shoved along right up to the steps of her carriage. Pushed by a bulging stomach, she narrowly misses getting smacked in the forehead by the bony elbow of the grandmother in front of her. She has looked at them often, on café terraces, surrounded by their suitcases and their laughter, under the departure boards, heads tilted back, standing in line, their mouths half open, by the platform entrances, being met, embraced, surprised, kissed, tears streaming down their cheeks, by the ticket machines, puzzled, conscientious, examining the front and back of their tickets again and again, and she had thought them so happy, so serene, so charming. And now to her great disappointment they are behaving like vulgar métro passengers instead of appreciating how lucky they are to be setting off in a straight line and not travelling round in circles. And even if he's not by her side, even if she's starting to get worried, a wave of joyous excitement washes over her as she steps into the carriage. She wants to talk to them, to shower them with smiles, but they're all busy attending to their suitcases and their tickets. Everyone is blithely bumping into everyone else.

Modern is the word that comes to her as she surveys the interior of the carriage. The floor and windows are clean, the seats comfortable, the lighting low, the colours match. It feels as if she has shrunk and stepped into a model. Her seat is next to the window. Perfect for watching the landscape rush by. She stows the sports bag on the overhead luggage rack, imitating a young woman she has seen doing the same at the far end of the carriage. She decides to keep her handbag on her lap. A man has put a briefcase under the seat next to hers, has sat down, and without giving her a glance or exchanging a word has opened a thick book. *The Best Marketing and Communication Techniques.* Several people hurry by on the other side of the window. She wonders why there are no seat belts on trains. A sensuous voice she doesn't recognize announces that they are leaving. The platform glides slowly backwards.

Grey houses, shut windows covered by whitish curtains, long electric wires, the bare, black trunks of trees that seem to have been planted haphazardly to make it look as if they were spared when the city was built. A female voice announces the existence of a bar at the centre of the train and lists a whole range of sandwiches and refreshments. She is hungry but doesn't want to disturb her neighbour, who is engrossed in his reading. If he leaves his seat to go to the toilet, she'll take the opportunity then. Outside, the woods and the walls in the foreground are flowing by too fast for her to see them. Stretched between barely perceived poles, supple and sinewy telephone wires attract and repel one another. She has to look into the depths of the landscape to see the things she wants to see, for them not to disappear at each moment. She likes the gentle, barely perceptible motion of the carriage. He too is on a train, kilometres ahead of her, but on the same track, bound in the same direction. Her eyes close, she presses her handbag against her body. She is on a train, she is going away somewhere, he is at the end of the line, waiting for her.

A feeling that something has touched her. While opening his briefcase, the man next to her has jogged her with his elbow. She is awake now. He has stood up and, swaying back and forth, has walked down the aisle to the far end of the carriage. To her relief, she discovers that her handbag is still on her lap. On the other side of the windows, huddled rows of brick houses are slipping along, accompanied by murmurs and sighs, the zipping of zips, the rustling of pages and plastic bags. The people outside are as invisible here as they were on the outskirts of Paris.

London would therefore be nothing but a single long row of identical houses, all of them deserted. Her mouth is dry, her body is as stiff as the seat she slept in. The voice from the loudspeaker announces their arrival at Waterloo station. She remembers now that the same voice spoke while she was asleep. She hadn't managed to open her eyes then, to regain consciousness and understand what it was saying. Without her noticing, the train went under the sea, travelling through a dark tube to avoid the water by plunging below it. An under-channel crossing. She thought it was going to be a unique experience but, to her great disappointment, she hasn't felt a thing. Back when the tunnel was being built, she wondered if it would be possible to see anything through the walls, algae, fish, one of those marine creatures that live deep below the surface. Later, she'd been sorry to find out that the tunnel didn't pass through the sea but under it, through dense, blinding, solid, reassuring earth, the same earth in which it is customary to put the dead.

He is waiting for her now, somewhere inside the station. He probably walked around for a while to stretch his legs, then sat down in a café from where he could watch the fresh arrivals. Very soon, they'll be together again. She can't imagine anything else.

The jolt of the brake has sent the passengers tipping forward. She retrieves the sports bag, inserts herself into the Indian file shuffling its way off the train, and falls in step with the passengers trotting along at different speeds in the same direction. After the platform come level corridors,

followed by an inclined walkway leading to the customs
booths. Her country is a member of the European Union;
she is in London, hundreds of kilometres from home, to
meet someone who is her only reason for being here. She
doesn't know what she'll be doing in the hours ahead, any
more than what she'll be doing in the days ahead. She gives
no thought to what she has done before this, to the chain
of events that has led her to this place. Her two feet are on
the ground, at a precise point on the globe, but until she
crosses the London border, she will still be in a parallel
dimension, in the timeless space of the journey. She walks
past the booths, attracting no attention, free. She is on the
other side now. The other side of the sea, the other side of
a symbolic border, the other side of herself perhaps. She
walks down a wide corridor, passes through doors. Dozens
of anonymous people are gathered there, necks craning,
arms crossed. Their eyes see her, then turn, looking for
someone else, until they raise their arms and rush forward,
lips ready, to the elected being they've been waiting for.
She feels a slight contraction in her chest, which increases
the farther she walks. She can't see him. Not to the right,
not to the left, not on the chairs, not by the pillars. The
palpitations are constant now. An escalator takes her up to
the main concourse. So many people, never him. It feels
as if her head has swollen, her bags have shrunk. She
wanders around, retraces her steps, peers over railings,
gets up on tiptoe, walks in and out of cafés, shops, hidden
corners, scans, searches, turns places upside down with
her eyes. And then suddenly she stops, overwhelmed, for

she knows only one thing for certain now: he is not there, he is no longer in a place where she can reach him, except inside herself, inside her body which is here, although she is alone.

She has sat down on the floor, against a wall. At the gare du Nord, she had seen them sprawled out like this in some out-of-the-way corner. They would settle down on the filthy floor amid streams of spilt liquids and pieces of crushed chewing gum, exposed to the freezing, dusty drafts, in the middle of the frenetic crowd intoxicated by the thought of departure. They'd stretch out under the reproving stares of the busy people to show they had no strength left, not even to go a few metres farther along to find a bench or the cushioned seat of a drinks stand. She'd assumed they were homeless or broke, waiting to sneak on to a train without a ticket. Now she is in the same position, no higher than a man's knee, like a dog. An ethereal female voice starts talking above their heads. She can't follow the words but knows that the voice is announcing the next train, the time, the number, the departure or arrival platform. An Englishwoman is sitting behind a microphone and performing the same task she does in Paris. Later on, she will leave her office and might walk past her, she with her ass glued to the floor, and glance at her briefly, wondering what that woman with a sports bag can possibly be doing there by herself. And then, all of sudden, a silhouette, a familiar gait, the fleeting certainty that. But no, her hope collapses like a botched cake and she sinks back into her hole at the sight of the atrociously unfamiliar face.

And so it continues, as she lets herself fall into the trap, tortured by the thought of his presence trying to incarnate itself in one of the bodies around her, a body that is never the right one. In the end, she becomes hypnotized by the parade of passing shoes. She would like a hand to touch her on the shoulder, for it to be his, and for that to be the end of the matter. The episode would become a little story they could spend the rest of their stay looking back on with laughter. But nothing of the sort happens. No one recognizes her, and she recognizes no one. She is in an unfamiliar city, and there is no place in it for her except with him.

Trains are leaving in the other direction, their noses pointed straight at Paris. There is nothing to stop her from taking one. Her bank account would go into the red, but in three hours she'd be back at the starting gate, where her old habits would be waiting for her. She would push open the door of her apartment and use up the last of her strength pretending nothing had happened. But going back is worse than staying put. She lacks the courage to make the trip, and when she returns, to confront the deluge of too many questions, the necessity of acting on what she discovers, whether he is in Paris or not. By staying, she will be able to pretend that their trip was not a total failure, she can give herself a small breather before being forced to swallow the truth in one gulp.

Every thirty minutes she has stood up, patrolled the station on her stiff legs, searching for the slightest clue, then returned to sit down in the same spot again, this corner of wall and floor. After seven hours of surveillance rounds, she leaves the station, slightly dazed, hunger in her belly. The night is pierced by the glow of headlights and street lamps, not very different from the ones in Paris. In front of her is a stretch of pavement, a succession of roads and a staircase leading down to a grim-looking underpass that she feels incapable of entering. A black vehicle in the shape of an estate car with the word TAXI lit up on its roof. She signals to the driver, who pulls over on the other side of the street. The traffic doesn't slow down. After several attempts, she manages to cross at a run. She climbs into the taxi, which strikes her as over-spacious, more suited to bearing coffins than upright living people. Far in front of her, the driver has said something. She can only see the back of his head. Ho-tel. She articulates the word clearly, hoping to compensate for her lack of a British accent. An incomprehensible question from the driver, who turns round with a not very friendly look on his face. She wants to tell him that she's had a hard day, that he could at least be polite, but all she has at her disposal is the word *hotel* and whatever patience she has left. Eventually, the driver takes off with a comment that ends in a sigh.

The bridge they take stretches across a wide river. Along its banks, lights from buildings of every kind, glass towers, domes, stone facades, historical moments captured in the dominant materials of their days. She has never seen such a jumble of heights and styles. She never would have guessed that London looked like this. After the bridge, she closes her eyes. She doesn't know where this man is taking her; she has entrusted herself to him, has given him the task of deciding what her next stop will be. If he pulls over and orders her to get out, she'll do it because she will have nothing to say to him, no recourse to language to defend herself. She can gesticulate and utter sounds, but she will never convince him of anything by the precision and sharpness of her words. She hasn't felt so vulnerable in a long time.

The taxi has pulled up outside a building with a white front, its entrance flanked by two columns. On a small metal plaque on one of them, she reads Beaumont House. She is ready to get out when the driver cuts her short. He says only one word, *money.* She understands, but she realizes to her horror that she has no money on her, at least not the right sort. Nevertheless, she takes her purse from her bag and from her purse a twenty-euro banknote, which she holds out to the driver as innocently as she can. He shakes his head. She pretends not to understand. *Pounds, not euros, pounds, not euros,* the man says, hammering out his words, completely exasperated. Her head is going to explode. She so wishes he were with her, he could explain the problem to this idiot. She would like to sleep and forget everything. Her eyes close, her body topples sideways, and she feels the cold leather of the seat pressing against her cheek. To stay there, stretched out forever, rocked by the motion of the taxi taking her through London for all eternity. The door by her head has been flung open, a chill draft tickles the roots of her hair. The driver bombards her with words, demented, meaningless words, and drags her out of the car. She is standing on the pavement, her sports bag and handbag at her feet. The taxi has disappeared.

She has to ring to be let in. When she hears the buzzing in the lock, she pushes the door. A voice calls out, she follows it. She enters a small lounge furnished with two floral-patterned armchairs and a drinks machine. No one. Jutting from a wall, she spots a small wooden counter with someone sitting behind it, a thin woman with short, sad hair, and a pair of glasses perched on the end of her nose. The woman is hunched over a magazine and fiddling with a bunch of keys. Behind her is a room filled with two paper-strewn desks. As she goes over, the woman gives her an odd sort of elongated smile before she starts to emit, as if in a nightmare, monstrous, incomprehensible words. *Ai-don-un-deur-stin-de.* The woman appears to grasp the message, holds up an index finger with a pointed nail and raises her eyebrows questioningly. She responds by tucking in her thumb and showing her four other fingers. She'll be staying here four nights. The woman goes to rummage in a drawer and comes back to show her a bank card. She takes hers out of her purse and hands it over.

Flesh-toned tights and grey mules precede her up the stairs, which groan beneath a thick layer of carpeting. At the top, the woman opens a door: a tiny room just large enough for a toilet. They then take a second, narrower staircase that leads straight up to the first floor. They reach a landing where there is barely enough space for the two of them. There are three doors, one of which is the door to her room. The woman pushes the light switch, motions her inside, says a few words with her stiff smile, and withdraws after placing the keys on the night table. She hears the door close, the woman's faint cough, then nothing. Her first silence in the weak glow of the ceiling light. For a moment she remains where she is standing, looking around the characterless room, which doesn't have a single redeeming feature. Walls that are too bare, a ceiling that is too high, robbing the enclosed space of any sense of protection, a yellowish wardrobe and desk, which have been touched by too many hands but have never belonged to anyone. In one corner is a dismal sink; on the other side, an ugly and cumbersome plastic shower unit. And floating in the midst of it all, the mingled odours of a cleaning product, the starch from the sheets, stagnant water, enclosed air. First, open the window – or rather, in this case, pull up the window. As she leans over the railing, she sees that the hotel looks on to a small park. The fragrant humus is a relief, an olfactory balm, and for several minutes all she wants is to breath in its smell.

She opens the wardrobe doors, the desk drawers, all of them sadly empty, all waiting to be filled to give the occupant an impression of being at home. If he had been there, she would have removed her few things from the sports bag for the sheer pleasure of storing them next to his. Alone, there's no point. The television set is shut away in a special cabinet opposite the bed. She turns it on, flicks through the channels with the remote control: an English version of the same cathode-ray-tube mush. She has no desire to know what is happening in the immense else-where, the opinions of strangers, the dramas of invented characters. In any case, she doesn't understand a thing. She switches off, the screen swallows back its images, the deluge of aural soup comes to an end. Barefoot on the bed, curled up in a fetal position, she looks for a way to stop the current of speculation that keeps bringing her back to the same question. Why didn't they find each other? She has two answers and can't decide between them: an unfortu-nate cluster of circumstances or the result of an intentional act. She swings from one to the other, going back and forth as monotonously as the pendulum of a clock. Unlucky, cursed, predestined, irresponsible, she tries out these adjectives on herself in an attempt to explain her role in what happened. She has missed her entrance cue, the play will go on without her, she is standing in the wings, flabbergasted that she has failed at the very moment when she most needed to prove her competence. There ought to be a special probe to inspect the inside of her head, that undifferentiated, infinite space that sits miraculously within the confines of her skull. She isn't sure, but there might be something like an immense clod of dust jamming up a tiny gear. Something not quite right, as they say. She thinks she ought to be thinking about something else, but in thinking this she can't help thinking about the matter she is thinking about. Try to get some rest. She slips a pillow under her head, a hand under the pillow. Find the best position for sleep. Images march through her mind; above all she must not focus on them. She hears the muffled hum of a car engine in the distance, she's almost there, she feels her consciousness melting away. But she has to reopen her eyes, brought back to reality by a noise that wasn't there before, a breathing, a panting, on the other side of the wall. And the more she concentrates, the more she hears it, rhythmical, provocative. Two people are getting it on in the next room. She doesn't want to know, she doesn't want to listen, she doesn't want to hear love, she doesn't want to know that it exists, she wants to be left alone. She could, but doesn't dare bang on the wall. Instead, she resigns herself to staying stretched out on the bed, staring up at the ceiling light that undulates through her tears, imagining that dozens of tiny elves have tied her body to the mattress.

She wakes up. The light from a street lamp is shining on the ceiling of the room, now plunged into darkness. She doesn't remember switching off the light. Her stomach gurgles. She thinks she hears the sound of a key in a lock.

She wakes up. Her mouth is dry. She gets out of bed and shuffles cautiously over to the sink. She brings her lips close to the tap. The water smells of bleach. Through the window, she glimpses a dark shape moving about in the park.

She wakes up. She can no longer ignore the promptings of her bladder. The door creaks as she opens it; the light makes her squint. She goes down the stairs as quickly as she can, afraid that she might meet someone. The timer light sounds like the chirping of a cricket. The floor tiles in the toilets are cold. She thinks she has stepped on something wet. She doesn't dare sit down on the seat and pees standing astride the bowl. She finds no paper to wipe herself with.

She woke up. Day had dawned outside.

She left the room, carrying her handbag with her. At the front desk, she saw a pair of hands poking over the counter; she didn't drop off her key. Outside, to her surprise, she noticed that all the houses around the park were identical, with their white facades, their columns, their raised front entrances, and their large windows. She wondered if the occupants all dressed the same, so as not to stand out. She headed right, although she could just as well have headed left. The few people passing by at that moment were all going in the same direction. She decided to do what they did; they obviously knew where they were going. She reached a crowded road, with shopfronts on either side. Unable to read the instructions, she had to try several combinations of buttons before she could withdraw four hundred pounds from a cash dispenser. She didn't know how much a pound was worth, but four hundred seemed to be an interesting number, probably because of the four. She then stopped in at some kind of café after reading, with the satisfaction of having understood, the word *sandwich* on the window. All the tables were empty, except for one, where a woman sat resting her elbows. She chose to sit as far away from her as possible. The place smelled of fried butter and cigarette smoke. A waitress took her time before coming over. She said, sandwich, and the waitress said something in response. She shrugged, the waitress returned with a menu, she pointed randomly at the first line. A few minutes later, a mound of bread, ham, and cheese landed in front of her. She ate because she was hungry, the sandwich oozed mayonnaise. She noticed that the other customer had the face of a witch and was rolling cigarette after cigarette, half smoking each one before stubbing it out in the ashtray, which she engaged in intimate conversation without uttering a sound, merely by moving her lips. She left, feeling rather ill, and set off in search of a supermarket. Since she was afraid of getting lost, she decided to keep to the main commercial street. She ended up going inside a place that went by the bizarre name of Sainsbury's, where she bought a dozen tomatoes, carrots, oranges and apples, a dozen yogourts, five packets of vacuum-packed cold cuts, and two cellophane-wrapped loaves of bread. It took her a certain amount of time and struggle to get it all back to the hotel, after she lost her way turning in to what she thought was her street. She made a dash for the stairs to avoid being spotted by the owner of the hotel. Back in her room, she put the yogourts and cold cuts inside two plastic bags, which she placed on the window-sill. The rest of the food she put away in the cupboard. She then brought a chair over to the window and settled down to observe the park and the street. The aim was simply to observe, perhaps even to comment on what she saw if she felt an inclination to formulate a thought, but above all not to reflect on anything that had to do with her. Seen from above, the people didn't look very different from the ones in Paris. She noticed a few squirrels in the park, as well as a bird she had never seen before. When the light started to fade, she was still in the same spot.

After eating a tomato and several slices of cured ham, accompanied by some bread and an apple, she lay down on the bed. She slept no better than she had the previous night and was woken up several times for no apparent reason. She didn't hear her neighbours making love, but when the door to the toilets was left open, there was the sound of water running in the flush. There was a murmur as well, as if two people were whispering somewhere in the room, unseen.

The next day, after some hesitation, she climbed out of her clothes. She took a cold shower in the plastic cabin. Removing some clean clothes from the sports bag, she rolled the dirty ones up into a ball before stuffing them into the desk drawer. Once again, she installed herself at her observation post, nibbling on bread and from time to time crumbling little pieces on to the windowsill.

Since moving into the room, she hasn't spoken. And now she feels as if her voice has been hidden somewhere inside her body, as if it were a living creature in the process of dying.

Later on, she heard a key in the lock. A young woman dressed in overalls appeared in the doorway and mumbled something with such ingenuousness that she immediately nodded in assent. The maid entered and began remaking the nearly untouched bed. She had done no more than cover herself with the blanket during the night when she felt cold. The maid passed a cloth over the night table, a sponge round the inside of the shower unit and the base of the sink, then picked up the white towel she had used to dry herself. She watched these efficient movements without seeming to disturb the maid, who mechanically went about her tasks as if no one else were in the room: her body was at work, but her mind was elsewhere. It occurred to her that she could offer her services to the hotel and in exchange live there for an indeterminate length of time. There would be no need for her to talk, she would learn the two or three English phrases necessary for the job, that would be enough. She could have another life, and far more easily than she had imagined before coming here. The maid put a clean towel on the bed before withdrawing in silence. She finished the rest of the bread, then went out.

The park gate was open, she sat down on a bench. The air was chilly, the sky grey and monotonous. Now and then, she saw the upper portion of a scalp pass by on the other side of the thick hedge. She drew circles in the gravel with her heels, stared at her hands, clicked her tongue, flicked non-existent specks of dust off her clothing. A squirrel with a frayed tail approached to within a metre of her feet. Up on its hind legs, it sniffed the air. She cleared her throat and spat, but her spittle fell short and the little animal bolted for the cover of a protective tree. She had absolutely nothing to do. She felt like a bored patient who hasn't the strength to do something to help the time go faster. She felt permanently out of breath, even though she hardly moved. Her heart was beating oddly, as if out of rhythm, as if she were constantly being dropped into a void. She tried to rekindle her enthusiasm. She was on a trip to London, there was an entire city around her to explore, she couldn't leave without finding out what Big Ben really was. But none of this inspired the smallest shudder of curiosity. She had to face the facts: monuments or no monuments, she couldn't have cared less. She had not an ounce of willpower left. Just getting herself down to the park had required an effort.

Later on, she stood up and walked round the park, tearing off bits of leaves as she passed by, sprinkling them at her feet. She went over to a tree and let herself hang from the first branch she could reach. The bark grazed her skin slightly, but she jumped up, trying to get her legs high enough to hook them over the branch. But they fell back heavily to the ground, not making contact. After about fifteen attempts, she gave up: she no longer knew how to climb trees.

She would have done anything for him to be there. She would have done anything not to think about him. She would have done anything never to have met him.

Back at the hotel, she passed a man on the stairs. He didn't say anything and kept his eyes trained on his shoes; all she could see was the top of his shiny bald head. She had an urge to grab hold of him and shake him as hard as she could until he finally looked up at her and felt scared. As he went by her, she clicked her tongue against her palate. The man turned his head. C'est vous qui baisez toute la nuit? The man shrugged with an air of doubt and continued on his way down.

She finished the first pack of ham and devoured the second. She ate four yogourts and several pieces of fruit. She ate as much as she could until she could eat no more. It was then that she remembered the photographs. She took them out of the folder, which was still in her bag, and studied them for a long time. Now she was there, now she could recognize herself. She placed the three photos upright on the desk. She filled the sink with water and put them in to soak. She wanted to see if the images would dissolve and then be washed away when she pulled the plug. Sitting at the window, she waited. When she went to check, the black-and-white versions of her face were floating intact beneath the surface of the water. She took out the sopping pieces of paper and scrunched them into a ball, which she threw in the toilet.

That night she had a dream. She was a man and there was a brown paper bag over her head. His wrists had been tied behind his back, hands were firmly gripping his arms, forcing him to walk despite a leg stiff with pain. He could see blood dripping on to the dust between his filthy bare feet. There was a tiny hole in the bag, a peephole through which he was trying to look out at sections of the ransacked city. And then something happened; he reopened his eyes in the dream. He was free. He was hobbling along a road in the middle of a forest cut in two by a streak of limpid sky. Up ahead, by the side of the ditch, he realized there was a woman, her swollen belly protruding under her dress. She stood motionless, arms dangling at her sides. He had to take her with him, that was the only possibility, even if the presence of this unknown woman would slow down his escape. Hurry up, he told her, as if it were a threat. She began walking behind him, not saying a word. Suddenly a contraction rooted her to the tar-covered road, dappled with writing spots of sunlight. Her two slender hands supported the weight of her child. He went over to her; it's coming, she murmured.

Startled awake, she had to get up to drink some water from the tap. In the street, a man was walking by with a dog. Trotting along with its snout a few centimetres from the asphalt, the animal was tracking smells that emanated from steps or posts. At the other end of the leash, the dog's master would tug the unwilling animal away, then continue walking along with long strides. After the man and his dog left her field of vision, she went back to bed. For a long while she sought sleep behind her closed eyelids. Then she sensed him. He was standing at the foot of the bed, holding the TV remote control and manoeuvring it as if it were a magic wand that could cast visual spells. His lips were moving, but she couldn't hear him. He seemed impatient despite his kind look. Eventually she shrugged to let him know there was a problem. He fiddled with the buttons on the remote control and then suddenly, in mid-sentence, sound was added to the picture, exactly as if a plug had just been reinserted into a socket somewhere . . . would you like to watch? Slightly wary of this sudden apparition, she told him that she hadn't understood. What do you want to watch? She hadn't really thought about what she wanted to watch, he could choose, she didn't mind. You said the same thing yesterday, he remarked in a harsh tone. Confused, she said in that case she would like to watch a film. He pointed the remote control at the television, the screen remained blank, but he appeared to be satisfied. He lay down beside her and took hold of her hand.

Someone was knocking gently and insistently not far from her. She opened her eyes. The cleaning woman pushed open the door and froze when she saw her still in bed. Neither one of them could say a word. A few seconds later, she gestured for the young woman to come in. Embarrassed, the maid headed straight for the sink and began scrubbing without so much as a sideways glance. She got out of bed. She realized that she had gone to sleep fully dressed.

From the vending machine in the lobby, she bought an orange juice, which she went out to drink on the front steps of the building. Today was her last day. According to the ticket, she would have to leave early the next morning.

If she spent another day like the previous ones, it would be hard for her to keep a grip on her mind, which was beginning to show symptoms of weakening. What had happened during the night worried her, and she could feel a powerful urge rising inside her to act in an unusual manner, to go beyond the boundaries of what was rational and acceptable. For example, she could no longer see any valid reason for keeping silent when she was alone or for not breaking certain rules of decorum, such as not spitting or burping in the street, not scratching her nose or rump in public, not swearing up and down the avenue. To keep these impulses in check, she decided to take a walk. She would go without any particular aim in mind, and to guard against getting lost she would use the following method: she would pick a street that led away from the park and stay on it. If she reached the end of it, she would turn left. And if she reached the end of this second street, she would then retrace her steps. She would therefore turn only once, to the left, and would be sure to remember the way.

A light rain began to fall. She went back up to fetch her umbrella. The cleaning maid had gone from the room. On the bed lay a fresh white towel.

Hereford Road, the name suited her and she turned on to that street. Laden down with a heavy plastic bag on each arm, a woman was walking along, head hunched into her shoulders to protect herself from the rain. A black cat slipped out from under a car, cut across the pavement, and sprang up on to a low wall, where it settled, oddly indifferent to the weather. From time to time it was seized by a sort of nervous tic and would begin licking its fur, agile and diligent. She went over and ran her fingers between the ears of the animal, which arched its back as high as it could. Suddenly, in a single flash, the cat whipped round and bit her index finger. The pain caused her to let out a soft groan, her hand came down hard on the mouth of the cat, which, after toppling off to the other side of the wall, bolted away, its tail bristling. The animal's canines had left two small blood-incrusted marks on her finger. She licked it gently, listening to the water. Which flowed along the gutter, fell into the storm pipes, ran down the facades, streamed over the windows of buildings and parked cars, slid along the veins of leaves, dripped from the ribs of umbrellas, light, fluid sounds crushed by the tumult of the city. Wherever it had come from, by whatever path it had taken, the water was returning to the earth, forming into pockets of liquid connected by underground canals; the water, exploded into millions of particles, was now one.

Hereford Road led to a wider road with motorized vehicles moving in both directions. She turned left, as planned. A little farther on, she came to a park enclosed by railings that ran the length of the street. She put her head through two of the cold bars. She was a prisoner, and she dreamed of escaping into that world of green lawns and abundant trees, of going to sit down on a bench and waiting there, protected by her umbrella, for the day to end. To do nothing, to move only in order to breathe, that seemed the only way out for her. She felt drawn to this state of minimal functioning as if it were a drug that would cure her of her need to commit senseless acts. Yet she had to resist it. Another bout of prolonged immobility could have a harmful effect on her. She feared he would take the opportunity to return.

She started walking again. Each step left another portion of pavement behind her that reappeared, unchanged, in front of her. She was moving along a conveyor belt, her feet carried by the tectonic spinning movement of a universe whose gravitational pull had lost its power over her. She was walking without going anywhere, to stay on her feet in the midst of people who could move forward simply because they knew where they were going. She was walking to convince herself that she wasn't immobile. There was a time when she knew how to put her talent for motion to good use, to travel from Paris to London, to go from her apartment to the gare du Nord every day, to show up for their meetings. Now she should have struggled, broken the rules on purpose, shoved someone aside, spat on him, hurt him, performed some impulsive random act that would allow her to re-enter the flow of cause and effect, the altercations and frolics that pulled people along by the nose and gave them a sensation of being alive.

She would have liked to disappear on the spot, not to die but to disappear, in a puff of smoke, shrinking down to nothing or vanishing into thin air. No one around her would notice a thing. Suicide, a real suicide, seemed impossible to her. She would need to make an immense effort to achieve something she could just as easily attain through patience. She would need a method that was one hundred per cent foolproof, a powerful determination to overcome her own instinct for survival. And she wasn't even sure that it was actually death she was after, but rather a permanent state of profound indifference. Life consisted of performing a series of gestures and movements triggered by a reflex or a summoning of the will. To be spared, she concluded, it was enough no longer to want anything.

The rain had stopped falling. She noticed it because she was the only person still holding an open umbrella. She closed it and continued walking. At one point, she thought she heard someone calling her name. People rushed past her, their faces expressionless, paying no attention to her. She turned around: he was there again, his hair wet, his features drawn. I've spent the past three days looking for you. It was definitely his voice, but the man now coming towards her hadn't moved his lips. She shook her head and hurried into a shop. She had to speak to someone, but she didn't have the right words. She was sorry she had never learned English. She began walking up and down the aisles, between shelves crammed with objects, some vacuum-packed, others wrapped in plastic or stacked in tins. French, French, she repeated, first in a low voice, then more and more loudly as she penetrated deeper into the shop. People were beginning to turn round as she went by, giving her startled looks, which they quickly hid. And then, someone said, yes. A man wearing jeans and carrying a backpack was looking at her. Next to him was a woman wearing jeans and carrying a backpack, holding a clothes hanger and a long, beige, patterned dress. The man and woman appeared to be a couple. She assumed they were tourists, fellow countrymen, allies. With a bit of luck, they could even have come from the same city she did. She was so happy to see them, almost reassured. She went over. From where she was standing now, she could no longer keep an eye on the front entrance. Talk to me. Taken aback, the man and woman stared at her in silence. You don't understand what I'm saying, I'm asking you to talk to me so he won't come back. The couple gave each other a puzzled look, and turned their backs on her. Please, wait! She wasn't about to let them go that easily, finding others like them would be hard. Just as she was starting after them, the man turned around, grabbed her wrist, and pressed a banknote into her palm, giving her an embarrassed shrug. She looked at the note as the identically dressed man and woman walked off. She wanted to shout after them to stay and talk to her, five minutes would do. Then she remembered Paris and the night she received two hundred and fifty euros for passing herself off as someone else. Here too she could have invented a new identity for herself, told one of those lies that came so spontaneously to her. But she couldn't do it any more. Her old reflexes were gone, something had changed. As her true self, she was worth only five pounds. In the past, she probably would have found that amusing. No longer.

She was still walking down Hereford Road when he came back for a greater length of time. He began walking next to her in silence. Although she didn't dare turn her head, she could sense that he wasn't very well either. At a red light, he spoke to her. My feet hurt, do you want to stop for a coffee? She clapped her hands to her ears. If she didn't listen to him, he would vanish. But even through her palms she could still make out his muffled words. Stop sulking, I've told you I've been looking for you, isn't that enough? She couldn't allow herself to react. I've looked almost everywhere, you know, I was waiting for you to get in touch. If she gave in, they would quarrel and she'd never be able to get rid of him. Now that I've found you, you're not going to behave like a little girl, are you? Like a little girl. It was easy for him to say that. Let me remind you that you're the one who came late. She gritted her teeth, trying to focus her attention on a man who was covered in white makeup and pretending to be a statue. Around him were a dozen onlookers all waiting for that moment when an eyelid, a corner of the mouth, a finger would twitch. If it's because of what happened with that man. She stopped. She felt people pushing their way past her, but she couldn't move. She'd made a mistake, she needed to look him straight in the eye to put an end to this ridiculous comedy. His pallor, his stubble, and the dark circles under his eyes made him look ill. There were smudges of dust on his suit, the top buttons of his shirt were open. She'd never seen him in such a state, she almost pitied him. If he had actually been there, she couldn't have fought back the urge to take him in her arms and comfort him. Since you're not making the slightest effort, I'll come back when you're in a better mood. And, just as she was about to reply, he disappeared for good.

For several hours she followed the meanderings of the street, which seemed to go on forever. Hunger had taken hold of her stomach, and because her legs were stiff from exhaustion, she was gradually slowing down. She had lost awareness of her surroundings, then of her own body, as if she were constantly sliding outside herself. At the last minute, the sight of a particular object, sometimes real, sometimes without shape or consistency, or a barely formulated thought, would pull her back. In that way, she managed not to fall down.

The red colour had caught her eye. She didn't remember walking past other telephone boxes earlier, and it struck her that this particular one was meant for her. It was not an ordinary part of the urban landscape but a temptation, or rather a command to do what she hadn't dared contemplate until now: to call him at home. It went without saying that she would not ask a single question, she would simply listen to the voice at the other end of the line as if she were some kind of anonymous crank caller.

She went over to the empty phone box. After several tugs on the door, she managed to get it open. The enclosed space stank of beer and urine. She took a deep breath, went in, keeping her head down to avoid the stench, and let the door close behind her. A black can of Guinness and several cigarette butts lay strewn in the corners on the concrete floor. People had come here before her to shut themselves away in this confined space, to get angry, to get worried, to get happy at one end of a wire. She knew the number by heart, like those childhood recitations that can never be erased from memory. She still had some change. She lifted the receiver, put it to her ear, fed in the coins, and began to dial. That was when she saw the photographs. There were about a dozen of them, all roughly the same size. Each one had a name and telephone number at the bottom, in coloured letters. Most of the women were topless. Some of them also showed their naked buttocks in G-strings. All had struck enticing poses: a promising wink, a tempting pout, a display of admirable teeth. But what impressed her most was the look in the eyes, which revealed nothing more than what these women wanted to reveal. Their contortions were a stark contrast to what she was about to do. After looking carefully at each one, she put the receiver back on the hook, but she couldn't bring herself to leave the box straight away. When she felt up to it, she would go home.

There had only been two men in her life. And she had never understood what they wanted from her.

She remembered the back and forth movement and,

underneath, intentions that had to be deciphered to the best of her ability. The hand ready to caress ended up striking, the tongue ready to kiss ended up licking, the organ ready to penetrate ended up loving. But the brain meanwhile chose its favourite thought and refused with a thousand defences to face up to reality.

Her life had been a more or less happy or painful succession of things and people. Her mistake probably had been not to hold on to them. People had passed through her, over her, beside her, and then had left without her really knowing what she ought to have done to make them stay.

He too had passed, without any intention of staying. She could no longer understand how she could have believed otherwise for a single second. She had looked for him, wanted him, desired him, waited for him. She had given herself, had opened herself up as never before. He hadn't been able to say no, for he had never been the object of such intense interest. However, he had remained anchored to his own life, crippled by fear and powerless to escape. He had been the only one and would always be the only one, but she had to use what was left of her strength to stop him from putting her through this endless torture. She needed to kill all hope, all desire, all longing for him. He had to be no more than a memory that she would drag around and that would eventually become so familiar that from time to time she could forget it.

It was late by the time she arrived at the hotel. She put all her things away in the cupboard, including the umbrella. She kept only her money and her documents. In a few hours, she would take a taxi to the station. She would leave the way she had come. The sole proof of her visit would be a handful of personal effects inside a red-and-white sports bag.

Getting off the train. A clock reads 8:30 a.m. She follows the other passengers heading towards the exit. She no longer knows if she has gone away, or if she has been travelling for several years. In the main hall of the gare du Nord, nothing has really changed. But her perception of things isn't quite the same: the proportions of the setting seem to have been modified, the extras have been replaced to look even more like one another. Most of all, she has the impression that she hears herself talking all around.

When she catches sight of him at the foot of the stairs, she has to grip the handrail to continue going down, her body reduced to a pair of eyes atop a swelling heart. She looks down at the steps and begins to count them. When there are none left to count, she looks up. He's there, in the flesh, his lips pursed, his eyes fixed on her.

Ange is pregnant.

She feels the slapped skin beneath her hand. She realizes that she has just hit him. Hard enough to knock his head back. He is speechless, he doesn't move. She sees the red marks left by her fingers. She likes the way it looks. She turns her back on him and starts to walk away like a robot, heading in the direction of her office.

She settles down at her desk. In front of her is the text of the day's first announcement. She leans in to the microphone and speaks.

Ladies and gentlemen, I regret to announce that all departures have been cancelled. No trains are running. There's no point in looking at the person next to you, he's not responsible. I'm the one who made this decision for personal reasons. The details would take far too long to explain. I therefore suggest two things that in my opinion would be in your best interest: either go home or stay here with me in this austere train station. Let me tell you; you will find nothing at the end of those tracks, I've been there, I've just come back, and believe me, I know what I'm talking about. You'll find nothing but yourselves, the same as here. So you might as well spare yourselves the trouble and stay. And, if I could offer a piece of advice: try to talk to one another. It won't make a big difference, but it might bring some relief.

She feels herself being pulled backwards. An enormous hand is gripping her arm. Monsieur Merlinter is red in the face, and she becomes aware of the total silence in the room. You're completely nuts, get out. She looks him straight in the eye, and then all of a sudden, in front of her stunned co-workers, laughter takes hold of her, a real full-throated roar of laughter, rising up from her belly, irresistible, out of control. And as she is led outside, she is still laughing.

[VOICE OVER]

A NOTE ABOUT THE TYPE

Pierre Simon Fournier *le jeune*, who designed the type used in this book, was both an originator and a collector of types. His services to the art of print communication were his design of individual characters, his creation of ornaments and initials, and his standardization of type sizes. Fournier types are old style in character and sharply cut. In 1764 and 1766 he published his *Manuel typographique*, a treatise on the history of French types and printing, on typefounding in all its details, and on what many consider his most important contribution to the printed word – the measurement of type by the point system.

BOOK DESIGN AND PHOTOGRAPHY BY C.S. RICHARDSON